Too Late… I Love You

Kiki Archer

Title: Too Late… I Love You
ID: 16574176
ISBN: 978-1-326-28502-9

K.A Books *Publishers*

www.kikiarcher.com

Twitter: @kikiarcherbooks

Published by K.A Books 2015

Copyright © 2015 Kiki Archer

Editors: Jayne Fereday and Diana Simmonds

Cover: Fereday Designs

Kiki Archer asserts the moral rights

to be identified as the author of this work.

All rights reserved.

Author photograph: **Ian France** www.ianfrance.com

ISBN: 978-1-326-28502-9

For Jayne and Diana.
Thank you x

CHAPTER ONE

'If love is light why does it blind us? If love is free why does it shackle us? If love is honour why does it cheat us? If love is strength why does it break us? If love is fearless tell me why I'm so scared?'

Ryan dropped the manuscript on the table. "You did not write this."

Connie nodded. "I did."

"But you only got a Desmond from De Montfort."

"A what?"

"A 2:2 and it was in management studies or something random like that, wasn't it?"

Connie stood from the small kitchen table in her tiny London terrace and smiled. "Business entrepreneurship and innovation, actually. Tea?"

"Exactly, so where's this coming from? Mint please, I'm detoxing."

"I just thought I'd try."

"Why?"

The young woman lifted herself onto her tiptoes and reached over the array of baby beakers to the mugs at the back of the cupboard. "Noah's sleeping better in the evenings and I've finally got a bit more time to myself."

"Well get yourself out then! Come clubbing with me. See your friends. You're twenty-five, Connie. Get out there and get your life back. You're not some old writer like Enid Blyton."

"I think she's dead."

"Exactly."

Lifting her shoulders into a shrug Connie signalled to her surroundings. "This is my life, Ryan."

"No." He ran his finger down the manuscript and started to read. "*This* is your life."

'**Have you ever asked yourself why people fall in love? Falling hurts. Why not jump? Jump in love. You can control how high, how far. When you fall there's no control, you just end up down, defenceless. Love isn't the medicine, love causes the wound.**'

He paused and looked up. "It's hardly chick-lit, is it?"

Connie dropped the fragrant teabag into the mug of boiling water. "It's fiction."

"Ha! I read somewhere that a writer's first work is always autobiographical."

"Well that's just a story."

"About a woman who's not in love."

"You've only read the first page," she said, handing over the steaming drink.

He inhaled the minty aroma. "Thanks. Oh I really need this. I'm looking frazzled, aren't I?"

Connie studied her friend. He had never looked frazzled. Not once. In the twenty years she'd known him, since their first day at school, he'd been the absolute epitome of put-together. Well dressed, well styled, great hair. Connie smiled to herself. Unfortunately the hair had started to thin so he'd taken the plunge and gone for the buzz cut, and when that had failed to disguise the receding he'd shaved it all off.

Ryan self-consciously lifted his hand to his head. "I'm shining, aren't I?"

"No, I'm just admiring your style."

"I was thinking of upping my facial stubble. It might have a counter-balance type effect."

Connie sat down opposite him, adding a plate of biscuits to the table. "Don't. Didn't you see that article that said the average male beard harbours more poo than a toilet?"

"Miss Parker! You've been spending far too much time around nappies and small children. Such a word should *not* be used in polite conversation."

"Oh sod off, you bugger."

"But maybe I should keep it as it is." He ran his fingers across his smooth chin and up over his perfectly bald head, narrowing his eyes as if posing for some invisible audience. "I think the two diamond earrings give me an early 2000 David Beckham type look."

Connie nodded at his bald head. "It's shining."

"Ooo you bitch," he said, laughing out loud.

"Oh Ryan, you're perfectly preened, as always."

"And you're..." He paused, eyeing his friend carefully. "Your hair's got really long. You look liked a wild-maned unicorn."

Connie fingered her thick mass of blonde layers. "It's on the list, along with the shopping, the cleaning, the cooking, the washing, the losing of weight and the growing of inches."

"No, you're perfectly pint-sized."

She rolled her eyes. "Says Mr Perfectly Perfect."

"Could you please go and tell that to the elusive Mr Right?" He took a sip of his drink, gasping dramatically in appreciation. "Oh this is good!" He paused. "Talking of Mr Right, tell me about Mr Wrong. How's Karl? He's not read this, has he?"

"Read what?"

"Your autobiography." Putting on his best stern voice Ryan spoke with meaning. "I don't believe in love." He waggled his finger. "I've never felt the magic." He threw the back of his hand against his forehead, finishing in a dramatic climax. "Where's my soul mate – if soul mates even exist?"

"It doesn't even say that and it's certainly not my autobiography." Connie looked down and kicked her feet against the leg of the table. "And I *do* believe in love. Karl can read it if he wants to."

"He shouldn't."

She lifted her eyes to Ryan's clear gaze. "Why not?"

Ryan picked up the manuscript and cleared his throat, finding the stern voice once more.

'I don't dislike love, I just don't believe. The whole concept's a ruse. A lie. Swelled by emotions that fade. Desire, lust, intrigue. They're all temporary.'

Connie reddened. "That's not me. That's Bonnie Blythe."

"Bonnie, Connie, oh come on!"

"I knew I shouldn't have shown you."

"Oh darling I'm joking. It's amazing. I think I'm just shocked."

"At what?"

"The fact you're telling the truth."

"It's fiction. Of course I believe in love." She signalled towards the baby monitor that was resting quietly on the kitchen counter. "Noah's my life."

"And Karl?"

"We love each other."

"Are you *in* love?"

"Of course we are. We've got Noah. We're making this work."

"Look at me, lady. In the words of a great writer…." He tapped the pages and spoke with meaning.

'Love shouldn't be this hard.'

CHAPTER TWO

The small work station was nestled neatly between the collapsed ironing board and the folded down clothes horse in Connie's snug yet sufficient under-stair cupboard. She liked to squeeze onto the chair and pretend she was Harry Potter, creating magic in the confines of the metre-wide space. That's what it felt like. Her special nook where her secret life raised sparks of emotion and pangs of self-doubt, driven on by the desire for knowledge and insight. What would Bonnie do? What would Bonnie say? What path would she take?

Connie opened up the Word document and felt that familiar surge of adrenaline. Her fingers took over, tapping away, as she watched the words appearing on the screen, reading them for the first time and wondering whose they were and what they meant. This wasn't her life. These weren't her words. They were Bonnie's. Bonnie Blythe's.

'There are two types of women in this world: the ones who return their trolleys at the supermarket and the ones who don't. I'm sitting in my car studying one of the don'ts, wondering if I can be her. Just for one day. Free from the shackles of the social restraints that make me walk through wind, rain and reversing cars to put my trolley back. Free from the chains of social etiquette that see me clear my table at the fast food chain, no matter how full-up the bin. Free from the small voice in my head that keeps me chewing until I can safely dispose of my gum.

I study the woman. Her single bag of shopping already safe in her sports car. Her trolley discarded by the bollard. She's fast. She's smart. She's gone. I watch with envy as her car roars away. Why can't I be like her? Sashaying with purpose. Moving

through life with priorities at hand. Get in, get out, move on. I pull down the interior mirror and try to replicate her hair flick. It doesn't work with my short brown bob. Maybe I should dye it blonde, grow it long, wear it big.'

"You've already got big blonde hair, and no one wants to read about trolleys."

Connie spun around, knocking her knees against the cupboard wall, trying to cover the screen with her hand. "Don't Karl, it's not finished yet."

"I thought it was romance?"

"I don't know what it is, but the lady's not me."

The smart-suited businessman bent down and kissed his girlfriend on the cheek. "It's okay, I'm not looking. How's Noah?"

Connie leaned back and glanced past him into the kitchen at the baby monitor. It was still sitting quietly on the counter. "Sleeping. He went down at seven and I've not heard a peep since."

"You're getting good at this." Karl loosened his tie and reached for the blue bean bag in the lounge, dropping it against the wall and slumping onto it.

"He's three, and we're sitting in a cupboard after not seeing each other for however long. I think it's called getting through it."

"I'm in the hall. You're the one in the cupboard." He ran his fingers through his short dark hair and smiled. "For what it's worth, I think you're getting good at getting through it."

Connie studied his tired eyes. "Long day?"

"It's always a long day. Tell me about the brunette with the trolley fetish."

"I'm just filling the time." She reached back around and turned off the screen.

"You must be enjoying it though? You're always in there."

"Where else am I meant to be?"

Karl lifted his hands in defence.

"I'm sorry." She squeezed past the chair and sat down on the floor in front of the bean bag, taking hold of her boyfriend's hands. "It's just something to do."

"Why don't you go back to work?"

"And pay someone else to look after Noah? That's not happening." She tilted her head, causing her mass of blonde hair to fall over one shoulder. "He's my world. Why would I trust a stranger with him?" She stared carefully at Karl. "You wouldn't trust a stranger with him, would you?"

"Your mum's always offering to do more, and so is my mum. Or there are nurseries run by childcare professionals."

"No way!"

Karl rubbed his eyes. "So we do this. We spend my salary while you fill your time with trolleys."

"It's not just about trolleys."

"So tell me what it's about then."

Connie shook her head. "No."

"Please? I'm interested."

"No. You'll just think it's silly."

Karl smiled. "Are you blushing, Connie Parker? I promise I won't pass comment. You've been working on this for weeks now. Tell me about that brunette with the bobbed hair."

Crossing her legs underneath herself, Connie adjusted her position. "Okay. But you have to promise me you won't laugh."

"I won't."

"Right, she's called Bonnie Blythe."

Karl laughed. "She's Bonnie, you're Connie. That's interesting."

"No! Ryan thought it was all about me too, but it's not."

The beanbag suddenly made a sharp rustling noise as Karl shifted his position and sat up, a notable tension appearing in his shoulders. "What's he been reading it for?"

"He's my best friend."

"I said this before, Connie, and I'll say it again. I'm getting seriously concerned about the amount of time that man spends around here. We have to be careful about the wrong stuff rubbing off."

Connie threw her hands into the air. "Oh for goodness sake, Karl, I'm not doing this again."

"It's true. Kids are so susceptible at this age."

"Well if you're so worried why don't you spend more time with him?"

"With knobgobbler?"

"No! With Noah! Your son!"

"I'm busy working so I can provide for my son! We own this house, Connie, and yes it's small, but we own it, outright, and it's in London, and it may be our first, but it certainly won't be our last. Do you have any idea how many other people your age can say that?"

"Why do you always bring up my age? And I'd rather have a mortgage like most normal people so we could spend our money on holidays and weekends away instead."

"Investing in property is the sensible option and all the rest will come in time. Trust me, I know what I'm talking about. I was already employing over a hundred people when I was twenty-five and here you are choosing to sit in a cupboard and write about trolleys."

"And look after your son."

Karl was about to snap back when the monitor in the kitchen flared to life. Both froze, holding their breath as if the wailing would miraculously stop. Suddenly it did, but they stayed still for that extra moment as their eyes locked in the waiting game, softening into apologetic smiles as the silence continued, realising they'd had a lucky escape. "I'm sorry," said Connie with a whisper. "I don't want to wake him."

Karl kept his voice low. "We agreed this at the start and it's fine by me. I work and you do the childcare."

"I know."

"It just frustrates me when you act like this isn't enough. Like you want more."

"I'm sorry. It's just hard. It's the hardest job I've ever done." She nodded towards the small sofa in the lounge. "Shall we sit down and start again?"

"Sounds good to me." Karl took off his now crumpled jacket and followed his girlfriend to the sofa. He lowered himself onto the worn cushions and instantly grimaced as he pulled out a hard toy that had poked into his thigh. "I thought you were cleaning today?"

"I have cleaned today. He's three, he never stops playing."

"He should learn to tidy as he goes."

"Karl, I am trying my best."

"Is it me?" The eyebrows were raised and the voice was shocked. "Do I need to do more? My ninety-hour week that pays for absolutely everything, is that not enough?"

Connie closed her eyes and dropped her head back onto the cushions. "It's fine. I'm sorry. It's just been a long day. I'm blessed that I get to stay at home with Noah, and I'm thankful that you fund it."

"And you're happy?"

"Noah makes me happy every single minute of every single day." The smile came, as it always did whenever she thought of her son.

"And me? Do I make you happy?"

"Of course you make me happy." She paused. "Do I make you happy?"

"Yeah."

Connie laughed. "Yeah? Is that all I get?"

"Oh Connie, we knew how hard this would be. We're working. It's working. Let's just keep moving forward."

She softened her voice. "I know this isn't quite what you wanted, but—"

"Please, let's not rehash old ground. This *is* what I wanted. Yes, slightly earlier than anticipated…"

"You're thirty-two!"

"But we'd only known each other for two months and you're still so young."

"I'm twenty-five!"

Karl took a deep breath. "Why are we doing this?"

"Because we have a child together."

"No, I'm talking about *this*. Niggling at each other."

Connie laid her head on his shoulder. "It's me. I'm sorry."

"So get yourself out more. Re-join your squash club. We're doing really well, Connie. The business is good. It's great even."

"And who has Noah? The squash team train every Tuesday. You're not around every Tuesday. Their matches are at the weekends. You're never around at weekends."

"Collis and Killshaw Insurance is a twenty-four-hour business, you know this. Just get a sitter."

She prickled in her seat. "I don't trust anyone."

"Like I said earlier, my mum's always willing—"

"Especially not your mum."

"Your mum then."

"I don't like asking her too often. We need her to cover those client dinners where I get wheeled out to smile and look pretty."

"Start the squash. You'll feel better if you get fitter."

"Thanks."

"I didn't mean it like that."

Connie shrugged. "I'm happy with my writing. That's keeping me busy."

"But you used to be so sporty. What about some walking groups in the day? Or something like yoga where you can take Noah along?"

"No, those things are always so cliquey and we're out and about too much anyway. Tomorrow I'm taking him to the library at ten and the soft-play at eleven. Then we'll go for coffee and cakes at Mariano's."

"And yet you complain about your day."

"It's hard work with a three-year-old."

"Guess how my day went? I arrived at the office at six a.m., where I immediately replied to thirty-four new emails. I then signed three new clients. I had six different meetings before I Skype-toured a potential site for the new Manchester office. I think it was about eight p.m. when I was on my tube journey home that I first took a breath for myself."

"You enjoy your job. You live for your job."

"And you live for Noah, so we're all square." He leaned back into the sofa, stretching his neck out to the ceiling. "I just hate having this conversation every time I get home. Who works the hardest? Who has the most important job? I think we should just change the subject once and for all." He nodded. "Tell me about your trolley lady."

"No. You're not interested."

"I am."

"You're not."

"I am!"

She turned to him and narrowed her eyes with suspicion. "Really?"

"Yes!"

"Fine." She continued to study him as she took a deep breath. "But only because you're asking, and I'm not quite sure where it's going yet, but she's in her twenties. Bonnie that is." A small smile formed in the corner of her mouth. "She's a bit of a plain Jane. Brown hair, pale skin. Short. Lonely. Never found true love. In fact she's very sceptical about whether true love even exists."

"But she finds someone?"

The nod was quick. "I think so, but I just can't figure out who she'll fall for. I can't picture their face or their character traits, but anyway she's not there yet. She needs to find herself first and learn how to love who she is and what she's got." Connie stopped talking. "Why are you smiling?"

"Because you are. You're animated. You're talking about Bonnie like she's real. It's nice to see."

"Anyway, I want her to blossom. I want her to have her dream. Her fairytale."

"Is that what you want?"

"I've already got it." She scanned the toys that were scattered across the small coffee table and focused on the smiling photo of Noah on the bookshelf opposite the sofa.

Karl reached over and stroked her cheek. "You know you're not average like Bonnie Blythe, don't you?"

"The book's not about me."

He tried to move some of the thick blonde hair away from her face. "You've got a lovely button nose and sparkling blue eyes. You're cute, Connie. Really cute."

The hand was instantly batted away. "Cute? A man in his thirties doesn't want cute. I bet you never called Louise cute with all her tits and teeth."

"She's only got two."

"Teeth? I wish she did. She's got the type of teeth you talk to."

Karl laughed. "Too much of an American smile if you ask me."

"You weren't complaining at the time."

"Oh Connie, come on. She's my business partner."

"And there's history. But like you say, you don't want to have *that* conversation every evening either." She lifted herself off the sofa. "Anyway."

Karl rolled his eyes. "Yes, anyway."

"Would you like your lasagne in here or in the kitchen? Or would you like to go crazy and have it on the beanbag next to the under-stair cupboard?"

"We live in London, this place is palatial." He patted the cushion next to him. "Shall we just eat in here and snuggle up with a film? I know it's late but we could open a bottle?"

"Okay, sounds good." The wailing stopped her. From her position in the lounge she could look straight into the kitchen at the baby monitor that was now revving bright red in sync with the wails coming from absolutely everywhere.

"Does it have to be that loud?" asked Karl, rubbing his temples.

"It's important that we hear him."

"This place is tiny. We don't even need that monitor. Plus he's three. He should be self-settling by now."

She raised her voice through the noise. "Who said that? Your mother?"

"He's not stopping. Why's he not stopping?"

"Would you go? I'll sort the lasagne."

Karl reached for the television remote. "No, I've been working all day. You go. It only needs re-heating doesn't it?"

Connie stared at him in disbelief. "You've not seen Noah since the weekend."

"Exactly, so I don't want to see him like this. We need quality time, not telling off time. He'll only want you anyway."

"You don't need to tell him off, you just need to comfort him."

Karl switched on the news. "No, you're better at it than me."

"Twenty minutes in the oven, salad's in the fridge." She reached for the bannister and started up the stairs. "Go knock yourself out."

CHAPTER THREE

The noise in the large community hall was a fusion of high-pitched giggles and long drawn out wails complemented by the chatter of mothers who were programmed to tune out both. The building had been constructed the previous year at the same time as the huge new hypermarket, no doubt a clause in the contract forcing the big brand to *give back*, even though it was the one responsible for taking away in the first place; another green field snatched from the already greying area. Connie was there, as usual, in her corner spot on the plastic chairs, admiring her son as he raced around on the pedal-kart. At least the hall was of use to families, she thought, with playgroups like this during the day and youth groups for older children at night; not to mention the dog training, zumba and weight-loss classes that were mixed into the hall's schedule as well. Another plus was the newly bought equipment that was all still remarkably clean, especially in comparison to some of the playgroups where the toys were ancient and completely covered in bite-marks.

She stayed seated and listened to the noisy activity emanating from each of the play stations. On the left were the tiny arts and crafts tables, littered with poster paints, PVA glue, plastic scissors (that never actually managed to cut anything) and wads of multi-coloured tissue paper ready to be scrunched up and stuck down. In the centre of the room were the padded rainbow-coloured gym mats covered in soft-play blocks of all shapes and sizes. That's where she'd mostly find Noah, always jumping, always building. She'd often encourage him to move over to the station on the right where there were cushions, cuddlies and picture books galore, but he'd only ever stay there for a short story before toddling off and diving straight back into the blocks – unless the pedal-kart was free, as that took precedence over everything. The back of the room was cornered off for messy play and today it was jelly, with wobbling rabbits and teddies already whacked into oblivion by the tiny tearaways brandishing wooden spoons like warriors ready for battle.

Connie glanced at her watch and wondered where Ryan had got to. They had been attending this playgroup together ever since it opened last year and both knew it was the perfect place for in-depth gossiping given the fact that Noah would entertain himself for the whole two-hour session. Ryan was lucky enough to pick and choose when he worked, a perk of being a private masseur, and he'd never let her down, not once. She noticed the discarded pedal-kart and scanned the soft-play area, searching out the bright yellow t-shirt. It was one of her coping mechanisms: lower the threat of losing your child by dressing them in something glaringly bright. That way they were easy to spot and you wouldn't have as many heart-in-the-mouth moments where you thought they'd run off, or been taken, or simply disappeared without cause. Connie didn't like to think of her behaviour as neurotic. It wasn't. She wasn't a helicopter mother who was always hovering around her child. She'd let him have his freedoms, but only under her strictly controlled conditions. Some of the mothers were awful: grabbing the glue in case it was toxic, kneeling at the bottom of the blocks to break any falls, telling their offspring to slow down, be careful, stop running, in fear of their fun. Connie nodded to herself. She wasn't like that. She was getting it right. She was the mother sitting calmly in the corner, allowing her child to explore, to be social, to take risks, to feel free. She scanned again. *Oh god, where was he?* She jumped to her feet.

"Look who I found!" sang Ryan, dangling a giggling Noah upside down by the ankles.

Connie gasped. "I thought I'd lost him! My heart's racing!"

"I've just this second arrived. He saw me and toddled over."

She straightened her hair and composed herself. She knew it was wrong, but the fear of an impending disaster had always been there. From the moment he had been born, she had worried. She had worried about dropping the car seat on the way to the car. Falling down the stairs en route to a night feed. Having him snatched from his seat as she paid for the petrol. Accidentally throwing him off the balcony at the local shopping centre. The fear was endless and overwhelming, but she'd always kept it locked up, and only at times like this did her panic betray her.

Ryan lifted the little boy onto his smoothly shaven head. "Where's he gone?"

Noah patted the baldness. "Here!"

"There you are!" he said, sliding him down to his shoulders. "He can't get out, Connie. The doors are child proof."

"I know, I know. It's fine." She edged her way back to her chair knowing how important it was to give her son space and let him feel fear, but only when she was *sure* he was out of real harm's way. She took a deep breath and smiled at the little boy. It seemed to be working as he was the most confident, outgoing daredevil around, encouraged mostly by Ryan. It was only her nerves that suffered.

"Shall we go and build the biggest tower?" asked Ryan, lifting Noah over his head and back down to the floor.

"Noah build. Noah build."

Ryan saluted. "Okay big man, let me know when you're done and I'll measure it."

"No. Noah measure."

"Okay then, shall I just sit down?"

"Ry Ry sit down."

Connie watched as the mop of blond hair bounced away with the trademark marching walk, still often on tiptoes, that signalled her son was in charge.

Ryan patted his jeans pocket. "I've got the cash, can I get you a cuppa?"

Connie groaned. "What happened to Costa?"

"Running late sorry. This church hall type tea at ten pence a pop will have to do."

"Okay, but let's have a Mariano's after. I need my morning mocha hit."

"Let's do lunch there as well. I can't stomach any more of these offcut playgroup biscuits bought in bulk in a crappy see-though plastic bag from the Battersea market. They're simply not sustenance for a stallion like me."

Connie laughed as her friend twirled on the spot and pranced off towards the small hatch at the side of the hall, famous for serving watered down tea and cloudy coffee topped up with UHT milk. She watched as the eyes in the room followed him and smiled at the throng of women who suddenly found themselves parched. It had been the same since day one. Sex-starved new mothers appearing on-heat whenever Ryan arrived. They would follow him round the stations and try to flirt with him at the hatch, desperate to find out his story. Where was the ring? Who was the blonde woman? Wasn't he handsome? And why couldn't their partners be as good with their kids?

Connie couldn't help laughing as one particular woman strode swiftly across the hall, purse grasped tightly in hand. They'd nicknamed her Titty, for two obvious reasons. They were huge. Always pushed out, pulled up and on glorious display. No matter the season, Titty would trot herself out in a vest top. She had a huge array of colours, prints, fabrics; but only ever one size – too small.

Titty had been the first to make a full blown pass at Ryan, and almost twelve months on she'd not given up hope. Her flirting was constant and her inability to spot, or accept, his sexuality was strong-willed, to say the least. Ryan was gay, and – to Connie – obviously so. He chose, however, not to divulge this information, claiming he enjoyed the gossip his presence generated far too much to come clean. Connie turned to the hatch and stifled her laughter as she watched him performing. He seemed to be complimenting Titty on her hair and outrageously embracing her wooing. But Connie knew the truth. He'd be back over in a minute comparing her to an on-heat Jackie Stallone.

She paused her observation and scanned back to the blocks, finding the bright yellow t-shirt quickly and smiling. Noah was playing with a little girl kitted out in bright yellow dungarees and matching yellow jumper. Together they looked like they'd dressed for a rave. She must be new, thought Connie, confident that she could name all of the children even though she knew none of the mothers. It might have been different had Ryan not been there hiding her in the corner and gossiping non-stop. She shook her head. This wasn't Ryan's doing. Ryan was actually her saviour. *She* was the one who stayed quiet. It was *her* choice to hide in the corner. Ryan was just her excuse not to mingle, her reason for keeping the false friends at bay. Connie flinched as Top Dog shouted across the hall.

"Joshhhhhhua!"

That's how she knew the names of most of the children - from the sharp chastising shouts of their mothers. Top Dog was the main culprit, never moving from her seat in the centre of her harem, always disciplining her son in the loudest of voices. Ryan had nicknamed her Top Dog as she clearly took charge of the playgroup posse. If you were sitting in her circle then you were somebody. You'd probably have tattoos and scraped back hair just like she did, but at least you were part of it, part of the clique.

Connie glanced around and searched out the two women who'd never fit into that circle: Earth Mother and Crusty. Both social outcasts. Earth Mother for her sheer size and refusal to wear a bra; constantly breastfeeding her son Lucas, even though he was now over four. And Crusty because of the dandruff. A real nervous mouse, in a state of perpetual blind panic. Always re-adjusting the bumper helmet on her son's precious head. Ryan had claimed the helmet was Crusty's method of hiding her son's inherited dandruff affliction, but pairing it with the boy's on-wrist beeping tracking device it was clear that Crusty had issues.

Connie sighed to herself. These just weren't her type of women. She had friends, albeit ones she rarely saw any more, but she had them, and she liked them, and she didn't feel the need to mingle for mingling's sake.

"You always look like a little lost sheep whenever I leave you." Ryan sat down and handed over the unappetising tea.

"I'm scared someone might come over."

"You're not scared."

Connie nodded. "I am. These women *actually* scare me."

"Yeah, maybe Crusty should, and possibly Top Dog, but the rest of them seem okay." Ryan parted his lips, dropped his jaw and continued to talk. "It's about time you made friends with Miss Titty."

"Why have you done that with your mouth?"

"That's how she talks. Haven't you noticed? She always holds her mouth slightly ajar. It's the lips, they're so full of filler I don't think she can actually physically close them anymore, and on top of all that her skin tone's off the scale today."

"Tiger orange?"

Ryan laughed. "It's her hands, they're so patchy. How anyone ever thinks fake tan is attractive is beyond me."

"Says you!"

"I'm old-school sunbed, darling." He took a sip of his tea, swallowing quickly to disguise the taste. "Oh my goodness, we've got fresh blood."

"Where?" Connie scanned the room.

"Hotty with a botty, two o'clock. Can we name her?"

Connie struggled to see who he was staring at. "No. No more bitching. I'm always a bitch around you."

"You are not. You're nowhere near my level of bitchiness. Come on, let's watch her and name her."

"Where is she?" Connie searched again.

"There, bending down next to Noah. That girl in the yellow dungarees must be hers. Oh bless look, she's got the same hair as Noah."

Connie watched as the little girl with the bright blonde hair passed large foam blocks to Noah for his tower. "They look about the same age, don't they?" she said.

"No clue." Ryan wiggled his eyebrows. "Go and ask the mum. Quickly, Connie. Get in there before Top Dog sinks her rabid paws in."

Connie looked at the woman, taken aback by her sophisticated style. Most of the mothers at playgroup looked fairly bedraggled, but this woman was poised and together. "She's not got her daughter's blonde hair, has she?"

"That's stating the obvious. Is she Arab?"

"Ryan! She's not Arab. She looks a bit Italian maybe? Or Spanish? But I think it's definitely her daughter, look, you can see from their features." Connie continued to stare. The woman was elegant and refined and certainly not someone you'd expect to see in a local community centre built by the owners of Asda. "She's far too classy to be hanging around here."

Ryan nodded in admiration. "If her daughter's the same age as Noah then she's done well to lose all her baby weight."

"Every woman's lost their baby weight by the time their child's hit three. I'm the exception."

"You and Earth Mother."

Connie hit her friend on his shoulder.

"Watch it, you'll spill my tea." Ryan stopped laughing and nodded in the direction of the blocks. "Go on, Connie, be brave."

"No, I don't want to."

"Please? I can't come next week. I'm out in Malta, remember?"

"Oh damn, your conference." She shrugged. "It's fine, I'll skip a week."

"And miss out on Crusty's drama?" He shook his head. "You will not. I need a full update. What if Earth Mother wears something other than that tie-dye dress and those big walking boots? What if Top Dog gets another facial tattoo? What if Titty breaks one of her stilettos? You never know what we might miss. Go on, Con, she looks friendly enough." He paused. "In fact she looks a bit of a loner, like you."

Connie glanced back at the woman. There was absolutely nothing about her that screamed loner. She looked like a woman who had millions of friends, millions of men and millions of pounds in the bank.

"No ring." Ryan was whistling in discovery. "Divorced. That's how she's got the money for those Gucci jeans."

"You can't get Gucci jeans."

"No, not in Ethel Austin where you shop, darling, but you can in the places where she shops."

Connie laughed. "You're so mean to me."

"Oh you love me for it, and your style's nothing but unique." He nodded his head towards the woman. "Her style, on the other hand, is top drawer."

"What would I have in common with her? She's at least a foot taller than I am."

"I'm not asking you to seduce her. Simply say hello." He nodded. "Shall we call her Amal? Like Amal Clooney? George Clooney's new wife. Or what about Seductress, because of her eyes?"

"What eyes?"

"Oh Connie, your observation skills are soooo poor." He nodded again. "Her eyes, look. They're deep like the sweetest milk-chocolate and rich like the moist winter soil."

"You're so full of bullshit."

"Yet another reason why you love me so much. Okay, sod it, let's just call her Tight Arse."

"I thought you said she was rich?"

"No! Physically! Look at her arse. It's perfectly tight."

Connie blushed. "I'm not looking at her bottom."

"Oh sorry, I forgot. You're totally unable to look at another woman with lust in your eyes. One day, Connie. Trust me. One day."

"Muuuuuuuuuuuuuuumeeeeeeeeeeeeeeeee!" Connie jumped up. It was an innate ability for any mother to recognise her child's cry in the first millisecond of hearing it.

"Muuuuuuuuuuuuuuumeeeeeeeeeeeeeeeee!"

"It's okay, Noah, I'm coming, I'm coming!" She hurtled towards the blocks and swooped down to pick up her son, scooping him into her arms. "It's okay, sweetie, it's okay. Are you hurting?" She jigged him up and down as he caught hold of his tears.

"Liss bash Noah."

"Liss? Who's Liss, sweetheart?"

Connie stopped jigging as the woman entered her space. "I'm so sorry, I think it was Alice, my daughter. Is he okay? There was a tussle with the blocks."

Connie stiffened as the woman bent down and stroked Noah's head.

"Alice can be rather forceful at times. I really am sorry. It's our first time here and already we're causing a fuss." The woman paused and stretched out her hand. "Hi, I'm Maria."

Connie stood still, lost in the milk-chocolatey eyes of seduction.

CHAPTER FOUR

"She shook your hand, so what were her hands like?"

Connie inhaled deeply. The rich aroma of real coffee paired with the quiet buzz of the quaint little shop always worked to relax her. "They were soft."

Ryan wiped some mocha froth from the top of his lip and encouraged her with wide eyes. "How soft are we talking? Good hand cream soft? Or never worked a day in her life soft?"

"I don't know, just soft. Can we stop debriefing now?" She reached for her drink and blew gently. "Our encounter was momentary."

"Connie Parker, you seriously need to work on your sensuality skills. Did her touch make you tingle? Was her grip one of power and dominance, or delight and desire? You know you can sense a person's feelings towards you via their handshake, right?"

"She'd only just met me! She didn't have any feelings."

"Hotty with the botty's daughter assaulted your son. She must have felt apologetic."

Connie automatically glanced to the left at the small children's play area penned off in the corner of the room. It was one of the main reasons why she loved Mariano's. It had all of the features of other big brand coffee shops but was designed with mothers in mind. She spotted the yellow t-shirt and smiled at her son. "It wasn't an assault."

"Did she use two hands when shaking? That's a sign of apology," Ryan paused, "but it can also be a sign of falseness."

"She just introduced herself, said, *Hi I'm Maria*, and shook my hand. Okay?"

The pitch was high. "Okay."

Connie used her little finger to scoop away some of the froth from the rim of her mug before sipping again. She looked up to the Gustav Klimt prints that hung on the walls and focused, as always, on the one called *The Kiss*.

Ryan glanced at the vibrant image, aware of Connie's distraction. He watched her and tutted. "Look at you, lady, seductively sucking on your finger."

Connie reddened and wiped her hands on her paper napkin. "No, I just like that picture, and I had cream on my finger." She ignored the wiggling eyebrows and gave Ryan what he wanted. "Fine, we'll talk about her. But what sort of woman shakes hands at a playgroup anyway?"

"The type of woman who's too classy for Top Dog's gang and too clever for Titty's nonsense. I can't believe you just left her standing there, ripe for the picking. Didn't you see how Earth Mother and Crusty swooped in?"

"Noah wanted a drink. I said hello back to her, I told her not to worry about the tussle and then I got him his beaker."

"Well in two weeks' time I want a third wheel on our bike, please. We've been at that playgroup for a year now. It's about time we gathered our own gang. We could call ourselves the cool ones, or the normal ones," he paused, "and let's be honest, Maria's the only woman in the past 365 days who looks like she might actually make the grade."

"I told you, I'm not going next week."

Suddenly Ryan squealed silently, frantically shaking his head as he flapped his fingers, overcome by extreme excitement. "She's here!" he hissed.

"Who?"

"Amal Clooney! Seductress! Hotty with a botty! She can't keep away!"

Connie felt an unfamiliar surge of adrenaline dancing through her chest and instantly accepted how dull her life must have become to experience such a buzz at the fact the newcomer to the playgroup had shown up at the coffee shop too; but this was her life now and she was willing to embrace it. "Where?" she hissed in return.

"Behind you. Don't look. Don't look. She's scanning around. I think she needs a high chair."

"This one's Noah's."

"Alright, Miss Selfish! Wait, wait, it's okay, she's got one."

"Good, there are always loads in here."

Ryan continued his low-voiced reportage. "She's got a table, she's got a high chair. It looks like she's trying to get Alice strapped in, but nope, Alice isn't playing ball." Ryan sat up taller. "What's this? She's getting table service!"

Connie couldn't help it, she turned around. The barista was kneeling next to the high chair and handing over one of the large chocolate coins available at the counter for a ridiculously high price. "They never do that for Noah!"

"You never get him to sit down."

"Because he loves the playpen so much, and anyway he does sit down when I call him for snacks."

"Therefore you don't need the barista's help." Ryan looked over at the scene and shook his head. "Oh no, now *that's* not okay."

"What? Tell me. I can't keep turning around."

"He's brought over... what looks like..." he squinted dramatically, "no way, a caramel ice frappe!"

"For Alice?"

"No! Maria. He's got Alice a fruit juice." Ryan lifted his hand to his forehead and peeped, quite obviously, through his fingers. "Now there are two of them, fawning all over her, and look, the queue at the counter's started to build." He reached across the table and tapped Connie's purse. "I bet she tips well. Do you ever tip when you're here?"

"No, it's expensive enough as it is."

"Exactly my point. We need to go over. If she's in our gang we'll get much better service."

Connie took a gulp of her mocha. "Women like her don't mix with women like me. We're in different worlds," she paused and wiped the top of her lip, "and anyway, you already get preferential treatment wherever you go. Flying first class to Malta, aren't you?"

"You're not in different worlds. You went to the same playgroup and now you're both in the same coffee shop," Ryan winked, "and yes, of course I am, darling, but stop changing the subject."

Connie shrugged. "I hate forced friendships. I'm not going over."

"Muuuuuuuuuuuuuuumeeeeeeeeeeeeeeee!"

With one quick jump she was out of her seat and over to the playpen, kneeling next to her son and holding his middle. "Hey, big man, what is it? Are you okay?"

"Liss, Liss, Liss, Liss!" The little boy wiggled out of his mummy's grasp and took hold of the white picket fence that had been penning him in, jumping up and down as he continued to shout. "Liss, Liss, Liss, Liss!"

Connie glanced back at the table she and Ryan had just been observing. She lowered her voice. "Oh yes, good boy, that's Alice isn't it."

Noah got louder. "Liss, Liss, Liss!"

"Shush, shush, shush, shush, shush. Alice is having some lunch with her mummy. Would you like your snacks now?"

"Snacks with Liss!"

"No, no, no." Connie picked up her son and got herself out of the playpen. "Noah sit with Mummy and Ry Ry."

"Noah sit with Liss." The little boy shouted even louder from his now elevated position, waving frantically in the direction of his new friend. "Liiiiiiiiiiiiiiiiiiiiiiiiiiiiiiiiiiiiiss!"

Connie turned around in mouthing apology to everyone in the coffee shop, unable to avoid Maria's smiling eyes. She nodded back at them, turning instantly red.

"Come say hi," mouthed Maria, signalling her over.

She shook her head and pointed at her son before miming the act of eating as she signalled down to the high chair. Connie cringed at herself, always so rubbish at acting.

The beautifully shaped lips continued to articulate the words. "Come on." Maria was holding up her index finger. "Just one minute." She pointed down at Alice who was grinning from ear to ear and waving both hands.

Connie could tell that her cheeks were now crimson as she struggled to keep hold of her son. She hated moments like this, embarrassment and shyness always getting the better of her. She shook her head and tried to mouth back. "No, I'll..." It was too late. Noah had succeeded in wiggling himself free and was now marching, on his tip toes, towards Liss's table.

"Go get her, cowboy," muttered Ryan from his seat next to the show.

"Oh stop it," Connie hissed, finding her game face and following her son. Edging past the old couple who were eating their buttered teacakes and toast, Connie realised she was far too nervous to enjoy the aroma. It was her usual treat of choice whenever she came to Mariano's. A fruit teacake with butter and jam. Not today though. Today she had to make small talk with a woman of stature, a woman of presence, a woman whose calibre far outshone her own tiny light. Maria was a beacon, she was a match. Maria was a lighthouse, she was a torch – one of those crappy self-revving ones. Maria was a... Connie stopped herself. Maria was standing there smiling. *Speak, Connie, speak.*

"Sorry, Noah can be so loud. Don't let us disturb you. Noah say hello to Alice and let's leave Alice and her mummy to have their lunch in peace." Connie watched as her son reached onto the highchair and helped himself to a raisin. "Noah, no! They're Alice's raisins."

The dark-haired lady laughed. "It's fine, honestly."

"Sorry, he's..." Connie shuffled on the spot, finally lifting her eyes to Maria's.

The brown eyes smiled at the connection. "It's nice to see you again."

"Yeah, we come in here lots." Connie cringed at her sparkling wit and repartee.

"What do you think of it?"

"Hi guys, sorry to interrupt. I've just had a call from a client. I'm needed." Ryan stretched out his hand to Maria. "Ryan Morley, private masseur. You two met at the playgroup, didn't you? Connie can be incredibly shy, can't you, Con?" He nudged his best friend with his elbow. "It's alright if she joins you, isn't it? The kiddies will probably be off in the playpen soon so it seems silly for you two to sit all alone."

Maria returned the handshake and smiled. "I'm Maria."

"I know. Connie's already told me lots about you." He paused and nodded his head. "She was right. You do have the softest hands imaginable. Anyway, I'll go and grab the highchair and drinks." He turned to Connie and smiled. "I don't want you berating me for leaving you in the lurch."

Connie could feel the heat radiating out from her neck, face and forehead; even her earlobes felt as if they were on fire. "No, no, it's fine."

Maria reached out and touched Connie's shoulder. "Oh do, it would be nice to chat. Look at them, they look like twins."

Connie was unable to study the mops of blonde hair; all she could feel was the hand on her shoulder. She shifted slightly and took hold of herself. *Calm down, head up, act normal.* "Okay," she managed to say.

"Great." Maria clapped her hands together. "Can I get you a drink? A snack?"

Connie managed to breathe, pleased that the contact was over. "No, no, it's—"

Ryan cut in as he placed the highchair next to the table. "Your mocha's empty, Connie, and we were going to order some lunch."

Maria nodded. "So that's one mocha and what's Noah drinking?"

"No, no, he's got his beak—"

Ryan continued. "He loves the fruit juices, like Alice, and we usually let him share a panini. The ham and cheese one. Connie likes the toasted teacakes with butter and jam, and we sometimes let Noah choose a cake at the end."

Maria smiled. "I'll get a selection. Are you okay to watch Alice for a minute?"

Connie didn't realise it was a rhetorical question and stood frozen in shock as the woman with the penchant for leaving her daughter with complete strangers made her way to the counter. "She's left her kid with us!"

"She's only at the counter."

Connie continued to gasp. "She doesn't even know us! Who does that? I'd never do that. What if we were weirdos?"

"Speak for yourself."

"Plus she's one of those touchy feely type women. You know how much they scare me. Did you see her squeezing my arm?"

Ryan lifted Noah up and placed him in the highchair next to Alice. "She's just normal. You're the one with the issues."

"Please don't leave me. Say your thing's been cancelled." Connie paused. "You have got a thing, haven't you? You did get a call, didn't you? This isn't some stupid ruse to make me make friends, is it? It better bloody not be, Ryan. I'll come out in hives."

Ryan placed another chair at the table. "Sit down and act cool. She seems lovely. It'll do you good."

"Not when I end up in hospital suffering from palpitations it won't."

He reached out and held both sides of the blonde hair, cupping Connie's cheeks in his hands. "Chat. Make small talk. Enjoy the company." He kissed her button nose. "You'll be fab."

"They're the three things I'm most crap at."

"Connie Parker, you're a strange little beast." He smiled and pushed her down onto her seat. "Talk to Alice then, she seems cool."

Connie looked at the two highchairs and couldn't help smiling. Noah had taken charge of the raisins and was carefully sharing them out. "You owe me, Ryan."

Ryan shook his head. "No, I think it's you who's going to owe me. Right, I'm off. Say bye to Maria for me."

Maria stepped up to the table. "No need, I'm back. It was nice to meet you."

"Oooh you're like a midnight black panther, very stealthy." He nodded. "You ladies enjoy. Connie, I'll call."

Connie watched as her best friend strode away. She had no option but to fill in the silence. "That was quick service. They're usually so slow at the counter."

"Are they?"

"Yes, and the prices are simply outrageous. Their large drinks are the same size as the regular drinks in Starbucks yet they're much more expensive. Plus you only get a small slice of cake." She paused as a barista arrived at their table.

"Miss Mariano, did you want cream with the mocha?"

CHAPTER FIVE

Connie silently begged the ground to swallow her up. Here she was, less than thirty seconds in and already attacking the owner of what was actually her favourite ever coffee shop. "Sorry, I was just thinking of something to say. I really didn't mean it."

Maria pulled out the padded chair and sat down. "It's fine. It's good to get feedback."

"No, no, I love it in here. I really do. The prices are fine and the service is great. That children's playpen is simply genius."

The laugh was warm and endearing. "There's no need to go overboard."

"No, honestly. Noah loves the fact he can watch CBeebies in there without me moaning at him, and all the toys are fantastic. He can't get enough of the bead runners and the abacus, and that little slide's just perfect. It's so reassuring as a mother to know they're fenced in, and that it's at the back so no one's walking past who shouldn't be walking past if you know what I mean?"

"Do you always talk this fast?"

Connie flushed. "I'm sorry. I'm just trying to dig myself out of the hole I so gloriously fell into."

The laugh came again. "It's fine. You weren't to know, and like I said before, feedback's always important. I've been out of the business for over three years now." She looked at her daughter in her high chair and smiled. "I wanted to do the whole stay at home mum thing properly, so I avoided coming in."

Connie instantly warmed to the comment. "I'm a stay at home mum too," she said, smiling, "and if you *had* come in you'd have seen that I've been part of the furniture here for the past three years."

"So our paths were destined to cross."

The squeaking noise that came from Connie's voice box was mostly nervous fluster half articulated in an involuntary "Y-hah."

Maria smiled at the response. "So what did you do before you had Noah?"

Connie dropped her eyes to the table, trying to pull herself together. "I was a business development manager," she managed.

"And you'd develop my business by lowering the prices and increasing the staff."

"No!" Connie looked up in earnest. "I'm sorry. I really do love this place."

Maria reached across the table and squeezed Connie's hands. "I'm teasing you."

Connie couldn't hide her embarrassment. She sat still, looking at everything but the woman opposite her, turning to her son the minute her fingers were free so she could play with his hair and frantically ruffle the blond mop, waiting until the ability to converse returned to her. She finally coughed and managed to glance back. "So your real name's Mariano?"

Maria was still smiling. "No, it's worse than that. It's Maria Mariano."

Connie connected with the intriguing brown eyes. "Really?"

"Yes." Maria paused as the barista brought over their tray. "Thanks, Tony. Could we get some napkins as well please?"

Connie eyed the huge selection and reached for her purse. "Wow, thank you. How much do I owe you?"

"Don't be silly, it's on me," she said, cutting the paninis and placing small chunks onto both children's trays. "My father was Italian and my mother was English. They decided to raise me here but only on my father's condition that I stayed true to my roots," she laughed, "which is a bit of a joke really as we only ever went back to Italy twice and I can't speak a word of the language."

"Do you have any brothers or sisters?"

"No. My parents ran a bistro here in Shoreditch, just down the road in fact, with Dad's sister Maddalena. Their relatives would come over and visit a lot, especially my dad's brother Maurizio and their other sister Marcella. My dad was called Marti, and I think every single name in the Mariano clan for the past three generations has started with an M." Maria looked at her daughter. "I broke tradition by calling her Alice."

Connie laughed loudly. "I love that."

Maria smiled at the guard that was starting to drop. "Anyway, the restaurant was passed on to me when my mum and dad died."

"Oh I'm sorry."

"It's fine. They were old. One of those dying-within-weeks-of-each-other, broken heart type things. Well actually it was cancer for my mum, but anyway, these things happen."

Connie held her breath, mesmerised by this stranger's ability to open up so quickly. "You have a bistro as well?"

"No, I sold it and used the money to start Mariano's. I tried to hand the bistro over to my aunt Maddalena because she'd worked there most of her life, but she didn't want it. She helps out in here sometimes, but she's mostly down at the Covent Garden store."

"There's a Mariano's in Covent Garden as well?"

Maria nodded.

"Wow. Do you franchise?"

"Not at the moment, but that's the end goal ... or it was." She tilted her head from side to side in indecision. "Maybe. But if I do I'll be sure to call upon your business management skills."

Connie lifted an eyebrow. "I wouldn't. I only worked for a year before having Noah." She pointed at the plate with the buttered teacakes. "May I?"

"Of course. We should have some toast on the way too."

The fruity aroma was wonderful and Connie inhaled deeply, relieved that she was easing into the chat. "Is there a lot of competition from the other big brands?" she asked, this time able to look directly at Maria.

"Yes, but coffee's one of the fastest growing businesses. There's space in the market for all of us." Maria bent and moved her long brown hair away from her face, pulling the silky length over her shoulder as she nuzzled her nose against her daughter's cheek. "I've got Alice now and I think these three years away from work have made me look at life differently."

"Again, Mamma!"

Maria repeated the nose tickle. "Yes lady, you've changed my life haven't you?"

Alice giggled. "Again!"

"Noah do it!"

Connie watched as her son threw his face against his new friend's cheek. "Careful Noah."

Alice burst into fits of laughter. "Again, Noah! Again!"

Connie smiled. "I know what you mean though. I can't imagine my life without him. It's as if nothing really meant anything before, as if nothing was really real."

Maria's eyes were wide and the head nod was enthusiastic. "I know. It's like we're part of this secret group of people who've finally figured out what life's truly about."

Connie paused. "You'd really go that far?"

The endearing laugh sounded loudly. "I would. I'm serious. I know it sounds clichéd but they complete your life. They really do."

Connie saw the spark in the brown eyes and smiled. "Why don't some people get it? And by the way I love your laugh."

"You mean husbands and partners? And thank you, you're the cause of it."

Connie dropped her gaze to the table and played with the handle of her mug, trying desperately hard not to let her smile show too much. "Even some friends. So quick to get back to work. So quick to find time for themselves. So quick to palm their kids off to any Tom, Dick or Harry who'll have them."

"Like me when I went to the counter?" The lips turned wickedly at the corners. "You need to work on your whisper-voice."

"Oh no! I'm so sorry. It's me. I'm extreme. Yes, he's my life, but that means I literally have no life at all. I don't trust anyone, not even my mother and she's great with him. Ignore me. It's Ryan, he brings out my inner bitch."

Maria laughed. "So, who is Ryan?"

"Well he's not my partner."

"I gathered as much."

"Did you? Most people don't spot it." She picked up her mocha and took a slow sip, realising she was enjoying the fun conversation.

"The diamond earrings gave it away."

Connie laughed. "Not the impeccable grooming or designer attire?"

"Nope, the earrings."

"Bless him. He's been my best friend ever since school. He tries to spend as much time with us as possible."

"You and Noah?"

Connie nodded.

"No children of his own?"

"I thought you knew he was gay?"

Maria lifted her hands with indifference. "That doesn't matter these days."

"Ryan with kids? Ha, the thought!"

"Because he's gay?"

Connie paused, unsure if she sensed a slight edge. "No, because..." She glanced down at Maria's hand confirming the absence of rings.

Maria followed her stare. "Yes, I'm single ... and I'm a lesbian. I'm a single lesbian mother."

Connie's laugh was one of nervous anxiety. "Oh great! That's great! That's really great!"

"That I'm single? Or that I'm lesbian?"

Connie could sense the brown eyes pinning her to her seat. "I've just fallen back into that hole of mine, haven't I?"

Maria stayed quiet.

Connie took a deep breath. She shook her head at herself and leaned forward. "I am so sorry."

"I'm teasing you! It's fine! Are you always so anxious?"

Connie coughed. "Oh! So you're not..."

"Oh yes, I'm very much a single lesbian mother," Maria stroked her daughter's cheeks, "and I'm very proud of all of that."

Connie couldn't help it, the smile was infectious. "That's great!"

"Who are you convincing? Me, or you?"

"No, seriously, it's great." She looked at the woman carefully. "I just don't think I've ever met anyone quite like you before."

Maria reached across the table and tapped Connie's hand. "I'm not sure I've ever met anyone quite like you either."

CHAPTER SIX

Connie was sitting at the top of the stairs in her small terraced house singing the same song she'd sung every night for the past three years: *There's a hole in my bucket, dear Liza, dear Liza, there's a hole in my bucket, dear Liza a hole.* She had no clue why that had been her song of choice all those nights ago when she'd first stepped onto the never-ending parental roundabout of night-time soothing, but it was, so she sang it, religiously. Tonight's version, however, was quick and upbeat, and instead of sharpening the stone with a knife Henry went straight on to fetching more water. Connie knew she'd be caught out if Noah was awake, but if he wasn't then she'd save a good five minutes and be able to dash down to her cupboard more quickly. Her fingers had been itching all afternoon, desperate to type out their story. Bonnie Blythe was going to meet someone, in the supermarket, as she strolled around with the other woman's trolley. Connie thought back to her afternoon at Mariano's. It *was* true; you *could* meet someone interesting and unexpected in the strangest of places. She nodded to herself. Of course there was nothing romantic about her meeting with Maria, but the conversation had been sparky and at times quite intense; all the things she could use in her story.

She finished the final verse in her lowest and quietest voice and started her creeping descent of the stairs. He was asleep, he had to be; there would have been an outcry at the lack of Henry's knife sharpening and the absence of stones if he wasn't. She made it to the bottom step and paused once more, listening for any signs of movement. Nothing. She was safe, free, ready to dive straight back into the world on her screen where the characters seemed real and their stories so true. She slipped into the cupboard and switched on the screen. There it was: her domain. The one place where she had no limits or restrictions. The one place she actually felt free. Connie smiled to herself as she felt the wave of words surging through her fingertips. She started to type.

'Be yourself, they say. Originals are worth much more than copies. I wonder therefore why copies are made. Isn't it because the originals are so wonderful that they need to be replicated? I'd rather be a copy of something perfect than something no one actually wants. I stare at the space the woman's sports car has vacated. I'm going to be her, just for one day. I start my engine and move into gear, driving to where she once parked. I take her abandoned trolley and head towards the entrance, suddenly spotting her discarded receipt blown against the steel mesh. Bonnie Blythe, if you're doing this you're doing this properly. I nod to myself, ignoring the crinkling in my pocket from my own list of essentials. I lift her receipt instead. Shop like her, sashay like her, sod off like her. What a good plan.

I enter the warmth of the supermarket and flick my hair. She'd have flicked. I flick again. Maybe confidence is in fact an illusion. Maybe everyone acts. Maybe it's not about finding myself … Maybe it's about creating myself. I look at the receipt; a creation like her is a good place to start. First on the list: 1 x Maybelline Paint Me Red lipstick. I feel a pang of excitement and head towards the toiletries section. I only ever wear ChapStick, and that's always plain. I scan the selections, amazed by the huge variety of shades. There it is, Paint Me Red. I take off the top. I'm shocked by the intensely vibrant colour. I'd never buy this. I'd never even try this. I catch my reflection in the small tester mirror. It's full of fear. My plain face looks scared and my brown hair looks limp. I stare at myself. Just try it, Bonnie. Try it and buy it.

My sashay's definitely got sexier and my head's now held up high. I can feel the slight tackiness between by lips and can't help but pout. I scan the receipt again. Next on the list: 1 x Tampax Compak Lites. I strut to the feminine hygiene section and avoid looking down at my usual pack of night-time-plus-extra sanitary pads, reaching for the discreet box of tiny tampons instead. They're dropped into my trolley and I'm moving on, heading towards the fresh counter to pick up my 2 x monkfish fillets. I spot the sauce from the list: 1 x black olive fish dressing. I don't like fish and I never eat olives, but she does, and I'm her, just for today.

I look at the receipt and gulp. £14.99 for 1 x Blason Montagny Reserve. I'd never spend that on wine, certainly not on one bottle. I stop myself, always cautious and careful, so wary of cost. Not her. She lives the good life. She struts around in her lipstick, drinking fine wine and frying monkfish fillets with black olive sauce. I march to the drinks aisle and start my search, finally locating the bottle near the Champagne.

"That one's my favourite."

I turn around and see him. Tall, dark, talking to me.

"Really great with fish."

I take hold of my trolley for support.

He continues to talk. "What do you drink with your steaks?"

Damn, why couldn't the blonde bombshell have that on her receipt too? My eyes dart to the bottom shelf and spot the high price. "Cognac," I say.

The man laughs. "I like your style."

I watch his eyes glance over my trolley and am thankful for the tiny Tampax, not daring to think of his judgement had I purchased my usual super-plus-extra absorbency pads. I stop myself. I wouldn't have met him had I been shopping for me. I see him studying the fish and pre-empt his next question. "It's monkfish. It goes really well with the Montagny Reserve."

"And that's a black olive sauce I see?"

I smile and nod.

"I must try that one day." He steps into my space and offers his hand. "I'm Mark."

The shake is strong but the hand is soft. "I'm Bonnie. Bonnie Blythe.'"

The doorbell rang. Connie jumped up and clambered over her chair. She dashed through the lounge, hoping the caller wouldn't buzz again. They did. This time with an added knock.

"Muuuuuuuuuuuuuuuumeeeeeeeeeeeeeeeee!"

"It's okay, Noah, it's just the doorbell."

"Muuuuuuuuuuuuuuuumeeeeeeeeeeeeeeeee!"

Connie shouted back up the stairs as she opened the door. "It's okay, Noah."

"Is he not settled yet? He really ought to be in a routine by now."

Connie stared at her stern-faced mother-in-law. "He is. The doorbell woke him."

Evelyn bustled her way into the house and took off her rain mac. "Vivian's children could sleep through an earthquake."

Connie closed the door behind her uninvited guest. "That's worrying. They say you should get yourself under a table or into a doorway."

"Pardon me?"

"Muuuuuuuuuuuuuuuumeeeeeeeeeeeeeeeee!"

"Sorry, I'm going to have to go and settle him."

"I never have these problems when I babysit for Vivian."

Connie tried to remember the ages of Karl's sister's children, sure they were at least seven and eight. "Are you on your way over there?"

"I should be so lucky."

"Muuuuuuuuuuuuuuuumeeeeeeeeeeeeeeeee!"

"You're confusing me, Evelyn."

"Muuuuuuuuuuuuuuuumeeeeeeeeeeeeeeeee!"

"It's all this noise." Evelyn shook her tightly-permed grey helmet and frowned. "He really needs to stop being so demanding. Self-soothing and self-settling is a key element in a child's development. I was in nursing for forty years. I know what I'm talking about."

"Muuuuuuuuuuuuuuuumeeeeeeeeeeeeeeeee!"

"He was asleep."

"And why do you need that monitor? All it does is echo the racket around. Karl's right, there's simply no need." She sat down on the sofa. "I'm here to babysit."

"Muuuuuuuuuuuuuuumeeeeeeeeeeeeeeee!"

Connie tried to ignore her son's screaming. "We don't need a babysitter."

"Karl's taking you out. It's a surprise. He wants you to meet him at the Flag and Lamb at eight."

"Eight? That's in twenty minutes. I'm in my scruffs."

"I'm late. It couldn't be avoided. Malcolm needed his tea."

Connie bit her tongue. Malcolm was her mother-in-law's cat. "I don't think I'll have time to get ready."

"Well you shouldn't be in your..." Evelyn screwed up her already wrinkled face. "What did you call them? Scruffs? And what does that say across your rear end? Juicy?" She shook her head. "You must be careful not to let yourself go even further, Connie. No man wants a scarecrow as a house guest."

Connie quickly tried to flatten her hair. "I'm his partner, and this house is ours. I like to be comfy when I'm working."

"What do you mean working?"

She blushed. "I mean writing."

"Oh yes, Karl mentioned that as well. You must be careful not to let your," she quirked her fingers in quotation marks, "*little hobby* get in the way of your duties."

"Evelyn, your son gets a home-cooked meal on the table every single night that he's here."

"If you were more attentive and well-presented then he might be here more often."

"Excuse me?"

The silence was deafening.

Evelyn nodded. "See, I told you he'd self-soothe."

****

Connie marched into the Flag and Lamb with steam coming out of her ears. How dare Karl be so thoughtless? Sending his mother round unannounced and uninvited so she could spew her criticism at their perfect little boy. She scanned the modern bar and eaterie.

Because he *was* perfect. Noah was perfect in every single way. Evelyn had sat down and deliberately turned up the television's volume; of course he was going to wake up again, and no, there was no justification for Evelyn's subsequent stalk up the stairs and chastisement of Noah. *She* was the one responsible for the upset in the first place.

Connie slowed her march and cast her eyes across the couples dining at the tables and the singles drinking at the bar, her anger growing by the second. If Karl thought this evening was going to be relaxed and rewarding then he had another thing coming. How dare his mother be so bitchy? How dare she judge with such disapproval? How dare— Connie paused as her eyes found her man in the corner. He was sitting on the low sofas, head tilted back, smiling dreamily as he stared into space. Connie couldn't help it, he was a handsome beggar. She sighed and walked toward him. Maybe this *was* spontaneous and sweet. Maybe this *did* signal progress. Maybe he *should* be rewarded. She halted. The fucker was on the phone. She stopped and watched as Karl played with his hair, giggly and coy. She shook her head, the warm thoughts instantly freezing. Who the hell was he talking to?

Connie ignored the hovering waiter and stalked straight to the sofas.

"Hi."

Karl was obviously flustered and scrabbled with the off button of his phone as he scrambled to his feet. "Hey, Connie, surprise."

"Who were you talking to?"

"No one. Why?"

"You were and you didn't say bye. You just saw me and hung up." She folded her arms. "And I was watching you. Your face looked all goofy."

"And hello to you too." Her partner slumped back down onto the cushions.

Connie stayed standing. "Who was it?"

"No one."

"Yes it was."

"Connie, would you just sit down, please?"

"Why?"

"Because we're out. I've planned a nice night."

"For me? Or the person on the phone?"

"Oh for goodness sake, would you just grow up?"

The familiar stab of guilt that jabbed her conscience caused her to shift her weight on her hips. It was always the same whenever her age was in question. "I'm just asking who it was."

"No you're not. You're accusing me." Karl held out the phone. "It was no one. See for yourself."

Connie glanced around the room expecting all eyes to be focused on her. They weren't. She ignored the outstretched offering and sat down. "I've just had a hard evening."

"Why? What could possibly be hard about it: your boyfriend's taking you out, the babysitter's sorted, so have a good time?"

"That's not quite how your mother delivered it." She rubbed her face and looked up at the ceiling. "I was in my scruffs. I was already settled."

"You're twenty-five, Connie. Maybe it's me who's bringing out the worst in you. You used to be so much fun." He sat forward in his seat, looking pensive. "Having Noah seems to have cut off your lifeline."

Connie's eyes flashed with passion. "He *is* my lifeline. He's my life, Karl." She nodded quickly. "And he should be your life too."

"That doesn't mean we have to stay in every single evening sitting around in our scruffs."

"You don't have any scruffs."

"Exactly."

She smiled, picturing him in his royal silk pyjamas. "I should get you some scruffs. Some Donnay joggers and a McKenzie hoody."

Karl grinned. "Would they go with my Ralph Lauren socks?"

"I'd get you some white Dunlop ones instead."

He reached out for her hands. "This is the Connie I love. You're witty and funny, and I want to get *us* back."

"There are three of us now."

"No. If we don't have an *us*, then we don't have a family."

Connie shook herself free from his fingers. "Is that a threat?"

"No, it's..." He shifted in his seat and scratched the back of his neck. "We didn't plan him, did we? It makes sense therefore that he shouldn't inhibit our plans."

"Karl! I can't believe you just said that. Noah's done nothing but add to our lives."

"What lives? We work. Well I do. And then we sort Noah, and that's it."

"We cuddle up on the sofa. We chat about our day. We do stuff on the weekends that you're free."

"What? The zoo? The park?"

"Yes!" gasped Connie, exasperated. "What is this, Karl? You want out?"

"No! This has all gone horribly wrong."

"What? Meeting me? Having a child with me?"

"Tonight. This surprise. I just wanted a drink with my girlfriend. I thought we could have a laugh, maybe go dancing," he smiled, "and then pick up a stinky kebab on the way home. You love to dance, Connie. We met on the dance floor, remember?"

"You hate dancing."

"Not with you I don't."

"People with young children don't go out. It's a fact of life." She looked around at the mix of diners for confirmation. "I bet none of these people have children."

Karl nodded towards the bar. "Those men do."

"Yes, but they've been let off their leashes so their wives can get five minutes peace."

Karl nodded again. "Fine. That old couple in the middle, see them? I bet they do."

"Yes, but their kids have grown up. That's why they're smiling." Connie signalled towards a young couple who were sitting across a table in silence. "They do." She watched them. "They look utterly miserable."

"They're probably just on a first date and shy."

Connie shook her head. "No. They've not spoken since I arrived and they've got the tell-tale eye bags."

"People who work hard have eye bags."

"Not the sort you can pull over your head and wear like a balaclava they don't."

Karl laughed. "Like ours you mean?"

"Hey! I wore concealer." She sighed. "I don't want us to end up like them."

"So let's make time for each other." He looked at her carefully. "And I noticed. You and your makeup look lovely tonight. You honestly do."

Connie took a moment to absorb the kindness before reaching into her pocket for her phone. There were no missed calls or messages from Evelyn so she smiled and made her decision. "Drinks and a dance?"

Karl smiled. "Drinks and a dance." He picked up his phone and stood from the sofa. "I'll go and order."

"And you need your phone for that, do you?"

He wiggled the mobile towards Connie. "I'm on call. I'm always on call."

The phone started to ring.

Both saw the name on the screen: Louise.

CHAPTER SEVEN

A week had passed since the disastrous date night and Connie still couldn't let things lie. She'd brought it up again at breakfast that morning, asking why he'd refused to answer Louise's call. If she *was* simply his business partner he should have no problem answering his phone and talking business. He'd chosen, however, to ignore the ringing, even though in his previous breath he'd claimed he was always on call. Connie had bristled at his combative accusation that she was stupidly insecure and demanded his phone. She was *sure* he had been speaking to Louise as she'd arrived at the Flag and Lamb, and his denial simply fuelled her quest for the truth.

"Prove me wrong," she had said once again that morning, fully aware that it would all be deleted by now, but wanting to restate her point. "If you have nothing to hide you hide nothing at all." It was then that Karl got up and left without a word of goodbye. That's the one thing he always did: kiss her when he left for work in the morning and kiss her when he arrived home at night. Not today though. Today he'd just grabbed his gear and gone.

Connie tried to pull herself out of the over-analysing by refocusing instead on the bustle of the community hall around her, wishing that Ryan was there by her side. He'd get to the point. He'd assign the blame. He'd make her feel better. She looked towards the centre of the room and smiled at Noah who was playing with the soft blocks, building towers and knocking them down. It was a game that could go on for hours. She scanned the rest of the room, her attention drawn to Earth Mother – rushing around in an agitated fashion. The large lady was kitted out, as usual, in a full-length tie-dye sack of a dress, accessorised with her trademark non-brand walking boots and hair rag that kept her wispy ginger locks away from her face. Connie shuddered. One of Earth Mother's long boobs was hanging loose over the top of the dress for everyone to see, even though her son was nowhere nearby. She watched carefully. Earth Mother seemed to be calling for Lucas, but only in her quiet whisper-voice. She was one of those women who spoke without actually engaging their voice box, someone who assumed their hushed tones invoked calmness and harmony, when actually their words just passed by unheard.

Connie eyed the hall for Lucas. She scanned the arts and crafts tables near the coffee hatch and the messy play at the back of the room, unable to spot the young boy. He was usually dressed in some sort of homemade brown corduroy outfit which could blend into almost anything, but his wild orange hair was hard to miss. Connie looked back at Earth Mother who was now teetering, tit still out, on her tiptoes in a poor attempt at a bird's eye view of the room. Connie stood up; she had to help. It was still early and most of the regulars had yet to arrive so she knew it would be easy enough. She walked towards Noah in the centre of the room and stepped over his block fortress, crouching next to him with a cuddle.

"Hey Noah, I love this. Is it a castle?"

"Noah's castle."

"Can I play in it?"

"No. Noah want Liss to play in it."

Connie looked towards the door where Top Dog and her gang were now making their entrance. "I'm not sure if Alice is coming today." She paused, hearing the disappointment in her own voice. No firm plans had been made after their Mariano's visit, but she knew, given the number of times she'd already checked the door, that she was hoping to see the intriguing dark-haired woman once more.

She turned her attention back to her son. "Noah, have you seen Lucas?"

The little boy nodded. "Lucas in wendy house. Lucas *always* in wendy house. Noah want Liss to play in wendy house."

"Thank you, my gorgeous boy. I'll come and play if Alice doesn't come today."

"No, Noah want Liss."

Connie stood up and ruffled her son's hair, looking over to the small plastic house. She spotted Lucas inside, bobbing up and down, deliberately dodging the eyes of his mother. She smiled to herself; he was probably avoiding the ever present tit, thrust into his face at every possible opportunity. She glanced at Earth Mother who was quite ashen. Connie waved; she had to. She waved once more, finally gaining the flustered lady's attention, and pointed towards the little boy's hide-out. Earth Mother fanned her face and bustled her way over, bouncing her on-show bosom up and down in the process.

The voice was hushed. "Oh thank you, is he in there? Oh yes he is, isn't he. What a terror. Thank you."

Connie didn't hear a word of it. "He's in the wendy house."

"Thank you so much, thank you, thank you."

Connie spoke loudly. "It's a horrible feeling when you think you've lost them."

Earth Mother nodded in agreement. "I always stick to schedule."

"Pardon?" Connie couldn't hear her.

Earth Mother stepped in closer. "Snack time. I always stick to schedule."

Connie looked at the large clock hanging on the community hall wall. It was only five past nine and the children didn't sit for snacks until ten. "Snack time?" She hoped her firm voice would encourage a louder tone but Earth Mother simply came even closer and took hold of the loose breast, lifting it up with a smile. Connie coughed, unable to avoid the weathered looking teat. "Oh right."

Earth Mother presented the breast to her like a prized slab of meat. "Did you breast feed?"

Connie couldn't take her eyes off the udder. "Umm, yes, for just over a year."

"Oh well done!" Earth Mother stroked the toughened skin with her thumb. "Lucas is four now, but the longer the better they say. He loves his booby-dooby time. Now, where is that rascal?" She raised her voice slightly. "Lucas. Booby-dooby time. Here's the booby-dooby. Lucas?"

Connie watched as Earth Mother hurried off towards the wendy house but was unable to hide her distaste as the woman got on all fours, causing her boob to scuff the floor, back and forth.

"Why do I always miss the action?"

Connie spun around, instantly greeted by a warm kiss on both cheeks.

Maria was smiling. "How are you, Connie?"

"I, umm…" Connie fell over her words as she inhaled the sweet yet delicate scent of Maria's cherry blossom perfume. She'd smelt the same intoxicating fragrance at Mariano's last week and had gone home and Googled perfumes that contained cherry blossom, confident after a while that Maria must either wear Jo Malone or Guerlain. Ryan would know, he was good at things like that; in fact he'd probably chastise her for thinking that a woman like Maria would own perfumes that were easily Google-able from Fragrancenet or The Perfume Shop. Maria would probably have them handmade for her in some Indian palace or other.

"Connie?"

"Sorry, hi."

"Has that onslaught of breast got you all of a tizz?"

Connie couldn't help but glance at the open neck of Maria's fitted black shirt. "No, I…"

"Oh don't look now but the other one's popped out."

Connie snapped out of it and turned around to see Earth Mother still on all fours but with both breasts dragging along the floor as she chased, unsuccessfully, after her son. "I … wow … it's… It's just too early in the morning for that, isn't it?"

Maria smiled. "I'm a lesbian. I love it."

"Really?"

"No! Of course not. I like breasts, but not covered in floor grit."

Connie self-consciously lifted her hand to her multi-coloured cardigan, aware that the buttons could gape. She paused, registering Maria's comment. "Floor grit?"

Both women looked back at the scene and grimaced.

"Yes, floor grit. That's got to chafe." Maria turned away from the boob show and pointed at the plastic chairs over in the corner. "I hope you don't mind, I've put my bag with yours. I assume you're sitting in the same place as last week? Is Ryan here?"

Connie studied the fascinating features. "You're good with names. He'd be flattered. But no, he's not."

"I make sure I remember what's important. The rest of the time I'm a bit of a ditz."

Connie knew there was no possible way the woman standing in front of her with such poise and self-assured elegance was in any conceivable shape or form a ditz.

"Really?"

"Baby brain. Didn't you get it? I did. That's why I stayed off work so long. I was in no fit state to make any decisions. I once brushed my teeth with haemorrhoid cream."

Connie laughed. "Really?"

"Yes, and by the end of the pregnancy I was addicted to Tums. I literally suffered from every single ailment going. If you could get it, I got it."

"Swollen ankles?"

Maria nodded. "Check."

"Varicose veins?"

"Like a road map."

Connie laughed. "Really?"

"Yes! I got the anaemia, the back pain, the itchy skin, the—"

"Well you look great now." She blushed at herself for butting in.

Maria smiled. "Why thank you. But the baby brain still lingers."

"You're sure you can remember where we're sitting?"

Maria linked Connie's arm and started to walk. "You're funny, aren't you? Come on, let me show you the way, blondie."

Connie reddened even more. "Blondie?"

"It's better than shorty."

"Now that's low."

"I know. Is there a joke in there too?" Maria squeezed Connie's arm tightly into her own body. "Sorry. I'm giddy. You're the first adult I've spoken to in two days."

Connie laughed. "I have days like that. Stop walking so fast. You've got much longer legs than me. I'm only average remember."

"You're far from average."

Connie stayed silent, unsure how to reply, just relieved to have made it to the chairs so she could free up her arm. She looked towards the serving hatch for distraction. "Can I get you a tea, or a coffee?"

"As long as I can get you a real one in return from my place after we've finished here?"

"Mariano's?"

"Yes, or you and Noah could come back to mine? I'm easy, whatever you think."

"Mariano's sounds great." She looked back at the closed slats. "Oh sorry, they're not serving yet."

"Sit down then and tell me off for teasing you. It's far too early for nicknames."

"Ryan and I are ahead of you there. We've given every woman in here their own special nickname."

Maria pulled her chair closer and nodded towards Earth Mother. "I bet she's called Titty."

"Nope." Connie found the woman she was looking for and tilted her head her way. "*She's* called Titty."

The brown eyes widened at the tighter than tight vest top. "Gotcha."

"Your Titty's called Earth Mother."

"Nope. My titties are Perky and Pert."

Connie's cheeks flared as her eyes were drawn once again to the open-necked shirt. She swallowed quickly. "I mean the breast-feeder in tie-dye."

"I know you did." Maria waited until Connie looked at her. "You're far too easy to tease."

"No, I... I just don't click with people very often."

"Do we click?"

Connie smiled. "You've been here five minutes and already you're talking about your haemorrhoids and booby names."

Maria nodded. "We've had coffee so we're officially friends."

"You own a coffee shop. You must therefore have hundreds of friends."

"Maybe. But don't you find things change when you have children? Your childless friends are somewhat interested at the start, but that soon tails off, and your friends with their own children are busy drowning in motherhood just like you are." She pointed at her blonde-haired daughter who was now playing nicely with Noah. "But look what we get, so it's fab, and we love it, and we never ever moan." Turning her attention back to Connie she smiled. "Come on, give me a nickname."

"Okay, Salvador."

"I'm Italian, not Spanish."

"No, like the artist. Salvador Dali."

"Really? He's one of my favourites. I love art and paintings and I've got a special thing at the moment for sketches."

"The décor in Mariano's is amazing. I've often just sat for ages looking at the walls while Noah's playing." She smiled gently. "Anyway, I'd call you Salvador because what you see isn't quite what you get. You're curious, like his paintings."

Maria maintained their gaze. "And what do you see?"

Connie studied the refined woman sitting next to her. "I see an achiever. Someone who's got it all figured out."

"How? Why?"

"Your clothes, your hair. You're preened, you're together." She self-consciously fingered her messy blonde layers. "You look after yourself. You take care of your appearance. You have a three-year-old. How's that even possible?"

Maria laughed. "Trust me, this is a new occurrence. I've spent the last few years in pyjamas."

"See, that's hard to believe. You're Salvador because the whole concept of *you*, talking to *me*, is bizarre. I thought women like you preferred the company of men. You know the sort: powerful, intelligent—"

"I'll stop you right there. I *have* told you I'm a lesbian, haven't I?"

Connie couldn't stifle her laughter. "Yes, a number of times. But maybe I mean women like you don't usually talk to women like me. But you *are* talking to me, and you're friendly and fun, and we're getting on ... I think. Are we?"

"You shouldn't be so unsure of yourself."

"I'm just not particularly social, that's all."

"Should I go and talk to Loose-Titty-Tie-Dye instead?" Maria pointed to the arts and crafts tables where Earth Mother was now breast feeding her son on full display like a life model for the budding artists. "What do you call her friend? The one that's always with her? Is she called Jumpy?"

Connie followed the stare to the little boy in a bumper helmet who was being scooped up and away from the scissors. "That's Crusty."

"Oh no, now that's cruel. Jittery, or Skittish, maybe. But Crusty?"

"It's the flakes of skin. They're falling off her all the time and if you're sitting next to her at snack time your biscuits get an extra frosting."

Maria couldn't maintain a straight face. "You and Ryan are cruel. I'm not sure I want to be part of your mean-girl gang. Maybe I should go and join them over there. They seem to have a nice little group going on."

Connie looked at Top Dog and her gang of tattooed tag-ons. "They wouldn't let you in."

"Why not?"

"Your hair's not greasy enough."

"Ooo, you *are* a bitch, aren't you?"

"No, I'm joking."

Maria laughed. "So am I! I do have a tattoo though."

"Really?"

"No."

Connie couldn't help get drawn into the giggles, smiling with warmth at the enchanting woman's energy. "It wouldn't surprise me if you did have a tattoo, maybe tucked away somewhere private. I'm far too squeamish but I did have my belly button pierced once."

"Is that the craziest thing you've ever done?"

"Probably."

Maria leaned over and shook Connie's knees. "I do like you, Connie. You really are good fun."

"Honestly, I'm not."

Maria laughed loudly. "See what I mean?"

CHAPTER EIGHT

'You've captured my interest. You've occupied my mind. Your words penetrate my every thought. Your insights resound with such meaning. It's like you know me better than I know myself. How can this be when we've only just met?

Some say a door slightly ajar is more intriguing than one fully open, but you're fully open and I'm fully intrigued. You chose me. You talked to me. You wanted to know more. Why?

Stop questioning, Bonnie; just go with the flow.

Mark smiles with sincerity. "This date has been lovely. May I see you again?"'

The mobile phone vibrated gently next to Connie's keyboard and she stopped typing. Number unknown. She left the phone where it was and looked back at her screen, re-reading the last sentence. She paused, glancing down at the caller and wondering if it might be...

She lifted the phone and answered quickly. "Hello?"

"Hey, Con!"

"Oh, hi."

"Sorry, were you expecting someone better?"

She pushed herself away from her work desk and swivelled round on her chair. "No. It's good to hear from you. How's the conference?"

"Hot!"

"In what way?"

"All ways. Temperature. Masseurs. How was the playgroup?"

Connie laughed. "Ryan, you're phoning me from Malta to ask about playgroup?"

"Yes. It's the highlight of my week. I've missed it more than I imagined."

"It was normal."

"Oh, Connie, you have to give me more than that! Was hotty with a botty there?"

"Who?"

"Don't play dumb with me, young lady. Amal Clooney. Miss Mariano! I've been dying for an update."

She closed her eyes and smiled to herself. "She might have been."

"She was, wasn't she!? And you two spent the whole time gossiping, didn't you!"

"Maybe."

"Is she as fabulous as first thought?"

"She's intriguing."

"Oh Connie, steady on love. She'll only break your heart."

"Stop it, Ryan. She's intriguing because she's interested in me. She must have such an amazing life full of amazing people—"

"You're a bit of blonde fluff. She's a lesbian. Of course she's playing all pally. It's the first step before she pounces. Plus it's pretty slim pickings at that playgroup. I'd talk to you over Top Dog and Crusty."

"No, we get on well, that's all."

"I bet you do. Have you found out how old she is?"

"Thirty-five."

"Nice. Experienced."

"It was fun. We swapped numbers."

"YOU DID WHAT?"

"Ryan! Noah's asleep!"

"He can't hear me! You swapped numbers?! The woman who hates making friends, hates even talking to new people, swapped numbers? Wait a minute, you thought it was her on the phone! You did, didn't you? When you answered?"

"I did not."

"You did! I could tell by the tone of your voice."

Connie leaned back in her chair and glanced along the hall towards the baby monitor in the kitchen. "I need to go. Noah might wake."

"No he won't. Talk to me. I'm not back until Sunday. What else is happening?"

"Bonnie's met someone."

"Who?"

She pulled herself back towards her computer. "Mark."

"No, who's Bonnie? And who's Mark? I go away for a week and you transform your friendship circle! What's got into you?"

"Bonnie from my book."

"Oh sorry, I thought we were talking reality?"

"It is real for me." She smiled. "Bonnie met him in the supermarket. He's tall, dark, handsome, well-to-do."

"Like Maria."

"No! He's a man and they've gone out on a date. They got chatting down the wine aisle and clicked straight away."

"Is Bonnie intrigued by him?"

"Yes, she's…" Connie paused. "I can hear you smirking. I know you think my book's nonsense."

"No, darling, it's not that. It's… Never mind, tell me more."

She turned herself back towards her screen. "The problem is, Bonnie isn't quite being herself and she starts to worry that Mark won't like the real version of her."

"Are you being yourself with Maria?"

"What's this got to do with Maria?"

"It's just a question."

"Of course I am. When am I ever anything other than myself?"

"When you're with Karl. How is that knobsack by the way?"

"Still at work." She lowered her voice. "We had a horrible date the other night. He arranged for his mum to come and babysit, which was horrific enough in itself, but then I had to meet him at the Flag and Lamb and when I arrived I caught him on his phone. I'm sure he was talking to Louise."

"That bitch?"

"I don't know, maybe. But anyway, his phone rang again later on and it was definitely her."

"Did he answer?"

"No."

"You need to check that phone."

Connie shook her head. "I tried but now that's made me the person he always accuses me of being. Insecure. Needy. Infantile."

"Oh darling, you need to get out."

"No." She sighed. "He's a good guy. We're making this work."

"Saying things over and over won't make them real."

"I know, but I love him and I love Noah, and…" She stopped. "Why are we talking about this when you're millions of miles away?"

"Because I'm all you've got."

"Nope," she smiled into the phone, "I've got Maria now."

"Ooo you little vixen. Go on then, call her up. Bore her with all of your whining."

"Will do, speak soon."

"Wait, wait, wait! Seriously, Connie, you have her number?"

"Yes, she put it in my phone today."

"WHAT? She actually physically took your phone and input her number?"

"Yes."

"She wants you."

"Oh stop it, Ryan."

"She does. It's powerful. It's confident. It's her way of saying I'm here, I'm ready, let's go. You should text her."

"No, I'm busy."

"Doing what?"

"Writing."

"And tomorrow?"

"I'm off to Bounce-a-rama."

"Invite her. That's perfect. You can roll around together on the inflatables."

"I'm not a lesbian!"

"Ooo how prejudiced. You *can* be friends with a lesbian you know."

"I know."

"So invite her."

"I might."

"Just type: Bounce-a-rama tomorrow at ten a.m. Les be friends."

"I'm going. I'll speak to you soon."

"Okay, but before you go, repeat after me: Karl's a cocksucker."

"No."

"Do it, or I'll keep teasing you about the Connie, Bonnie, Maria, Mark love quadrangle. Karl's a cocksucker. Say it, Connie."

Connie laughed. "Karl's a cocksucker."

"Again."

"Karl's a cocksucker." She froze, feeling the firm hand tightening on her shoulder.

"Give me that fucking phone."

CHAPTER NINE

"I said, give me that *fucking* phone."

Connie pressed the receiver into her lips and spoke quickly. "I've got to go."

"Don't you dare." Karl grabbed the mobile from Connie's grip and snarled into the mouthpiece. "Who the fuck is this?"

"Karl, leave it." She watched as her boyfriend's forehead flared with anger. "I was messing around. Please, let's not wake Noah."

Karl ignored her, listening to the caller's response instead. "Ryan? You fucker. I should have known it was you. Fact is you're the actual cocksucker, mate, not me. Now piss off and leave us both alone." He hit the red button and stared down at the wide eyes in front of him. "What the hell are you doing, Connie?"

"He's in Malta. You know what he's like, he's always messing around."

"You told him I was a cocksucker."

"He made me say it."

Karl shook his head in disbelief. "What?"

"He was just teasing me."

"He told you to call me a cocksucker so you did it?"

She stood up and tried to reach out for her boyfriend. "He's just an idiot."

Karl stepped backwards. "I think I'm the idiot here. Seriously, how old are you?"

"I'm old enough to know better. I'm sorry."

"Don't bat your eyes at me, Connie. That doesn't work anymore. Just grow up and get a life."

"Where are you going?" She watched as he made his way towards the front door. "Please, Karl, I've made us a curry. I want to make up for this morning. I shouldn't have brought up that Louise thing again. I really am sorry."

"I'll eat out." He threw the mobile onto the sofa and stalked out of the house.

"Don't slam..." Connie shuddered as the door slammed. She stood still and waited for the inevitable holler.

"Muuuuuuuuuuuuuuuumeeeeeeeeeeeeeeeee!"

"It's okay, sweetheart. It's just the door. Mummy's here." She stayed quiet and hoped for the best, relieved with the silence that followed. Waiting for a further minute she finally dared creep towards the sofa. Sitting down slowly and clenching her fists she let out a long silent scream. What was she doing? Why was she getting things so wrong? How could he tell her to get a life when this *was* her life and she was trying her *best* to lead it? To own it. She shook her head. To want it. She lifted her phone and started to type.

I'm so sorry. I'm an idiot. I'm immature and can get carried away being silly. Forgive me?

****

Karl loosened his tie in the warm evening sun. The start of the summer had been typically British with wind, rain and sleet the dominant weather for most of May and June, but as July had finally come into focus the sun had shone and London's propensity for high-collared black trench coats was slowly being replaced by a sea of tan-coloured macs. Karl took his off and threw it over his arm, walking as fast as he could with no intention of stopping no matter how many times his phone beeped. How dare she betray him like that? How dare she indulge that wanker's behaviour? He crossed the road and ducked into Hoxton tube station, making his way down to the platform. It was late but he'd head back into work. He'd eat at his desk. He might even stay there all night. Checking the overhead announcements board he saw that the next tube was due in three minutes. He sat down on the cold metal bench and stared up at the white arched ceiling, sighing in confusion. What was he doing wrong? How else could he please her? Wasn't it enough that he was there? Present. He'd stood by her. What more did she want? What more did she need? Karl closed his eyes. What did *he* want? What did *he* need? His message tone beeped twice more as his phone connected to the underground's Wi-Fi. Taking it out of his pocket he ignored the texts and dialled a contact instead.

"Hey. Are you still at work?" He waited for the response. "Great, I'm coming back in." He paused, biting on the inside of his lip. "And you're right." He spoke with a smile. "We want the same thing."

****

Connie checked the clock on the wall. It was almost midnight. She reached behind the sofa and found the fleece blanket that had once served as Noah's first play mat. Pulling it over herself she typed out one final message.

Please, if you don't want to sort this out, if you don't want to make this work, then let me know and we can stop wasting each other's time.

She reread her words, desperate to press send, but unable to touch the green button. Instead she deleted the message and started again.

I know I don't deserve you. I know I don't deserve us. You've given me everything. A house, a home, a family. I appreciate it all. But I want you ... and I want you to want me too.

She tapped the green button and watched the message fly away, hoping it would bring him home soon.

****

"Surely you're going home soon?" asked the woman sitting upright on the high-backed chair.

Karl pushed the box of takeaway noodles across the desk that was the main feature in his large centre room office and dropped his head onto his outstretched arms. "What does it say again?"

"Sit up, you're not drunk."

He tilted his head to the left and then the right, looking out of his tinted panoramic windows at the clusters of empty workstations that surrounded them. "I think I am."

"Then you're a lightweight. You've only had one bottle."

Karl stayed where he was, dropping his face onto the expensive suede desk pad. The lights in the office were low but still he chose to shield his eyes from their glare. "Read it again?"

The female voice spoke more firmly. "No. You heard it the first time. She says she's sorry, she appreciates you and she wants you. All of the things that *you* should be saying to *her*. All of the things that matter. She's the mother of your child, Karl, and she wants you. She wants you home."

He dragged himself up onto his elbows. "What if I want you, Louise?"

"Right, that's it. I'm calling you a cab."

The sorrowful speech continued. "We had it, didn't we? That thing? That spark?"

Louise Killshaw stood from her seat and straightened her skirt, pulling her jacket from the back of the chair and taking out her Collis & Killshaw security pass which she looped round her neck. "Go home, it's late." She tightened her long dark ponytail and combed her fingers through her blunt fringe.

Karl watched her. "We did, didn't we? We had fun?"

"No." The upscale businesswoman pushed the mobile phone back across the desk to its owner, who left it stranded, not interested in reading the message for himself. "At some point you need to grow up and take responsibility," she said.

"How shit's that?"

"That's life."

"What if I don't want that life?"

"Oh Karl, why do you have these ridiculous self-doubting self-pitying breakdowns? You did it when we secured these new offices, remember? Worrying that we'd be over-stretched. And then when Noah was born, claiming he'd be better off without you."

Karl threw his hands over his ears. "Alright, alright."

"No. Life's simple. This new venture in Manchester is simple, and you're the perfect man for the job. You know it and I know it." She picked up her bag and tucked it neatly into her shoulder. "If you don't want Connie, you tell Connie."

"And I'd get you?"

"Oh Karl, you are drunk." She moved the chair back into its original position in the corner of the precisely decorated office. "You'd never get me. And can we clarify one final time that you never really had me. I'm your friend, your business partner of ten years, and now apparently I'm your confidante." She paused. "Your date night the other night, did you do what I said? Did you take flowers? Did you shower her with fine wine and affection?"

"No, we went to the Flag and Lamb and it sucked."

"If you don't listen to me then you need to stop asking me." She checked her watch. "I really need to go."

"Fancy man waiting up for you is he?"

"No. I work hard. I get home late. I like to relax."

"I could come? We could relax together?"

Louise walked round to the other side of the desk and crouched, connecting with Karl's tired eyes. "You've had your sulk. Go home, say sorry, and suck up that so called shitty life that most people actually dream of."

"It wouldn't be shitty if I had it with you."

"I told you. Never. Going. To. Happen."

CHAPTER TEN

"Thank you so much for inviting me; this place is amazing!" Maria gazed in disbelief at the brightly decorated warehouse jam-packed full of inflatables. "I didn't know places like this existed. I've been to all the regular play centres with slides and tumble gyms and things, but never anything like this. It's incredible."

Connie pointed to the back of the Bounce-a-rama building. "That whole area is one big inflated pillow. Noah loves that best. Then over there to the left are the three standard bouncy castles."

"They're hardly standard; look at them!"

Connie laughed. "You seem excited."

"One's a pirate ship, one's a Barbie castle and the other's a train. Who wouldn't be excited?"

Connie smiled, finding Maria's enthusiasm contagious. "It gets better. On the right over there by the café are the castles with slides, and behind us there's a tunnel maze which is actually pretty dark." She dropped her bag onto the table. "We get to sit in the middle here so we can see exactly where they are and what they're up to."

"Great layout, but I'm not sitting down."

Connie looked the slim woman up and down. "You're hardly dressed to go crazy."

"You only messaged me an hour ago. I was on my way out."

"To the opera?"

Maria lifted her hands to her white jeans, white shirt and blue blazer. "I'm never taking you to the opera if you'd wear something like this. I was off to a meeting."

"At Mariano's?"

She removed her jacket and threw it onto the table. "They've survived for the past three years without me. Missing one meeting won't make any difference." Holding onto the back of the chair she kicked off her heels. "I can't believe how quiet it is here."

Connie looked over to the inflated pillow where Noah and Alice were already bouncing around. "The mornings are reserved for children aged one to three. Then at twelve the four and five year olds can come in. Then after school it's a free for all. I brought Noah once and the big kids were far too rough for him. There won't be more than five mums here this morning."

"Really? And we can bounce?"

"As long as it looks like you're helping your child."

"She doesn't need help. I'm off. That slide's got my name on it." Connie laughed. "Maria!"

"What? Come on. No one's checking."

"Don't you want a coffee first?"

"No! Be there or be square."

Connie watched as the naturally poised woman dressed all in white with silky dark hair threw herself up the steps to the bouncy slide. She glanced back at Noah and Alice who were perfectly happy jumping together and rolling around. "Oh what the hell," she said, giggling and crouching to untie her laces.

****

"So, how did it go?" asked Louise.

Karl looked up and saw the tits and teeth peering around his large office door. "How did what go?"

His fresh-faced business partner stepped into the room sporting a pin-striped trouser suit and a higher than usual, but still perfectly straight, ponytail. "Oh, Karl! You've got the same shirt on as yesterday. You didn't go home, did you?"

"I did," he lied, rubbing his face and pulling himself further under his desk.

"No you didn't. You've got stubble. You never have stubble."

"I fancied a change."

Louise moved to the corner of the room and looked into the bin. "Our takeaway's still in here. The cleaners haven't been in. They probably saw you snoring away and left you to it."

"I've got work to do."

"You've got a hangover."

Karl adjusted his laptop screen and ran his finger over the mouse pad. "Seriously Louise, you need to leave me alone."

"Hey macho man, that's not how it works. You can't ask me to spend my life with you one minute then palm me off the next."

"I did not—"

"Yes you did. Maybe not in so many words, but that's what you alluded to. And you didn't even confirm your decision on the Manchester office. On the phone you said you wanted what I wanted, and we both know that I want you there."

"Can we not rehash my drunken ramblings, and I don't know what I want."

Louise reached for the high-backed chair and parked it in front of his desk. "Why didn't you go home?"

"Seriously, don't sit down. I haven't got time for this."

She sat down and crossed her legs, twitching her elevated foot up and down, flashing the red underside of her Louboutin heels. "Yes you have. Tell me what's happening." She glanced at the wall clock before focusing back on the task in hand. "Tell me."

"I need to finish the Richardson claim."

"What? You haven't finished the Richardson claim?" The long dark ponytail swayed from side to side as she shook her head. "That was due Monday!"

"I know, so please, if you'll leave me to it?"

"I'll finish the Richardson claim for you. You take yourself home, freshen up, apologise to Connie and get back in time for the Manchester investors' meeting at four."

"I can't."

"Why not?"

"She won't be home. She takes Noah to Bounce-a-rama on Thursdays."

"And your pride doesn't want you to show up all grovelly in front of her friends?"

"She goes on her own."

"So go! Take flowers. Tell her you're sorry. Sort yourself out and get back here looking the part."

Karl scratched his stubble and checked the clock. "You don't mind?"

"You're useless when you're like this. I manage you like I manage all our company's employees. I know how to bring out the best in you and this is for the best. You need to get yourself sorted." She nodded. "And anyway, we're partners; it's what partners do."

Karl smiled. "You'd make a good—"

"Change. The. God. Damn. Record."

****

"Be there or be square? Who actually says that anymore?" Connie was sitting next to Maria at the top of the tallest inflatable slide that looked out across the echoing expanse of the brightly coloured warehouse.

Maria brushed dust off her white trousers and smiled. "I do. I also say you shouldn't miss moments. Life's short. People spend too long waiting for that special day, that special person, that special moment. Waiting for a time when they think everything will finally fit into place. Life's not perfect and that time might never come, so you make your own happiness, you fulfil your own dreams. You enjoy every day for what it is: unique, special and only lived once."

"Oh, I thought you'd want to come back again next Thursday?"

Maria laughed loudly. "Yes I do, and I'd like many more moments like this." She grabbed hold of Connie's hand and flung herself off the slope, pulling Connie down with her.

Connie wailed as she sped after the woman, coming to a rather awkward stop at the bottom of the slide with her face somehow plunged into Maria's ample chest. She pulled back quickly. "I'm so sorry."

"I'm not, I'm a lesbian, it's fine."

"Oh, I..." Connie jumped up and dusted herself off.

"I'm teasing you. I love having a woman's face in my cleavage. Now help me up, would you?"

"Sorry, I couldn't stop myself."

"That's what they all say."

Connie flared with colour. "Sorry, I..."

"Come on, I'm older than you, I need a hand."

"Right, sorry." She took hold of the soft fingers and pulled.

Maria rose from the floor but prolonged the contact, holding onto the hand and smiling at Connie. "Thank you. I'm sorry. I'll stop with the teasing. Let me get you that coffee."

"No, it's fine. You're funny. It's... I can just get awkward sometimes, that's all." She paused, aware that her rambling wasn't needed. "A mocha would be great." She watched as Maria walked to their table for her purse. Her white jeans and white shirt were now scuffed with dirt, and her silky brown hair was slightly more wayward, but still she looked preened and perfected, like an Arabian princess at an evening soirée. Connie snapped herself out of it and turned towards the inflated pillow. Noah and Alice were now chasing a new boy around. She walked their way and watched them for a while before gaining their attention.

"Are we ready for snack time yet, guys?"

Noah shook his head. "Noah and Liss chase Doo-Doo."

"Doo-Doo?"

"Yes, Doo-Doo." Noah pointed at the new boy and bounced after him.

"Alice, would you like some snacks?"

"No, I chase Doo-Doo."

Connie smiled and waved at the new little boy who seemed to be enjoying himself too. "Hello, I'm Noah's mummy; what's your name?"

The little boy giggled his way past his two new friends. "Doo-Doo."

Connie laughed. "Okay then. You guys come over when you're ready for a snack. We're just sitting in the middle. Can you see where?" All three children ignored her and continued their game so she spoke to herself. "*Yes, Mummy. Thank you, Mummy. See you soon, Mummy.*"

"No one's listening to you." Maria handed over the steaming mug of coffee and waved at her daughter. "Alice, are you okay?"

"Yes, Mama. Go away, please."

"Right." Maria nodded. "That's both of us told. Shall we sit?"

"With pleasure; I'm exhausted."

"No you're not. We haven't even done the dark tunnel maze yet."

"I've never done the dark tunnel maze."

Maria placed her drink on the table and sat down. "I'm good with dark tunnels."

Connie laughed. "Another lesbian joke?"

"No, I'm talking about Italy. One of the things I do remember was the drive over there through lots of really long dark winding tunnels."

"Oh sorry, I…"

Maria pulled back a chair for the blushing blonde. "Of course it's a lesbian joke. Us lady lovers enjoy exploring dark tunnels."

Connie couldn't help but grimace.

"You pulled a face! You're one of *those* straight girls, aren't you? I'll have to listen to your endless tales of male sexual relations but the minute I want to divulge anything all-female you'll clam up."

Connie placed her mocha on the table and sat down. "Clam up? Surely there's a lesbian joke in there somewhere, isn't there?" She smiled. "Anyway, people with three-year-olds don't have *relations.*"

"Don't they?"

"Well they have birthdays. You know the type," she mouthed the words, "where you're obliged."

Maria laughed. "It's my birthday soon."

"Should I oblige?" Instantly Connie tried to cover her face with her hands. "I'm so sorry. I have no idea where that came from. I try and keep up with your joking and the wrong words fall out of my mouth."

"That's the best offer I've had in years."

Fanning her face Connie continued. "I don't even talk to my real friends like that."

"Real friends?"

"Sorry, I mean…" She lifted her mug and took a large gulp, scalding her tongue and spilling some froth. "Oh look at me. I'm all of a dither."

"All of a dither? Who says *that* nowadays? And why aren't I a real friend yet?"

Connie placed her mug back on the table and tried to cool her cheeks with the backs of her hands. "Don't you think it's strange how we're chatting? Like we've known each other for years?"

"We're in week two. We click, that's all. Our friendship's developing."

Connie shrugged. "But *how* do we click? How is it possible? You're like some mature, sophisticated international business woman, and I'm just a short, plump mother of one."

"You're not plump," Maria enforced her words, "*at all.* And I'm not sure how I've ever acted mature and sophisticated. Didn't you see me on that pirate ship?"

Connie laughed. "It's your presence. There's just something about you. It's something that usually scares people like me off women like you. You have that sort of air of togetherness."

"You *can* be together and still have good fun."

"I know, but it's like I was saying before. What you see isn't quite what you get with you. You dress beautifully. Your hair's always perfect. Your figure's incredible. You've got businesses. Your life's on a path." She paused. "But then you're all chatty and open and you can get giggly and," she crinkled her nose, "a bit silly sometimes. It's just not what you'd expect when you look at you."

The soft lips turned at the corners into a thoughtful smile. "Perspective's funny isn't it. Everyone always thinks the grass is greener on the other side, but no one's living that perfect life. The key is just to water the grass on your own side of the hedge."

"I live in a barn."

Maria laughed. "Well it must be a beautiful barn *conversion* with huge sash windows and a paddock at the back because what I see is a free spirit who's friendly and fun and loving her life."

Connie sighed and dropped her eyes to her mug. "My partner Karl didn't come home last night. I'm not loving my life and I'm anything but free."

"Oh, I…"

"Sorry, I shouldn't have said that. You bring out the fun me. I don't want to drag us both down."

Maria tilted her head to the side. "I'm a lonely old lesbian with no real friends. Does that help?"

"Ha. A little bit. But I know you're lying."

"Well I'm friendly with lots of people: my employees, my neighbours, the mums at the groups. But my real friends have moved on with their lives. I see them now and again, but it's never the same. It's not their fault. They've got partners and only need to dip in and out every so often. But I do miss their company."

"You must have one best friend though? Women like you always have that one posh person they lunch with, gossip with and shop with."

"Oh I have those, but they're typically false and quite bitchy."

"So why suddenly turn up at the community hall playgroup? Did you want to enhance your social group with women like Crusty?"

Maria shifted in her seat. "No. I had one best friend. Phoebe. We'd known each other since school. She thought I was doing the wrong thing when I said I wanted to raise a child on my own. She tried to talk me out of it, told me I was selfish." Maria paused. "I really needed her, but she walked away. She couldn't support my decision and I lost her."

"What a bitch."

"Not really; people are entitled to their own opinions. But I'd heard on the grapevine that she'd got married and had a baby and I just thought she might be there. I guess I wanted to show her how well I was doing and how precious and perfect Alice is." She smiled. "I've been trying a new group each week for the past couple of months now. I only came back to the community centre so I could see you again."

Connie rolled her eyes. "Yeah right." She sipped on her coffee and thought out loud. "Don't you have her number though? Can't you just call her?"

Maria shrugged. "I think I'm a bit proud. I want to accidentally bump into her and make her realise she's wrong without having to say a single word." She nodded towards the giggles coming from the bouncy pillow. "Alice is the one thing I know I've got right. The one decision I know was my best."

"Don't worry. I'll find her on Facebook. I'll stalk her for you." Connie snarled. "We'll show her. She'll be grovelling to have you back, but I'll be there wagging my finger saying nuh-uh she's mine now." The laugh that Connie loved to hear rang out once more. "It's true," she said with a smile.

"And what do you want me to do for you?" asked Maria.

"Just hanging out like this is great. It takes my mind off things."

"What's your partner's name again?

"Karl."

"I could tell Karl he's a twat for leaving you home alone."

The voice was low and irritated. "I'd rather you told Connie that private lives should be kept private."

Connie spun round and looked up at her boyfriend. "Karl! What are you doing here?"

"Wasted journey I guess." He shoved the bunch of flowers onto the table. "I'll get back to work."

"Wait! Noah's over there."

Karl glanced towards the bouncy pillow and scratched on his stubble. "No, he's having fun. I'll see you at home."

"Now?"

"This evening. I'll be late." He turned around and stared at her coldly. "Oh, and Connie, if this is what you do all day then I think it's about time you went back to work."

Maria waited until the man was out of earshot. She whispered quietly. "Do you want to come and play in my field for a bit?"

CHAPTER ELEVEN

Upon lifting the lid of the slow cooker, aromatic steam wafted up Connie's nostrils. She inhaled the lemon and garlic scent and smiled to herself. Surely this would soften him? She'd ripped the recipe out of a battered copy of the Sainsbury's magazine that had been propped alongside other equally-as-old issues of Reader's Digest and WellBella in the newspaper rack at the dentists. That's how her day had progressed: fun with Maria, chastisement from Karl, then praise from the dentist. Noah's teeth were in perfect condition and he'd opened wide whilst sitting still throughout the whole ten minute ordeal; quite a feat according to Dr. Singh who actually had an acute fear of three-year-olds himself.

She had then rushed to the supermarket, picking up the chicken breasts, the expensive bottle of white wine and the other ingredients that would make her apology even more noteworthy. She inhaled once more and used a wooden spoon to coat the breasts with more juices. The recipe had guaranteed a "succulent mouth-watering melange of chicken, lemon and garlic, served best with mushrooms and rice". She looked at the clock and checked the time. It was nine p.m. already; how much later was late? She'd already pre-fried the mushrooms and given some to Noah on toast for his tea. The sizzling could often set off the smoke alarm and the last thing they needed was a crying child to contend with, so she'd pre-empted the drama and cooked them first. She'd also laid up to avoid the clinking of cutlery and the crashing of plates. Nothing was going to distract them from their discussion.

Emptying the pan of mushrooms into the slow cooker and stirring them in, she nodded to herself; because it *would* be a discussion. Yes, she'd probably have to make a long-winded apology first, but then they'd discuss. They'd hash it all out. She replaced the lid on the cooker pot and looked around at the room. It was still a small and basic kitchen, but the candles looked pretty and the lighting was low. Re-straightening the napkins and glancing back at the clock she knew there was nothing more she could do until he was home. Maria's advice had been to ignore him and make him see sense. How dare he come in, catch the tail end of a conversation that wasn't even Connie's fault, then rebuke her in front of a stranger. In Maria's opinion it was *he* who should be apologising, not her.

Connie sighed and crept into the lounge, thinking about turning on the TV. She shook her head. It was too big of a risk. If Noah was up when Karl came home then he really wouldn't be happy. She turned instead to the cupboard under the stairs. Bonnie wasn't calling her but there was nothing else to do. She paused. What if Karl and his mother were right? What if the whole thing was just ridiculous? Did anyone truly want to read about trolleys, supermarkets and people pretending to be people they weren't?

She sat down and stared at the screen. Maybe Bonnie would get her comeuppance? Maybe Bonnie would learn that there's no virtue in living a life that's not really yours. She lifted her fingers to the keyboard, all too aware of that feeling.

'There's a fine line between being yourself and bettering yourself. People have to change if they want to grow, don't they? And growth's what life's about, isn't it?

My reflection in the mirror's confusing me. My makeup's brighter and my hair's bigger, but my eyes are the same: shy, unsure, hesitant. I step closer and stare. Who am I trying to be? What am I trying to prove? I snap myself out of it. *Bonnie, you're doing this.* Mark's the first person to take an interest in god knows how long, and this is what he wants. This is who he wants. This is the person he met down the wine aisle with the monkfish in her trolley. Big, bold, brash and bolshie. The type of woman who reapplies her red lipstick whilst she's wining and dining. The type of woman who orders the salad and leaves half

on the plate. The type of woman who cares about wine lists and not about cost. That's what I'm doing. That's who I am.

I hear the beep of a horn and race to the window. A sports car or a luxury 4x4? I hide behind the curtain and take a look. Maybe he's ordered a limo? I stare again and wait for the beep. He'd insisted on driving so he must want to show off. I feel a buzz of excitement as the horn sounds again. My eyes follow the noise. *What's that?* A Ford Fiesta? He's driving a Ford Fiesta? What's he doing driving a Ford Fiesta? I drive a Ford Fiesta! People like him don't drive Ford Fiestas! He spots me and waves at the window. I draw back, thrown by this insight.

By the time I arrive at his car he's out with the passenger door open.

"Hi Bonnie, great to see you."

"You too, Mark." We share an awkward handshake.

"Shall we?"

I look at the open door and worry that my heels are too high to make an elegant entrance into the car. "Thank you," I mumble, as I struggle in.

Mark shuts the door behind me and moves around to his side. He climbs into the clapped out old banger and turns his body my way. "We don't have to do this."

I frown. "What do you mean?"

"The second date. The meal out. I'm not what you're wanting. I'm not what you thought." He sighs. "I saw it in your eyes when you looked out of the window. I need to be honest with you, Bonnie. I never approach women like you. I don't know my fine wines. I don't know my monkfish. I was bluffing when I spoke to you and I hardly ever eat steak." Mark shrugged. "I saw you and I liked you. You can't blame a bloke for trying. I bustled my way through our last evening of drinks but I can't keep this up. I'm just me, Mark, a regular bloke with a really crap car."

I stare at the handsome man sitting next to me. "The monkfish was nasty. Can I go change my shoes?'"

Connie pushed herself away from the screen and smiled. Bonnie *would* get her happiness and Mark *would* be her perfect companion. They'd laugh about their meeting and tell each other the truth, slipping into a perfect harmony of compatibility and togetherness. That's all people ever really wanted, wasn't it? Someone to get on with. Someone to be real with. Someone they didn't seem to constantly disappoint. Connie touched her phone to look at the time, her eyes drawn to the two flashing messages she'd somehow managed to miss. One was from Karl, simply saying: *Looking more like 11pm.* The other was from Maria. She smiled as she opened it.

I hope your barn's not become infested with rats and therefore uninhabitable. If that happens please remember that my field is big and green and always welcoming to a bouncy Shetland pony and her young foal.

Connie hit reply. *You think I'm a Shetland pony?*

The ping back was almost instant. *Yes, slightly short and very fluffy. What animal am I?*

She stifled her laugh. *I think Ryan was right when he described you as a midnight black panther.*

The reply came quickly. *Aren't panthers dangerous?*

You could be VERY dangerous. Connie blushed the minute she'd sent it.

??? Whatever do you mean ???

She closed her eyes and scrunched up her face. What did she mean? What was she saying? She typed quickly. *I open up to you. I never open up to anyone. That might be dangerous.*

Oh, is that all?

Connie bit her bottom lip and smiled. Was Maria flirting? Was she flirting? She was about to reply when another message pinged in.

You must open up to Ryan?

I do, but not in all ways. Ryan and I have some weird history that's far too long, complicated and embarrassing to go into, but yes, he knows bits.

I like knowing bits.

Connie smiled and replied. *I'm enjoying getting to know bits about you too. Today was fun.*

It was. Would you like to come for a play date at mine tomorrow?

At Mariano's?

No, at my house. My coffee's just as good as Mariano's.

Connie heard the click of the door and typed quickly. *Sounds great, send through the details. Speak tomo x* She put down the phone and jumped off her seat, rushing quickly into the lounge. "Hey, it's nice to have you home," she said, smiling at Karl.

"Is it?"

"Yes." She signalled towards the kitchen. "I've made us a meal."

"I've already eaten."

"Let's just sit and have wine then. I've set up the candles."

Karl ran his fingers through his short dark hair and shook his head. "I don't want this, Connie. I don't want any of this."

"It's fine, it'll keep. I'll just put the food in containers and the wine can stay in the fridge."

"No, I mean *this.*" He lifted his hands to their surroundings. "You clearly don't want it either and I've no clue what we're trying to prove."

"I *do* want this."

"No you don't. You're slagging me off to anyone who'll listen. You're rarely physical with me in bed."

Connie shook her head. "They're the only times I've ever said anything bad about you, and I was only ever joking." She paused. "And we have a three-year-old in the house. Things like that are difficult."

Karl slumped onto the sofa. "So I coincidentally walk in every time you bad mouth me, do I?"

"It wasn't bad mouthing, but yes, you do! And you can't blame me for," she blushed, "that *other* thing. You're always tired from work."

"No I'm not. But it doesn't matter. I've made up my mind. I think we should separate."

"What?" Connie shook her head in disbelief and knelt at his feet. "Where has this come from?"

"I'm not happy and if you're honest with yourself you know you're not either."

"Look at me." Connie took hold of his knees. "Why can't you look at me? We've got Noah."

He kept his eyes averted, staring into the middle of nowhere. "That's not enough."

"So you leave me? You leave us? You kick me out? You take my son? What does this mean, Karl. You're scaring me. I can't do this alone."

He finally looked down at her wide eyes and placed his hands on her shoulders. "You *have* been doing this alone. We both know that already. I'm bad at this. I'm just making things worse."

"You're his father."

"And financially I'll provide a great life for him." He sat up straighter and nodded his head slowly as if realising something for himself. "I've decided to take charge of the new office in Manchester."

"With Louise?"

"No, of course not. She'll be here at the London office. I'll work up there. I'll come back at the weekends and see Noah then. I'll get myself a flat. I'll sign all this over to you."

"We want you, Karl, not your money."

"You've never had me. Work's always had me, and if I'm honest, work will continue to have me. I'm Karl Collis of Collis and Killshaw. It's what I'm good at. It's what I know. I've learnt to play to my strengths and being a father just isn't one of them. We met in a bar. We had a few dates. You fell pregnant. None of this was planned."

"No! I gave myself to you."

"Only because you were fed up of waiting for Mr Right."

"That's so unfair."

"It's not. It's honest."

"So you just abscond?"

"No, if I commit to seeing him every weekend he'll get much more time with me than he's ever done before. Everything will work itself out."

"How can you possibly say that?"

"Everything will be the same, Connie." He smiled and tried to massage her shoulders. "Things will be better."

"For who?"

Karl's silence answered her question. She pulled herself upright and walked towards the stairs. "This is you, Karl. Not me." She held onto the bannister and narrowed her eyes. "You cock."

CHAPTER TWELVE

Connie kept a tight hold on Noah's hand as she pressed the doorbell once more. It was one of those posh ones with a round ivory button and black marble surround that chimed an old-fashioned "ding-dong" out of the house. She looked up at the building. Everything about it was grand. There were four sets of double windows layered one above the other with an impressive balcony at the very top. Adding this to the wide driveway set back from the road and the Shoreditch postcode, she knew this tall and imposing terrace had a two million pound price tag, at least. Connie made a mental note to check on Zoopla later. She stood still and waited, her anxiety rising by the second. Why was she here, standing gormlessly outside a mansion that made her own pitiful dwelling look like a self-build garden shed? This wasn't her world. She didn't belong. She could never invite Maria back to hers for a play date in her poorly decorated 3x3 metre lounge. Whatever would she think? Her panicked thoughts were interrupted by the click of the lock. She watched as the large round doorknob turned in slow motion then tried to catch her breath, somehow managing to hold it instead. Maria appeared, looking as majestic and radiant as ever.

"Connie, hi. How are you? Come in, come in." She smiled down to Noah. "Hi there, Noah. Alice is so excited to see you."

Noah shared none of his mother's apprehension and raced straight into the house, chasing an impatiently waiting Alice through the huge open-plan hallway with his own roaring greeting. "Lissssssssssssssss!"

Connie shouted after him. "Shoes, Noah!"

"It's fine, it's fine. Come in." Maria kissed Connie's cheeks and drew her into the house. "Did you find it okay? Of course you did, you're here, but you know what I mean. Can I take your coat?"

"Thank you, and thank you for having us."

"Pleasure, pleasure; please do come in. Let me get you a drink. I've laid out some snacks as well. Would Noah like a drink? I've set up the play room with puzzles and games so they should be fine entertaining themselves." She stopped and stared at Connie. "What are you smiling at?"

Connie eyed her with suspicion. "Nothing, but I've never seen you looking flushed before."

"I'm nervous."

She laughed. "Really? I thought it was just me?"

"Why would you be nervous?"

Connie shrugged. "Why would *you* be?"

Maria batted her on the shoulder. "Oh just give me your coat and come in."

"I am in."

"I mean come in and make yourself comfortable. Let me show you the lounge."

Connie handed over her jacket and took in the impressive expanse of the hallway with its large wide staircase and aesthetically curving bannisters. "Your house is just gorgeous," she said, smiling back at Maria. "Now tell me why you're nervous."

The endearing laugh made an appearance. "It's your first visit. Don't you get nervous when people come round to yours for the first time?"

"I don't invite them round to mine."

"Well you're inviting me."

Connie shook her head. "Nope. You've got more square footage in this entrance hall than I have in my entire house."

"Size doesn't matter, Connie. I thought you straight girls knew that?"

"My doorbell's plastic."

Maria gritted her teeth and shook her head. "Okay, you're right. If your doorbell's plastic then I'm not coming round."

"Good. We can host all of our play dates here instead. Which way am I going?" She puzzled at the choice of doors that led off from the hall, smiling as her host finally pointed her in the direction of a tall one on the left. She entered what she could only assume was one of the main lounges and gasped. "Oh good god, you could host the whole playgroup in here. This is huge!"

"Size does matter to you then?"

"If it's all gorgeous like this, then yes!" Connie couldn't take in the room fast enough. "Oh Maria, this is beautiful."

"Please, take a seat. I just want you to be comfortable."

"Let me take off my shoes."

"No, honestly it's fine. The floors are oak, your shoes are no problem."

Connie bent down and untied her laces. "Fine as they might be I want to do one of those skids that Tom Cruise does in *Risky Business*."

"Doesn't he wear just his underwear in that scene?"

"Done."

"Oh Connie, you're great." Maria was laughing again. "I've been smiling since the moment I met you."

"You know what?" Connie pulled off her shoes and looked up at her beaming friend. "I think I have too. But shall we have a coffee first, before I strip off?"

"Still nervous?"

She tucked her shoes against the skirting board. "If I *ever* had to get naked in front of you I think I'd have to blind you first with a flashlight."

Maria looked down at Connie's jeans. "Is that a torch in your pocket or are you just pleased to see me?"

"Does that work with lesbians?"

"*Everything* works with lesbians."

"Really?"

"And I bet you look lovely naked."

"No, honestly I don't."

"And of course we like protruding bits. We just don't like them when they're attached to men."

Connie's cheeks flared. "Okay my nerves have officially gone, overtaken instead by embarrassment."

"Sorry. I forgot you don't like the uncomfortable lesbian banter, do you?"

"No, no, I do, I love it."

Maria smiled. "You *love* it?"

"I didn't mean it like that. Oh look, you're making me all nervous again." Connie tried to ignore the teasing and walked instead to the tall window that was streaming glorious summer sunshine into the room. "It's just strange how we get on so well. I worry when we're apart about our differences, but the moment I'm with you it's like we just fit. We get along, no matter how mismatched we truly are."

Maria joined her in the warm spot and stared out towards the street. "I think we're perfectly suited."

Connie turned around. "Really?"

Maria nodded and kept their eyes locked, maintaining the connection. "Yes. And you shouldn't worry. The two pieces of a jigsaw that actually fit together are the ones that are totally different."

Connie studied the smiling brown eyes. "I love that."

"Think about it. It's true."

"Can I steal it?"

"What do you mean?"

She reached into her pocket for her phone. Opening up the notes app she started to type. "Say it again, about the jigsaw? I always write down interesting things that I hear."

Maria moved to the sofa and sat. "You've never got your phone out before so is this the first interesting thing I've ever said?"

Connie laughed. "No."

"Why do you write them down?"

"For my book."

"Really? A novel? You're writing a novel?"

Connie nodded and sat beside her friend on the plush white sofa. "And I'd love to use that jigsaw thing."

"You never cease to amaze me, Connie, do you know that? I think you've progressed from a violinist to a harpist, there are that many strings to your bow."

Connie winced. "I don't think I'll use that one though. I think that saying is meant to be about archers and how they can still take a shot at their target if their string breaks." She nodded to check that Maria was following. "Because they'll have a spare."

Maria laughed. "See what I mean?"

****

Karl rubbed his face with both hands. It was mid-morning and he'd yet to attempt any work. "Fuck it. I've done the wrong thing, haven't I? I shouldn't have slept on the sofa and I shouldn't have come in early today. I should have stayed at home and talked things through."

Louise, who had been listening to this ramble for almost an hour, got up from her seat. She coughed once and stood beside him, towering over his desk in her super-high heels and imposingly sharp dress suit. "Karl, you HAVE to get yourself together. I've been listening to this for far too long. We've got the Richardson meeting in twenty minutes and you look rough."

He sat up straighter in his seat. "We can't all be naturally slick like you."

"I'm professional, not slick, but yes we can. I'll get you a coffee while you go freshen up in the men's."

"I'm essentially walking out on my family. Who does that? She called me a cock. She's right. I'm—"

"NOW!" Louise's ponytail swung with the force of her words.

"Alright, alright, I will. Just one thing. Give me your summary. You're the queen of summaries. I listen to your summaries. Your summaries are always spot on."

Louise fingered her blunt fringe. "Fine. Tough love time, Karl." Her pacing began as she outlined the points on her fingers. "You're not married. You didn't want the baby. You only asked for a second date because you found out she was a virgin and thought it would be a challenge."

Karl swung himself forwards. "NEVER repeat that! I was drunk and sounding off! We had good chemistry; she was fun."

"You've been drunk far too often recently, and as fun as a blonde bit of nonsense can be you never imagined it would lead to you trapped in this monotonous family-man twilight zone. This is the here and now. It's not working with her, but what *is* working is the business. We're on a roll, Karl. We're expanding. We need you."

"*You* don't need me."

"No, not here, you're right. But I do need you in Manchester. Call it a trial separation with Connie if you like. Once everything's up and running we can replace you with someone else if that's your final decision." She walked to the window and tapped on the smart glass, changing the tint to transparent. Pointing at the desks of workers taking calls and typing away she turned to Karl and growled. "But you do realise how many of those people would love to be you?"

He rubbed his eyes at the sudden influx of light. "I don't care. They can be me. I'm done being me. Being me's shit."

"*You* started this business. *You* built it from scratch. *You're* the one who'll expand it."

"No, this is all you and we both know it."

Louise shook her head. "It's both our names on the letterhead."

"You badgered me into this. You've driven everything from day one."

"Well let me badger you now." She tapped the glass once again and as soon as they were hidden from the rest of the office she strode towards him, placed her fists on the desk and leaned forward to eyeball him. "Stop. Whining. Get. A. Fucking. Grip."

****

Connie scooped the last grains of couscous onto the Peppa Pig spoon and held it in front of her son's mouth. He'd been successfully feeding himself for the most part, but she wanted to show off his completely clean plate. She'd never given him couscous before and was surprised at how happily he'd eaten it. He'd been known to have rather dramatic meltdowns in the past when presented with strange food. Swede was strange because mash shouldn't be orange. Broccoli was strange because you shouldn't eat trees. Eggs were strange no matter how they were presented, and fish was just strange *"cos it stinks."* Connie had fully expected Noah to come out with such a gem as Maria offered him the plate of couscous and chicken, but he'd looked at Alice, seen her tuck in, and done exactly the same.

She smiled at her son. "Well done, Noah. You're all finished. A completely clean plate."

"I have a clean plate too," said Alice.

Connie nodded at the little girl. "Yes you do, don't you. Well done both of you. Was that delicious, Noah?"

The mop of hair moved up and down enthusiastically. "Kiss kiss like sand. Noah like sand, and Noah like kiss kiss."

Alice laughed loudly. "Couscous! Not kiss kiss!"

Noah laughed loudly. "Kiss kiss!"

Maria smiled at the giggles and stroked their matching blonde heads. "You two are just adorable."

"Can I get down, Mama?"

"Yes of course you can." Maria unbuckled the booster seat and helped her daughter from the chair.

"Noah down too!"

Connie shushed the shouting. "You have to ask nicely."

"Pleeeeeeeeeease."

Freeing her son, Connie watched both children race back towards the playroom. "When did Alice start using I and me instead of her own name?"

Maria reached over and ripped a chunk of tomato and olive bread from the tear and share loaf. "I'm not sure she's ever used Alice."

"When's her birthday again?"

"September 8th."

"Noah's is September 18th. But she seems so much more advanced than he is."

"They're all different," said Maria, adding butter to the bread and speaking between mouthfuls. "Noah's physically more capable than Alice."

"No, she's a good little runner."

Maria laughed. "They're both perfect." She dabbed the corner of her mouth with a napkin. "And I'm glad we approve of each other's offspring. I'm dreading starting nursery in September." She signalled to the spread of food lying in front of them on the large wooden table in the middle of the old-fashioned rustic kitchen. "Please have some more to eat."

"No, I'm good thank you, but I'm dreading it too. Will you send her to a school-based nursery?"

"Yes, she's on the list for Maple House."

"The private school?"

Maria nodded.

Connie sighed. "We're in the catchment for Five Ways. Currently in special measures."

"Oh no. That's awful. Isn't there anywhere else?"

"Not in our area and we definitely can't afford Maple House prices."

"It's actually quite reasonable. They take them from age three to eighteen so they don't get stressed about moving up to a big school."

"I loved my first day at the local comp. I got to wear a blazer and have my own locker."

"Oh bless you. Did you do well at school?"

Connie stood and began to stack the children's plates. "I did okay."

"Please, I'll do that."

"No, no it's fine." She paused and smiled. "What do you classify as doing well?"

"Well you obviously did do well because you ended up at university."

"I went for the booze."

"You did not."

"I did. My degree's a bit rubbish."

"A degree's a degree."

"Is that why you want to send Alice to Maple House? So she does well academically?"

Maria got up off the beautiful hand-carved bench and took the plates from Connie. "Let me do this. I'll stick it all in the dishwasher and we can retire to the lounge to discuss education and politics and possibly even religion."

Connie pretended to look at her watch. "Is that the time? I need to go."

Maria laughed. "No! I have food prepared so you can stay for tea as well."

"You don't want us here all day."

Maria smiled. "Maybe I do." She turned back to the dishwasher that was hidden discreetly inside a large oak cupboard. "And I know that Alice does too."

"Noah still naps at half one."

"Alice will occasionally. We could try them together?"

"I feel like I'm imposing."

Maria returned the food to the fridge that was also hidden behind a panel of intricate carvings. "What do you usually do when he naps?"

"Collapse."

"So let's collapse together then."

Connie smiled. "We'd be frauds! We've not done anything. They've entertained themselves all day. He's honestly so much easier when he's got someone to play with. Maybe I should have another baby."

"I think about that sometimes too, but maybe we could just save on the nappies and borrow each other's for now?"

"Instant siblings?"

Maria smiled. "Now wouldn't that be nice?"

CHAPTER THIRTEEN

Pulling herself into her workstation, Connie threw out her arms and stretched wide so that both hands were touching the walls on either side. She was glowing. The day had been perfect. Relaxed, enjoyable and thoroughly good fun. Noah and Alice had napped for two hours, giving her and Maria time to debate the pros and cons of private education with the resounding conclusion that happiness was key. Maria wasn't sending her daughter to a private school for the perceived better education, but rather the smaller class sizes which she felt would reduce the risk of bullying. Connie had done her best to assure Maria that her daughter would be fine wherever she went as times were changing and acceptance was commonplace. And while Maria had agreed to an extent she had maintained that the fee-paying school's close-knit family atmosphere might be more welcoming to a young girl with a single lesbian mum and no siblings. Connie had laughed and suggested that Maria might not be single for her entire life and that more children might one day appear, which in turn led Maria to announce her news.

Connie dropped her hands back onto her lap and shook off the memory. Maria had a date. Tonight. With a woman. Connie tutted to herself; of course it was with a woman. Maria was a lesbian. A lesbian who was going out tonight with another lesbian. She fiddled with the mouse. Why did the thought of two gorgeous women (because Maria's date would most definitely be gorgeous) intrigue her so much? Would they pull back each other's chairs like Maria had done for her at Bounce-a-rama? Would they split the bill equally? Would they laugh and chat? Would they get along as well as *they'd* been doing all afternoon? Connie pulled herself out of the spiralling bad mood.

She couldn't be jealous. That didn't make sense. She nodded. It must just be intrigue. Intrigue and nosiness. She took a deep breath and closed her eyes. The vision of two women kissing came into focus.

"Oh for god's sake, Connie, come on!" She clicked on the mouse, bringing her screen back to life. What was happening? She scanned the last sentence. Oh yes, Bonnie and Mark had just returned from a wonderful date. Bonnie was happy. Mark was happy. Everyone was happy. She sighed. She'd spent the whole day ignoring the facts. Karl was leaving her and he'd made up his mind. She checked the time; it was gone eight already and she had no clue when he'd be home, or even if he'd be home at all. There had been no messages, no voicemails, just the memory of his words ringing in her head: *I don't want any of this.*

Connie rolled her eyes. They hadn't been ringing in her head. She'd hardly thought about him all day. The events of last night had been neatly tucked away while she enjoyed a thoroughly nice time with her friend. It hadn't been a conscious decision not to tell Maria about it, it just hadn't come up, and anyway she'd only have spoilt the mood. She closed her eyes once more and thought back to the grand house and the warm and inviting lounge with its huge windows and shiny oak floor. Sitting on that sofa she'd felt comfortable, not at all how she thought she'd feel in a million pound property with its million pound furnishings.

She smiled and reached for her phone, opening up the notes app and re-reading the words. She lifted her fingers to the keyboard and started to type.

'I never believed in soul mates, in one key for each lock. Keys can be copied and locks can be forced. I never accepted the notion of a magical path guiding me to my fate. If fate knows best why does it wait so long? People settle for people. They give up on the fight. The twists and turns in the road can no longer be stomached and the height of the walls gets too tall. We're overpowered. We stop. We accept. We curse ourselves for believing in that fateful twinned soul.

But what if it's real and we've been approaching it wrong? We shouldn't be looking for that perfect match, or that complete

compatible. The two pieces of a jigsaw that fit together are always totally different. There is no perfect person, just that one person who'll fit you perfectly.'

She smiled. Maria was right. Some people just worked. Bonnie and Mark worked. Her friendship with Maria worked. Connie heard the front door and turned around in her seat. Karl was standing there, looking tired and drawn. She had to face facts. She didn't work with Karl, at all. Standing up slowly she walked towards him and gently wrapped her arms around his shoulders.

"You're right," she said, "it *will* be better."

CHAPTER FOURTEEN

Maria checked her watch. It was eight fifteen and there was no sign of her date. She had suggested they meet at the Hawksmoor steakhouse in Spitalfields, her absolute favourite eatery from her life before Alice. A life where she had dinner dates, and invites to cocktail parties. A life where she felt relevant, and in the know. She glanced around at the clusters of tables arranged closely together under the low-bricked ceiling. She'd never been here and not been noticed. People would recognise her as the daughter of the ever-exuberant Marti Mariano, owner of the Italian Bistro down the road, then, in her own right, as Maria Mariano, owner of the new coffee shop down the road. Not today though. She'd been out of the loop for too long. She reached into her bag for her phone. But Alice had been worth it. She had been worth everything.

There were no missed calls so she resisted the temptation to phone home once more. She'd already made two calls en route and another once she'd arrived. Aunt Maddalena had made it very clear that she was to stop phoning and get on with her evening. Her father's sister had always been rambunctious to the point of unruly, making for very interesting family gatherings when the rest of the relatives came over to stay.

Maddalena had never married or had children of her own and Maria was sure she was her way inclined; but at seventy-two it wasn't the kind of thing you could ask such a woman. She'd babysat for Alice on a number of occasions, but mostly after lights had gone out. Alice loved her Great Aunt Maddalena and would certainly not settle if she'd known she was there. One time Alice had woken in the night and Maria had come home to find the pair of them playing pirates in the lounge with cushions thrown onto the floor, a blanket draped between two chairs and Maddalena swimming around like a shark on her stomach.

"Maria?"

Maria shifted out of her memory and smiled at the woman standing in front of her. She looked exactly like her profile picture, which made a nice change from her two previous dates. It wasn't that she was on a mission to find a partner, she just felt it was time to move on with her own life. Alice was three and she knew she had to peep back over the parapet of nursery rhymes and nappies into the adult world. Meeting Connie had reignited her taste for female company and she hoped this woman would prove as fun and flirtatious, but without the added issues of a boyfriend and straight inclination.

The woman continued to talk. "I'm sorry I'm late; I've had a nightmare at work. I hope I haven't kept you too long?"

"It's fine. I used to come here all the time. It's been nice to sit back and remember." Maria stood and pulled back her date's chair. "Shall we?"

The woman took off her suit jacket, displaying a slender waist and crisp white shirt that was tucked neatly into her knee-length skirt. She smiled a dazzling smile. "Are you recently back in the area?"

Maria mirrored her date and sat down. "No. I had a little girl. My hands have been full."

"Sorry?"

"I've been a stay at home mum."

"You have a daughter?"

Maria nodded, confused. "Yes."

The smile had gone. "Oh. Right. Okay."

"You sound shocked?" Maria crossed her legs under the table and studied the professional-looking woman.

"I don't remember it being on your profile."

Maria nodded again. "It is."

"Oh. Okay." The pause was awkward. "Is there another mummy? Or a daddy on the scene?"

"No. Just me. Is that a problem?"

"No, I… How old is she?"

"She's three."

"But you're in finance, right?"

Maria shook her head. "Nope. I own Mariano's coffee shop down the road."

"Oh. Right. Okay."

"Have you confused me with someone else?"

"No, no, I'm…" The woman sighed. "Things have been so up in the air at work that I've been skim-reading all the un-essentials and trying to focus on the important tasks in hand."

Maria laughed. "And here we are on that un-essential date."

"No, I didn't mean it like that." The woman paused and smiled. "I'm sorry. Can I start again? Let me get you a drink?"

****

The atmosphere in the small terraced house was calm and the quiet, kind whispers were welcomed by all. Karl rubbed the back of his girlfriend's hair and hushed into her ear. "Say the word and I'll stay."

Connie's head was resting on his shoulder. She shook it gently. "You were right. Things will be better. I'm sorry for storming away last night."

"No, I should have followed you up and I shouldn't have run off to work this morning."

Connie pulled back and looked at him. The dark circles beneath his eyes were ageing him badly. "It's given me time. Come on. I miss your smile. Sell me the schedule."

"There doesn't have to be a hard sell. I'll stay. I'll do whatever you want."

"I want you to be happy. You were right. You're young, you'll find someone new. You'll live the life you were meant to live, not the one you were forced into by me."

Karl straightened. "You're not saying this because *you* want to find someone new, are you?"

"No, *you* wanted this."

"Only because…" He massaged his temples and held onto his words. "No. You're right. We both know this is for the best. I'll be moving up to Manchester next weekend. We're renting a flat near the offices."

"You and Louise?"

"No, the company. And why would you say it like that?"

"I'm just asking."

He couldn't help himself. "No, you're asking in that tone of voice."

"I am not."

"You are."

Connie scrunched up her face. "And here's why we're doing this. We're squabbling. We're always squabbling."

"You squabble, I don't."

"Yes you do."

"No I don't."

Both managed to smile, with Connie giving in first. "I'm sorry."

Karl sighed. "No, I'm sorry too." Then he nodded, as if solidifying his plans. "I'll work up there all week and come home on Fridays. I'll stay with Mum at the weekends."

"I bet she's thrilled."

"She is."

"I know! I wasn't being sarcastic. Evelyn's got her little boy back from the wild-haired hag who trapped him with a child."

"She likes you, Connie."

"No she doesn't."

"She does and we'll come next Saturday morning to pick him up. He can stay the night with us and I'll bring him back on Sunday. Or he can stay here Saturday night and I'll come back for him again the next day. It's up to you. Or we can do something together. Whatever you think will work best."

"Shall we play it by ear?"

Karl smiled. "Thank you."

"For what?"

"For just being you. And I'm not a bad man, Connie. I'll still be there for my son whenever he needs me."

"I know."

****

Maria watched the woman's dark ponytail swing from side to side as her story reached its finale.

"So anyway, he's gone home tonight to tell her he's staying and that his family comes first."

Maria frowned. "But it doesn't?"

"I'm not sure." Maria's date paused and leaned in closer. "I made the drunken mistake of kissing him once. Office Christmas party, far too much booze. Anyway, I've not heard the end of it since."

Maria smiled. "Must have been a good kiss?"

"It should never have happened."

"No, I meant..." She turned her attention back to her plate. Connie would have quipped back. She'd have got the flirtation and replied with one inappropriate innuendo or another. Maria cut into her steak and wondered how to continue the conversation. The Hawksmoor was buzzing and the food was divine, she just needed that extra bit of sparkle from her very gorgeous date to enhance the evening. Maria decided to add a teasing edge to her tone. "Does he know that you're gay, or is kissing male colleagues a habit of yours?"

The reply was as blunt as the woman's fringe. "You're not in the bash-a-bisexual brigade are you?"

Maria smiled even wider. "I don't mind bashing a bisexual."

The expression softened as the woman finally got the joke. "I just like to keep my work life and home life pretty separate; not that I get much time for a home life with the business the way it's been."

"But you've been working together for ten years?"

Louise Killshaw nodded.

"And this..." Maria wiggled her fingers. "This... this... what's he called?"

"Karl."

"This Karl doesn't know that you're gay, or bisexual, or that you date women or whatever it is that you do?"

"I do date women and, no, I don't know if he knows." She smiled. "What I do know is that I'm enjoying *this* date with *this* woman."

Maria looked over at the plate opposite. Her date had ordered a salad even though the Hawksmoor was known for its steaks. She wondered how much enjoyment anyone could ever actually get from a salad. "Really?"

"Really."

Reaching for her wine glass Maria imagined what Connie would have chosen had she been there: probably the rib-eye steak with lashings of Béarnaise sauce or the fillet with smoked Stilton hollandaise. She froze, suddenly making the connection.

"Are you okay?" asked Louise.

"Your company's an insurance company, right?"

The woman nodded. "That's right."

"And Karl's girlfriend? She's called Connie, isn't she? And their boy's called Noah?"

"Oh god, you don't know them do you? I really shouldn't have said anything. Do you know her? Are you good friends?"

"It's fine." Maria remembered that morning and Connie's arrival. She'd been her usual bubbly self, and she'd certainly not mentioned Karl or any impending separation. She felt her heart drop, realising she was hurt that she didn't know more. "I don't know them that well at all."

"But you know *of* them?"

"I know Connie from playgroup." Maria frowned. "This definitely happened last night?"

"Yes. He told her he'd had enough. We've got offices opening in Manchester and he's going to front the whole process." Louise shrugged. "But he left work tonight saying he was heading home to plead for forgiveness. I really shouldn't have said anything, but you know how it is, leaving work and letting off steam."

"Noah's the same age as my little girl."

Louise spoke quickly, desperately wanting to cover her indiscretion. "Even more reason to give them some space. They've got lots to sort out."

Maria looked down at her plate, her appetite suddenly gone. "Do you know Connie well?"

"I've met her on occasion. Such a shock when they got together, I never thought he'd be the type to settle down. But anyway, Karl said she was distraught when he told her he wanted out. That's probably the reason why he's backing away from Manchester." She lowered her voice. "I think Connie can be somewhat temperamental. She's young."

"You can't be that much older than her, can you?"

"I'm thirty-two like you."

"I'm thirty-five."

"Oh. I must..."

"So, who is this mystery thirty-two-year-old woman who works in finance and doesn't have children?"

The teeth were out in impressive force. "I don't know, but I'm glad she's not here. You might be the best wrong button I've ever pressed."

Maria shrugged. "You have to press the right buttons with me."

The knife and fork were laid down and the intense look across the table was meant with sincerity. "I'm sorry. I was late from work. Flustered. This stuff with Karl was racing around in my mind. I spoke before I thought. I let off steam." She looked down at her plate. "But my worst mistake was ordering this salad because I thought you'd judge me if I ordered the steak." Louise picked up a lettuce leaf with her fingers, dangling it with dismay. "And then you ordered the steak after me and now I'm sitting here salivating because it looks utterly delicious." She paused and looked up at Maria. "Can I start again?"

Maria laughed quietly and nodded. "Okay then. Three questions. Ask me three questions."

"About you?"

"About my life. Things I might like to talk about."

"Okay, well I now know that you're thirty-five, and I now know that you own Mariano's coffee shop. So I guess I'd like to find out:

One, why you're blind-dating. Two, how you ended up with your own coffee shop. And then three, I'd just like to check one final time that you're not going to tell Connie and Karl what I said. I hope you can understand that the chances of me going on a date tonight with someone who knows them is so slim, and I was just chatting away about my work day without even thinking."

Looking across the table at the pretty woman sitting opposite her, Maria could do nothing but exhale her disappointment. "She's called Alice. My daughter's called Alice."

CHAPTER FIFTEEN

Connie's dour mood was made even more obvious by Ryan's dazzling Malta tan and over excitement at being back at the playgroup. She frowned at him. "You're acting like this is the most enthralling place on Earth."

"But they've got a new ride-on!"

"They always get new ride-ons."

Ryan nodded towards the centre of the room. "But that one's got a horn!"

"Ryan, you missed one week." She looked around at the mixture of frantic mothers and hyperactive children. "We're at the crappy community centre. You've been to Malta. This shouldn't be a highlight."

"Oh but it is, and we've got so much to talk about."

"I'm just a bit tired."

"Darling, I bought you Dior!"

"I know you did, thank you." She glanced once more towards the entrance.

"A Dior scarf. It's Dior, darling! You do realise the attention it'll bring you, especially from…" He paused, following Connie's longing gaze. "Oh god, I get it now. She's not here, that's the reason for your ghastly depressing face."

Connie turned back around. "I haven't got a ghastly depressing face, and I've no idea who you're talking about."

The perfectly plucked eyebrows rose two inches. "Your hair's been brushed and you're wearing blusher. Last time you wore blusher was at our Year Eleven prom."

"It was not."

"At least you've held off on that god-awful blue eye shadow this time."

"Oh stop it, Ryan."

"And that top's new. I've seen all of your tops a billion times over and that one's definitely new. It's still too baggy for you, but at least it's got a pretty design on it. Honestly, Connie, when are you going to start wearing fitted clothes that actually show off your cracking little figure?"

"I prefer it when you talk about my ghastly face."

He nodded towards the entrance. "We're forty-five minutes in. If she was coming she'd be here by now." He gasped. "Wait! There's someone coming!"

Connie spun back around. "Where?"

"There! Oh, hang on, it's not her." He squinted. "Looks like more fresh blood though. Maybe you could show your blusher and scarf off to this new hotty?"

Connie looked at the woman who had entered the hall, hushing a red-faced girl who was screaming to get out of her pushchair. "She's not hot."

"Ooo so you *can* pass judgement on a woman's desirability?"

"Of course I can."

"And she doesn't do it for you?"

"No."

"What does do it for you, Miss Parker?"

"Maria's my friend. How many times do I have to say it? She's my friend." She paused and shrugged. "Or was."

"How many days now?"

Connie lifted her eyes to the ceiling as if counting backwards. She didn't need to, she already knew to almost the hour. "Five days."

"So you last saw her at the *amazing* play day at her house on Friday?"

"Stop being sarcastic. It was amazing."

"I know, you told me." He scraped his chair closer to Connie's knees and inhaled deeply, adding weight to his instruction. "Just text her."

"No. When I left her house she said she'd call me about doing something this week. But she obviously went on that date with that perfect lesbian and forgot all about me."

Ryan sniffed with indifference. "No, she's probably still shacked up with her in bed. That's what lesbians do. They hook up, spend a week shagging nonstop, only pausing to order in food and sex toy supplies, then they decide who's going to move in with whom."

"They do not."

"Connie my dearest, they do. On the plus side it's only a matter of time. When she's stopped shagging she'll give you a call."

"And I'm meant to be grateful for that am I?"

Ryan sat taller in his seat and tilted his bald head. He looked bewildered. "Darling, you're not her wife. What's got into you? You get one friend and suddenly you turn all single white female?"

Connie fidgeted in her seat and sighed. "I just hoped she'd be here."

"Why?"

"Because I've not heard from her, and she's been here for the past two weeks."

"Is that all?"

"I like her company. We've had fun. It's been nice. And yes, maybe you're right. I *have* missed having friends and maybe I *am* taking a while getting used to the rules again."

"Darling, with true friends there are no rules. There's no second guessing. There's just friendship." He nodded. "You just know."

"So Maria and I aren't real friends then?"

"No, you're probably not."

"But *she's* the one who keeps talking about us being real friends."

Ryan rubbed his own temples. "Oh god, darling, this is boring me now, and I never thought I'd say this, but can we talk about Karl instead?"

Connie tutted. "No."

"Good, sorry, you're right. I don't know what got into me. A momentary lapse of judgement. The last thing I want to do is talk about that man. Two days left though?"

"He's moving up this weekend and he's back next weekend."

"Noah okay?"

"He's fine."

Ryan exhaled, relieved. "Good, that's all we need to say on the matter, now go chat up that new woman."

"No."

"Not exotic enough for you, like Maria?"

Connie widened her eyes at the scene across the hall, drawing Ryan's attention to it. "No, it's her exorcist child that's putting me off."

****

Maddalena shooed Maria from behind the counter in the Covent Garden branch of Mariano's coffee shop, forcing her towards the tall stools even though she was half the size and more than double the age of her niece. "Out, out, out."

"No, let me relieve you for a bit. Why don't you have a quick play with Alice in the pen? She loves coming in here to see you."

The old woman tightened the bow at the back of her black barista's apron and shuffled back towards the cakes counter. "You make bambini playpen so good, no bambini need grown-ups."

"Well sit down then. Get yourself a coffee. Take a break for a minute." Maria knew what was coming. Her aunt Maddalena would thicken her Italian accent and furrow her weathered wrinkles further, transitioning into the mafia aunt she never dared mess with as a child.

"I say out! *Fuori*, Maria!"

Maria decided to try her luck. "How about I sit down with you? We need to talk about the shop."

The old eyes squinted with suspicion. "The shop don't need you. We be working well since you gone." Maddalena folded her arms and tapped her toe in her well-worn slip-ons. "Is that why you come, Maria? To tell me you back? Why you not work in Shoreditch, closer to home?"

Maria smiled and softened her voice. "No, Aunt Maddalena. I don't know what I want, that's why I want to talk to you. You've done a fantastic job here."

"Done?"

"You're doing. Please, five minutes? Even if we just talk about keeping things exactly as they are."

"We keep things same?"

"Yes, exactly the same."

"*Grazie a Dio!*" The old woman lifted her hands and looked around at the room that was running to perfection with a steady buzz of customers and an efficient array of staff. "Everything perfect. You not change things when everything perfect."

"I know."

"We do weekly meeting at your home, like usual. It work for past three years. I know business, Maria. You know I know business. I ran bistro of your father for decades, god bless you, Marti, with your lazy Italian," she used her finger to outline the cross over her heart, "but good-natured soul." She closed her eyes and tilted her head up to the Lord. "*Che Dio vi benedica.*"

Maria dared to place her arm around her aunt's shoulder and gently guide her away from the counter. "Aunt Maddalena, this place is yours, we both know that, and I'm more than happy with the way everything's going." She pulled out a chair and encouraged her aunt to sit. "It's just Alice. She's getting older and she'll be in nursery soon. I need to do something more with my time, with my life."

Maddalena realised she was being forced into her seat and bundled her way back up, waving her hands at their surroundings. "You have two Mariano's! You huge success! You want for nothing!"

Maria gently pushed her elderly, yet feisty, aunt back into her seat. She waited for a moment to check she was staying put before sitting next to her and reaching out for her strong, wrinkled hands. "I love you, Aunt Maddalena. Maybe I just came in today because I'm feeling a little bit bored."

"No, you come today to go behind counter. You not go behind counter. What change? Usually you sit and drink coffee while Alice play in bambini pen."

"Yes, usually I do. But Alice is ready for nursery. She's ready for more." Maria nodded. "So am I."

The hands were snatched back and the arms were folded. Maddalena looked away from her niece. "You own shop. You free to come and go when you please."

"I know you like running ship around here and I'm not going to change that. I just don't know whether I should look into opening another branch, or maybe working in Shoreditch permanently."

Her aunt shook her head. "No. Tony good manager. You boss, Maria." She shook her head again. "Maria Mariano not need to work shop floor."

"Dad always did."

"Pfft. He just get in way like you do. Mariano's not restaurant. Coffee shop simple. Press buttons for drinks, scoop out cakes."

Maria smiled. "So why do you like working here then?"

"I very good with customers. They like little old Italian lady."

Maria laughed. "They certainly do."

"I know what you need." The thick accent became even more gravelly. "You need lady."

"Pardon?"

"You heard me. You need lady friend. Never liked last one, or one before that. You need nice one."

"I'm looking, Aunt Maddalena."

"I babysit whenever you need. Not all dates be bad like last one."

"She messaged me and asked if I wanted to see her again."

Maddalena banged her fist on the small round table. "No! You say she not ask about Alice. No good. No good at all. You say she no good. I know she no good."

"She had me confused with someone else; she wasn't aware of Alice at the start."

"She date too much then. You need nice lady."

Maria smiled at her animated aunt. "She was pretty."

"Pfft, look at me. Pretty lady be wrinkled and short in no time. You need good heart. Good heart last forever."

"You've been okay on your own."

"I never find good heart."

Maria couldn't help it. She spoke quietly. "Or pretty lady?"

"*Non capisco.*"

"Maybe you never found—"

The voice was louder and the accent was thicker. "*Non capisco. Ho bisogno di tornare al lavoro.*"

Maria watched as her aunt stood up and shuffled away from the table, still chattering under her breath. Everyone knew that when the *non capisco*, the *I don't understand*, was muttered, then all bets were off and no more discussion would be had. Maria smiled to herself and looked over at the large playpen where Alice and a few other children were seemingly engrossed in an episode of *Peppa Pig*. She turned her attention back to the counter where Maddalena had slotted herself between the three other baristas and was already working in sync once more. She sighed. Maddalena was right. No one needed her and no one was missing her. Closing her eyes for a moment she absorbed the quiet buzz of the shop. She was free to travel down any path she chose, but with no destination in mind it was hard to move away from the crossroads. She smiled. Connie would be able to make some sort of quote out of that. Opening her eyes she reached for her phone, scrolling down to Connie's name. But she stopped, remembering Louise's advice. Maybe Louise *was* right. Maybe Connie and Karl did need time. If Connie wanted her involved then she'd have involved her. But she hadn't, so she probably didn't. Closing the contact, Maria opened Louise's message instead.

****

"Oh my good god, she just bit him!"

Ryan gasped at his friend's shock. "Who?"

"Exorcist girl. She just bit Lucas. And look, poor Earth Mother's just hovering around. She doesn't know what to do."

"She needs to tell her off, or go and tell the mother!"

Connie continued to watch the action at the wendy house. "Exorcist girl's mother is pretending she didn't see. She's walking away. I hate it when they do that."

"Earth Mother needs to say something. Look, Lucas is crying. Crikey you can see the red mark on his arm from here." Ryan flinched.

"Bad?"

"No, she's getting her tit out. *This* gay man does not want to see *that*." He paused. "But really, she should say something."

"Earth Mother doesn't raise her voice when she's forced to speak normally, so she's hardly going to cause a scene with that new mum."

"Oh, darling, no!" Ryan was peeping through his fingers. "Lucas is on the udder and that girl's just bitten him again!"

Connie stood up. "I'm going over. I bonded with Earth Mother last week. I'll come to her rescue."

"Wait, here, take the Savlon." Ryan reached into Connie's bag for the small first aid kit she'd carried everywhere since the day Noah was born. "Will he want a plaster too?"

"Give me the whole thing. I'll try and make a real song and dance about it so the mother sees."

"Connie Parker, I'm away for one week and you suddenly grow a huge pair of bollocks. I must leave you alone more often!"

"Give me the latex gloves as well. Crusty's just joined them. I don't want her flaking all over me while I administer treatment."

"You're still a bitch though."

Connie marched over to the wendy house, deliberately looking over at the new woman who was now head down on her phone in the corner. It had happened once or twice to Noah, with children being rough or saying mean things, and Connie always confronted it. Yes, she may be naturally quite shy in her own life, but if anyone ever dared mess with Noah, god help them.

She crouched next to the biter. "Excuse me, young lady, would you please leave Lucas alone."

Crusty, who was standing behind Earth Mother, started to giggle, and Crusty's son, Lucas's best friend, wobbled his head around in his bumper helmet and added his knowledge to the event. "New girl called Tabitha." He spoke with a lisp as he pointed at the little girl. "Tabitha thop biting."

Crusty controlled her nervous giggles and timidly echoed her son, bending to address the new child. "Yes please, could you go back to your mother, please?"

The wild girl snapped her teeth together at Crusty, causing her to fall backwards from her crouched position. "MY wendy house!"

Connie moved even closer. "It is NOT your wendy house and you DO NOT bite."

The girl snapped her teeth at Connie, but Connie stayed put, executing her best death stare. "NO BITING."

"Waaaaa-aaaa!" The little girl raced away, straight to her mother.

Crusty's giggles were now rather panicked. "She'll tell!"

Connie tried to ignore the slurping sound coming from Lucas and the udder, taking the lid off the antiseptic cream instead and squeezing some onto her own hand as a form of distraction. "Her mother won't come over. Didn't you see the way she disappeared when the girl started biting?" Turning her attention to Earth Mother she looked from Lucas, to tit, to floor. "Is he okay with Savlon?" she said to no one in particular.

"Thank you." The voice was hushed. "That's very kind of you."

Connie applied the cream whilst trying not to see the undulating breast. Instead she looked up at both women. "I'd go and speak to her if I were you. She can't have her daughter going around biting people."

Crusty looked frightened and Earth Mother whispered something too quiet to hear.

"Would you like me to go and have a word?"

"No, no, no, no." Crusty was shaking her head and Connie found it hard not to imagine a snow globe.

"Okay, well give me a shout if you need anything else." She watched as both women fluttered with embarrassment, but nothing more was coming from them so she walked back across the hall to Ryan. "They love me," she said, feeling every bit the hero.

"Darling, they don't." His eyes didn't move from the wendy house.

"They do."

"No. Look. They don't."

Connie turned around to see Crusty and Earth Mother in earnest conversation with exorcist girl's mother, shaking their heads and pointing her way, giving her up and ratting her out faster than a convict with a deal on the table. "They're telling on me!"

"Yep, and exorcist girl's mother is heading this way!"

Connie stayed standing, she wasn't tall, but she didn't want to be sitting when this new woman attacked. "Hi," she said brightly as the lady arrived, led by the gnashing of her daughter's teeth.

The woman's voice was quieter than expected. "I'm sorry to interrupt but Tabitha said you shouted at her."

"I raised my voice slightly because she bit that little boy Lucas over there. There's a real mark. I had to rub on some Savlon."

"They didn't say anything about a bite. How peculiar."

Connie nodded. "Unfortunately she did. She bit him."

"Fat lady shout!"

"Tabitha, we don't use that word."

"Daddy call you fat!"

"Tabitha, will you please..." The woman looked at Connie apologetically. "Sorry, she's going through a phase."

Trying to ignore her hot cheeks, Connie stayed firm. "She bit."

The woman looked down at her daughter. "Tabitha, did you bite?"

"NO! NO NO NO NO! Lady SHOUT!"

Connie nodded. "Yes, because you bit."

"Lady FAT! Mummy FAT!" Tabitha stamped on her mother's foot and marched back to the wendy house.

The woman looked as if she was about to burst into tears. "I'm so sorry. I'm struggling. I don't know what to do anymore. I have to keep finding new playgroups because she's just so awful."

Connie didn't know what to say. "It's...."

"Hi." Ryan stood up and offered his hand. "I'm Ryan. We're no experts but we'll give you advice if you want it, won't we, Con?"

Connie nodded, still dumbstruck by the little girl's appalling behaviour.

"I think I'm beyond help," said the woman, sighing under the weight of her failure. "I'm Phoebe, by the way."

CHAPTER SIXTEEN

Connie waited for the woman to disappear before quickly twisting to Ryan. "It's Phoebe!"

"Yeah, that's what she said. Poor woman's at the end of her tether, but wouldn't you be if you had an exorcist daughter like that?"

"No! Maria's friend Phoebe." Ryan still looked mystified and Connie spoke as quickly as she could. "Maria said she had a best friend from school, some woman who was always there for her, but didn't agree with her when she said she wanted a daughter. Didn't think it was right raising a child all alone, or something like that. But it has to be her. She looks about the same age as Maria, doesn't she?"

"She's called Phoebe. Lots of people are called Phoebe."

Connie pulled a face. "No they're not! I need to take a picture of her. I need to send it to Maria."

"I thought you weren't contacting Maria?"

"This is different. If this woman dared to get on her high horse about how shit Maria would be raising a child then she needs to see the truth."

"What? That she's shit? I think she knows that already."

"No, that Maria's amazing. You've seen how advanced Alice is. You've seen—"

"Connie, it's probably not her."

"But it might be."

"And that's your route back in?"

"No! I just hate it when people judge others. Maria's an amazing parent and this woman needs to see it. Maria said they used to be best friends. Maybe they can patch things up."

"Then you'll really be out of the loop."

"I don't care. I want to find out." She handed Ryan her phone and leaned conspiratorially closer. "When she comes back, let her walk as near as possible so she gets in the shot. Then I'll stand up and pretend I'm posing for a photo. You make sure you get her in the background."

"Oh Connie, darling, you're so sweet."

"No I'm not, I'm just nosey. Wouldn't you love it if this woman had the perfect husband, the perfect family life, yet the wildest most totally uncontrollable daughter, while Maria has the more unconventional home life but her parenting's all figured out?"

"The husband's obviously not perfect if he's calling her fat."

"I know but… Quick! She's coming!"

Ryan waited a moment before lifting the phone. "Photo of your new top, Con?"

Connie jumped up and smiled. "Ooo great!"

The woman blinked at the flash.

"Sorry," said Connie, smiling. "I nearly bumped into you there. Ryan's been away for the week. He's obviously missed me."

"How long have you two been together? Are you sure you don't mind me joining you? No one's ever been this kind before."

Connie pointed at the spare chair. "Please. And please come again next week. You can't keep moving playgroups, it might be one of the reasons why your daughter feels unsettled."

"I gave up second guessing my daughter the minute she was born."

Ryan leaned forward. "Err, I know you like to keep up the illusion Connie, but you can't tell people we're together."

"Sorry, no," She squeezed the firm thigh. "Ryan and I are just friends."

"But parents?"

"No, I'm…" Connie couldn't find the right words to describe her current status.

Ryan filled the silence. "Well I'm gay, and Connie's going through a separation."

Pulling her thick blonde hair over her shoulder, Connie shrugged. "I guess I now say I'm single." She took a deep breath and announced it properly. "I'm a single mum."

Phoebe murmured. "What I'd give to be single."

"Really?" said Ryan and Connie together. "The grass is never greener," continued Ryan.

Connie smiled, remembering Maria's analogy about her paddock and barn conversion with beautiful sash windows. "Excuse me a minute." She stood up. "Ryan, could you watch Noah for me, please?"

****

Ducking quickly out of the community hall, Connie sat on one of the comfy chairs in the small reception area. She clicked on her phone and studied the picture, stretching her fingers to enlarge the image of Phoebe. It was slightly grainy, but her face was easy enough to see. She pressed on the forward arrow and sent via text, adding the caption: *What do you think?*

The grey speech bubble appeared, signalling that Maria was typing and she felt a burst of adrenaline at the instant response, watching her phone as if willing it to react. The bubble turned to green and the message pinged through.

I think you look beautiful and I love that pretty top. Is your hair different?

Connie felt her heart beat even faster. Maria hadn't even looked at the background, she'd chosen to look straight at her. She replied quickly. *No, I mean the woman.*

Yes, beautiful. But like I said the other day, your style's unique. It's what makes you you. You're already all woman x

Connie was flustered; her fingers hit the wrong keys and autocorrect turned the nonsense into more nonsense. She deleted and corrected before pressing send. *In the background. The woman. Is it Phoebe?* She tried to calm herself, but it was too difficult. Maria hadn't just responded, she'd responded instantly, with affection, or was it flirtation? She read through the thread again, aware that Maria's response would be long because the grey typing bubble kept appearing, disappearing, then reappearing once more. She held her breath as it finally flashed through.

Oh my goodness!!!!!! Yes, that's Phoebe. She's at the playgroup? Have you been talking to her? Does she have a child? Boy? Girl? What are they like? It's too late for me to come over, is she coming next week? Could you invite her to Mariano's? No, forget that, she won't come. Just see if she'll do playgroup next week. I'll come, or you could take Alice for me, or...Oh Connie we need a plan!!! I know you're going through a difficult time at the moment, don't ask me how I know, but I do, and I know you chose not to confide in me, which I respect, but I'm here for you if you need me. I feel silly now for thinking you were sending me a picture of you.

Connie replied quickly. *I didn't think you'd want a picture of me. Have we got our wires crossed?*

Yes. I want you.

Connie studied her phone, unable to breathe. How had this gone from a picture of Phoebe to that simple sentence that was now sending ripple after ripple of emotion through her body? Connie read it again. *I want you.* It said: *I want you.* Maria had just written: *I want you.* Connie jumped as her phone pinged again.

Sorry, that sounded wrong. I mean I want you to want me to be there, to confide in, to do playgroups e.t.c

Trying desperately hard to ignore the chaotic thoughts and feelings racing around her mind, Connie got up. She knew she should speak to Ryan, she should get his advice, she should plan her reply. Instead she abruptly sat back down and ignored herself typing the words. *I do want you. You were meant to be calling.*

Sorry. I thought you needed some space?

From you? Why?

No...ahhh, long story. Come to mine after playgroup?

Connie smiled. *Okay.*

CHAPTER SEVENTEEN

Ryan bustled Connie to the side of the wide doorstep. "I'm not standing behind you like some lost puppy."

"You shouldn't even be here."

"I'm carrying Noah and anyway we always do things after playgroup. You're not dumping me for anyone, no matter how hot," he raised his eyebrows at the imposing building, "and no matter how excruciatingly rich they are."

"I'll press again. The house is so big she probably hasn't heard it."

Ryan gasped as the grandiose doorbell sounded once more. "Of course she'll hear it, it's echoing out here. She'll be checking her hair, or make up, or... Oh wow." Ryan's attention was distracted by the colourful window box to the left of the doorstep. "Are those snapdragons? Look at this, Noah. These flowers actually snap." He crossed the gravel to the tall window, showing Noah the flowers.

Connie turned back to the door, breathing deeply to control the nervous energy racing around in her chest. It failed. The door opened and Maria's beautiful face greeted her. Both women stared, lost in the moment, smiling with relief evident in their eyes. Connie wasn't sure how long she stood on the step, just looking at the smile, but she knew that Maria was looking too, and she knew that Maria was hugging too, and she knew that they were holding each other, locked in a moment of revelation. They liked each other. They needed each other. They'd stop with the insecure second guessing.

Ryan coughed. "You're right, Connie, I shouldn't have come. Here, take Noah."

Maria pulled away from the embrace, noticing Ryan for the first time. "Sorry, no, it's fine. Hi. How are you? How was Malta? Come in, come in."

As Maria turned back into the house Ryan took the opportunity to glare at Connie. "*What. The. Actual. Fuck?*" he mouthed.

"*What?*" mouthed Connie in return, aware that her face was on fire.

He climbed the steps and walked past her, whispering as he went. "Five minutes ago you didn't want me here. Now I know why."

Connie followed him in, ignoring the comment. "Shoes please, Noah."

"Lissssssssssssssss!"

Alice raced across the hallway towards her friend. "NOAH!"

Ryan watched as the two toddlers jumped up and down in each other's arms. "They look like you two," he said to both women.

Maria glanced at Connie, then back at Ryan. "I…" She paused, then went on hurriedly. "Come in, come in. Can I get you both a drink?"

Ryan shook his head. "Honestly, I need to get off." He turned back towards the door. "Connie, I'll call you."

****

Two hours had passed since their awkward arrival and Connie and Maria were standing in the doorway of Alice's bedroom, completely at ease. The soft pink lights were emitting a gentle glow and the dainty mobile hanging from the ceiling turned slowly as it played its lullaby, soothing the children to sleep. Both Alice and Noah were tucked up in the cot bed, cuddled into each other's arms.

"I can't believe they can sleep like this," whispered Maria.

"I know. It's always a struggle to get Noah to nap but he needs it or he's a real grump in the afternoons."

"I thought Alice had stopped napping, but look at her, she's out for the count."

Connie smiled. "It's all the running around they do. They tire each other out."

"The lullaby's not even finished and they're already asleep." Maria dimmed the lights even further. "I think you should bring him round every day."

"Would you like me to?" she asked, looking up suspiciously at her friend.

The warm nod was genuine. "Yes."

"You would not." Connie laughed quietly and looked away.

Maria waited until Connie turned back to her. "I would."

Standing still, Connie felt a rush of emotion overwhelm her. This beautiful woman, with whom she'd somehow managed to strike up a friendship, was looking at her, holding her gaze and smiling with such natural affection. "You'd tire of me very easily," she finally managed to say.

The brown hair moved about the slender shoulders as Maria shook her head. "I wouldn't. I love having you here."

Connie felt the charge of electricity course over her skin. The intense eyes were looking right at her and the beautiful body was just inches away from her own, open and unguarded. She reached out with her hand, connecting with Maria's waist. The tension was real. She stepped forward but suddenly froze as she realised what she was doing. She let her hand drop, forcing herself out of the doorway and back into the brighter light of the landing, cursing her own stupid crush. "Shall we... Shall we have that coffee now?"

"Wait." Maria grabbed Connie's hand and pulled her back into the soft light. "What were you going to do?"

Breaking the contact, Connie spoke to the floor. "Nothing, sorry, I think I'm a bit tired too. That lullaby's made me drowsy."

Maria stayed in the shadows and smiled. "We could always go for a lie down as well?"

Connie's laugh was nervous. "Ummm, now I know you're not being serious."

"Actually I..." Maria paused before shrugging her shoulders and joining her on the landing. "You're right. Coffee sounds great. Follow me." She led the way quickly to the curved wooden stairs, stopping once to look back at her friend. "We almost had a moment then."

Connie blushed as Maria's stationary presence forced her to stand still. "What do you mean?"

"You never touch me. You're not a touchy feely person," she smiled, "but you touched me."

"No I... Oh I don't know. It was just sweet seeing the kids sleeping like that."

"Is that what it was?"

Connie shifted awkwardly. "Or maybe I'm just trying to loosen up around you."

"Well I like that better."

"Or maybe I feel a bit drawn to you."

Maria's lips turned at the corners. "Really?"

"I'm talking because I'm nervous. Stop making me nervous. Stop making me talk."

"I'm not doing anything!" Maria laughed. "I'm just saying that it's okay to have contact between us. In my world it's normal."

"The lesbian world?"

"No. The normal world. The world where humans interact with emotion. The world where humans aren't guarded."

Connie linked her hand through Maria's arm. "The coffee's this way, isn't it?"

"We have progress! You linked my arm. Look at you being brave. The world didn't end. Progress, I tell you!"

Connie stopped and dropped Maria's arm. "But progress to what? Where do you want me to get to?"

"Just go with the flow. Stop missing moments." Maria locked their arms back together and started once more down the wide stairs. "Let our friendship evolve on its own."

"Says you who decided not to call me."

"Right. Coffee, chat, cards on the table. You've spent all morning choosing to play with the kids instead of setting things straight."

"I just love Hungry Hippos, that's all."

"As if!" They reached the ground floor simultaneously and Maria guided them through the farmhouse style door to the kitchen and finally loosened her grip. She pointed Connie in the direction of the long table and bench seats while she pressed buttons on the coffee machine and took some almond biscuits from a tin. "And ponies? You just had to join in with that game too, did you?" she added.

"I couldn't have Noah climbing on Alice's back like that. They needed me."

"Well they're asleep now, so let's start at the beginning. But let's sit in the snug and I'll bring your coffee over."

Connie headed for the small, chocolate brown corduroy sofa that occupied the big bay window. The sun was streaming in and the cushions were warm. She sat and watched Maria as she worked. "Anyone would think you're a barista."

"Sprinkles on your mocha?"

"Always," she said, smiling. Looking around at the pots and pans hanging above the large wooden island counter, she couldn't help but compliment her surroundings once more. "Your kitchen's so lovely. It's the type of thing you expect to see in an old farmhouse, not a townhouse in the centre of London."

"I renovated when I moved in."

"You designed this yourself?"

"No, I pointed at it in a brochure." She moved around the island and handed over a mug of fragrant coffee before sitting next to Connie in the sun. "Well this is cosy. Where do you think we should start?"

"You told me to let things flow, and they're flowing, so tell me about this house. Did you have someone else pointing at things in a brochure with you?"

Pulling one of her legs under her, Maria angled her body towards Connie's, enjoying the warm rays on her face. "Your real question is: Have I lived here with anyone else before?"

"Have you?"

"No."

"You've had serious girlfriends though?"

Maria lifted her mug and smiled. "I think you ask me lots of questions because you don't want to talk about you. Is that what you did last Friday?"

Connie looked over Maria's shoulder out the window at the same snapdragons that Ryan had been admiring earlier. "Okay, let's make a deal." She turned back to Maria. "We're friends who answer first time. We reply honestly, clearly, succinctly and we don't worry about what we say."

Maria laughed. "Do you think you can do that?"

"Yes. Do you?"

"Yes."

Connie smiled. "Well that's a good start then. So, tell me about your lovers."

The brown eyes glinted. "Lovers or girlfriends?"

"There's a difference?"

"Oh yes, huge, and I love how that's your first question."

"See, I'm going to bore you in no time. I have no juicy stories at all."

Maria nodded. "Okay so my first question to you is this: Do you have low self-esteem?"

"I thought this was meant to be enjoyable? And I asked you first."

"Clear, succinct, honest answers. I ask you because you're always putting yourself down. You've said you'll bore me and I keep saying you won't."

"Okay then, no. I don't think I have low self-esteem. I think I just get nervous around you and I start to question myself, that's all."

"Why?"

Connie blew carefully on her mocha. "We've been through this. Mismatched people, different walks of life."

"And we've been through the jigsaw chat as well, so let's move on. We're friends. We fit. No need to question the other."

Connie smiled. "Agreed. I like that. So lovers first, then let's move on to girlfriends."

"Steady on, we're only having coffee."

"Oh stop it," Connie laughed.

"Why? You like me flirting."

"Maybe I do."

Maria nodded. "Official question: Do you like me flirting with you?"

"Yes."

"Right." Maria sipped her drink. "Glad that's decided then."

Connie looked carefully at the beautifully intriguing woman sitting opposite her. "Are you avoiding the girlfriend chat?"

Shaking her head Maria exhaled her indifference. "Honestly it's not that interesting. I've had three long term girlfriends. I loved them all. But none of them ever loved me quite enough."

"Oh no, that can't be true."

"Were you going to reach out and touch my leg then?"

"No!" Connie laughed. "Well, maybe... But only because I felt sorry for you."

"Don't, it's fine. They were all good relationships, but I always wanted children. When it came to that point they all shied away. I can make it more heart breaking if it means you'll touch my leg."

"They can't all have been like that?"

Maria moved her hair away from her face, making the most of the sun streaming through the window. She nodded slowly as if coming to a decision. "I came to the conclusion that it was better to raise a child with one parent who truly loved them and wanted them, than two who were doing it half-heartedly, or forced into it."

"Do you know the dad?"

"Alice hasn't got a dad. She's got a donor."

"Oh right, sorry."

"It's fine, it's just important to get the language right. Yes, if the man who donated his seed lived with us then he would be called her dad, but he doesn't, so he's called the donor."

"Seed?"

Maria laughed. "Sorry. It's how I tell it to Alice. You need the seed of a man and the egg of a woman to make a baby, so Mummy asked the baby doctor to find a kind man who would donate his seed.

The doctor put the seed in Mummy's tummy, it met Mummy's egg and grew into you."

"You tell her that already?"

"You have to. Children are clever. They need to be empowered by knowledge. Alice needs to know. It's obvious that her family's different to others, and if I ever get another partner then it will become even more obvious. I want her to feel happy in *her* normal."

"She is."

Maria smiled. "Exactly."

"Does she ever ask about the donor?"

"Not really, but I make sure I talk about him. We have pictures from when he was a baby and so much of his family history."

"You have pictures?"

"Yes, that's where she gets her blonde hair from. He's a physiotherapist who enjoys nature and science." Maria laughed. "But he could have just made that up to make himself sound more appealing."

"What's he called?"

She shook her head. "We don't know, but he's identity release, which means Alice can contact him when she gets to eighteen if she wants to."

"Do you think she will?"

"Who knows, but she's not been adopted, her father's not abandoned her, she's got me and I'm her family and I hope she grows up secure in that knowledge."

This time Connie did reach out to squeeze Maria's leg. "She will. She is. You're an incredible parent, Maria, and she's wanted; that's all any child really needs."

Maria smiled. "And lashings and lashings of love."

"Don't we all want that?"

"Do you?"

Connie paused. "Actually no, I don't think I do. I think I'm quite independent."

"I agree. Behind that *look at me sitting all delicately in the sunshine with my blonde hair cascading around my shoulders waiting for my prince charming to come and rescue me from this bay window look,* you are."

"I'm a tough little cookie, you know."

"I know."

Connie smiled at the connection, enjoying the moment for what it was, two friends making the most of a rare break in their days. "Soooo," she said finally, "what's next? Shall we make it something lighter? Shall we talk about your lovers instead? How was your date?"

Dropping both feet to the floor Maria sat upright. "Right, well unfortunately that's not going to be lighter either."

Connie frowned.

"I'm not quite sure how it happened, but she knew you. My date. That's why I didn't contact you."

"What?"

Maria got up and placed her mug on the wooden island before returning to the sofa and angling her body even closer to Connie's. "She told me about your problems with Karl. I'd spent the whole day with you and you'd not mentioned it once. I questioned our friendship and thought it best to give you some space."

"Who the hell was it?" asked Connie, pushing back against the arm of the sofa.

"Louise."

"Louise? As in Louise Killshaw? Karl's business partner? All tits and teeth?"

"I think so."

"She's gay?"

Maria took the wobbling mug from Connie's hands and pulled herself back off the sofa placing it down next to her own on the island.

"She's gay?" asked Connie again.

"Bisexual I think."

"Oh great! Wonderful! I spent my life worrying about Karl and Louise and now I'll do the same worrying about you!" She drew her knees into her chest and looked out of the window. "Bisexual? Of course she's bisexual. She's one of those women who has to have it all. So she knows everything about Karl and I and she's talking to total strangers about us? Brilliant."

"She didn't know I knew you."

"That makes it even worse! What was she saying?"

"Look at me. I'll talk you through it. And what do you mean you'll be worrying about me?"

"No, I…" Connie sighed and slowly swivelled back around to look directly at Maria. "She's… I'm sorry. It's not you. She's just always been there, in the background. I always knew Karl wanted her more than he wanted me."

"But she doesn't want him."

Connie lifted her eyes to Maria's. "Because she wants you?"

"No."

"Are you seeing each other?"

"No."

"Might you start seeing each other?"

"No! She messaged me, but I've not replied. She wasn't the tiniest bit interested in Alice so I'm not interested in her."

"You're sure?"

"Yes! Why is this suddenly about me?"

Connie shook herself. "Sorry I'm… I'm sorry. She's just one of those people who's always there, lurking around with her big tits and big teeth."

"She had bad breath."

Connie gasped. "She did not!"

"Well no, but I thought it would make you feel better." Maria tried to get comfy on the sofa but Connie was sitting so upright that it was making it difficult.

"That's worse. Now I know she *doesn't* have bad breath. Did you almost kiss her? Is that how you know she smells great?"

"Guess what, my answer's no! Why are you focusing on the irrelevant things? Why aren't you talking about Karl? Louise said he'd been thinking about leaving, but then said he'd decided to stay and make things work. I'm pleased for you, Connie. It's good if he's going to try harder."

Connie folded her arms and studied the floor. "We've separated. He's leaving this weekend."

"Oh no, I'm so sorry."

"It's fine. I always knew it was coming. We've not worked for ages." She shrugged. "We were living a lie. I fell pregnant by accident. We'd only been dating for two months but we thought we ought to try and make things work." The laugh was quiet. "Those religious people should be criticising women like me, not women like you. Anyone can fall pregnant." She looked out the window and smiled at the snapdragons nodding in a sudden breeze. "Apart from gay people. They never fall pregnant by accident. They only fall pregnant when they really really want a baby. The child's planned and prepared for, and there's never any doubt."

Maria touched her finger to Connie's chin, refocusing the gaze on their conversation. "I doubt myself every single day. Am I getting things right? Should I look for a partner?"

"No, I mean Alice. She'll grow up knowing she's wanted."

"And so will Noah."

Connie shook her head. "Karl's not a natural. He says he'll have him most weekends, but I don't think he will."

"Noah's got Ryan."

"Yes but..." Connie shrugged and frowned. "Are bisexuals real?"

"Where did that come from?"

"Well we certainly need to lighten the mood now, don't we?" She stood up and retrieved their mugs. "I'd not finished, had you?"

"No." Maria took her drink back and smiled, patting the sofa and encouraging Connie to return and relax.

"Ryan tried sleeping with a woman once. Both of them were drunk. Consoling each other. He said it was the most weird, never to be repeated event of his life."

"Yes, because he's gay."

"But isn't Louise? She goes on dates with women, doesn't that make her gay?"

"Bisexual people don't change their orientation just because the sex of the person they're dating changes. They're bisexual. They like both."

"And she likes you?"

"Maybe."

"Of course she does. What's not to like?"

"Are you flirting with me?"

Connie laughed. "Do you want me to flirt with you?"

"Yes."

"Right." She mimicked Maria's previous response and sipped her drink, repeating the very same words. "Glad that's decided then."

Maria laughed. "She doesn't want him."

"We'd only been together for two months when Karl invited me to their work do. I said I couldn't come until later but I must have arrived earlier than expected. I found them snogging over a photocopier. He's always denied it, but I know what I saw. I sneaked out and asked Ryan to fetch me, but when I told him what had happened he went back inside and made a real song and dance about it, shouting in front of all Karl's colleagues. I don't know whether it was the fact I told Karl we were over or Ryan's dramatics that ended it. But it ended." She sighed. "And then a couple of weeks later I found out I was pregnant."

Maria smiled warmly. "And you've got Noah. So you wouldn't change a thing."

"I know." Connie paused before glancing around the kitchen. "You do have a monitor, don't you?"

"It's an in-house sound system."

Connie laughed. "Of course it is."

"We'll hear them when they wake."

"I hear the neighbours on mine. It's the cheapest one that Argos sells. It's only got one frequency so you pick up all the other monitors in the area."

"You do not."

"You do! Come round and listen."

"Is that an official invite?"

"No actually, you'll get cabin fever."

"Let's do Bounce-a-rama tomorrow and then let's go for coffee at yours."

Connie shook her head. "I only have Aldi home-blend instant and I am not serving that to Maria Mariano, owner of the greatest coffee shop in town."

"I like instant coffee and I like cosy spaces."

"Liar."

"I do. I'll prove it tomorrow."

"Bounce-a-rama, yes. My house, no."

CHAPTER EIGHTEEN

The gentle tapping drew Connie away from her computer and out of her under-stair cupboard. She crept towards the front door and opened it as quietly as she could. Ryan smiled and stepped inside. He knew the drill. Utter silence until they were on the sofa and sure that Noah wasn't disturbed. He took off his jacket and hung it on the bannister, pulling a chilled bottle of white from the inside pocket. "*From the shop,*" he mouthed.

Connie crept into the kitchen, trying her best to ensure there was no chinking and clinking as she took the glasses from in between all the other cups and baby beakers. She padded back into the lounge and whispered quietly. "It's fine, he's settled. He's been asleep for over an hour already."

Ryan lowered himself onto the sofa. "Have you been writing?"

Connie nodded as she unscrewed the bottle top and started to pour.

"Can I read it?"

"No, I've written lots since you last read it, it won't make sense."

He took the proffered wine glass and signalled towards her workspace. "I just want to read what you've written tonight."

Connie sat down next to him. "Why?"

"Because I'm your friend and I love you."

"I've not printed it off yet."

"I'll read it on your computer."

"No."

Ryan pushed himself off the sofa and walked towards the cupboard. "Please Connie," he whispered. "Let me read it on here?"

"No." Connie stood up and raced around to block his entry. "I thought you came here to chat?"

"I did, but I want to read what you've written today."

"It won't make sense."

"Read it out loud then." He reached down for the bean bag and planted it against the wall beside the open cupboard door.

"Why? I'll feel silly. You laughed at me last time."

"I did not. Please, Connie, just a little bit." He got himself comfy. "Indulge me."

Connie sighed. "Okay, but then we're drowning our sorrows in its crapness."

"Fine," he nodded.

Connie stepped over the chair and pulled herself into her computer. She scrolled up to the start of a paragraph and took a deep breath. "Just one section."

"Just tonight's work."

She started to read. Her voice was quiet and shy, but her words came out with ease.

'Why am I turning around? Why am I checking the number? I've been standing at the same petrol pump filling my car for the past five minutes. I've looked up at the number ten times already, so why am I turning around? I know what the number is. I'm at the counter, I'm ready to pay, yet I can feel myself turning around. Why am I turning around?

I turn around and look back at the large number sticking out over my car. "Pump number five, please." Why did I need to look? I knew it was pump number five. What could possibly have happened during my walk from the car that would have changed the pump number? It's the same on an aeroplane, or in the cinema. I know my seat number. I always know my seat number. I've studied my seat number. But at the last possible minute I check my seat number once more. Why can't I be sure? Why can't I just know?'

Ryan cut in. "Is this Bonnie talking?"

"I guess it's Bonnie thinking. I think they call it an internal narrative."

"Why's Bonnie unsure?"

She stayed facing her computer. "Mark's told her he's in love."

"And she doesn't believe him?"

"She's just questioning him, questioning herself."

"Why?"

"Because that's who she is."

Ryan shook his head. "That's who you are, Connie."

She turned around. "No, this is Bonnie's story, not mine."

"You're questioning your feelings for Maria and you're questioning her feelings for you."

Connie minimised the screen and stood up so suddenly she banged her head. "That's it, you're not hearing anymore."

"I don't need to. I saw everything I needed to know today." He dragged the beanbag into the lounge and followed Connie back to the sofa. "You held each other."

Connie grabbed her glass off the coffee table and took a large gulp of wine. "We did not."

"You did. You both did. There's an energy between you."

"There is not."

"Connie Parker, put your glass down and look at me."

"Not when you're towering over me."

"Fine." He sat, pulled her down and tried to snuggle up next to her.

Connie took another huge swig of wine.

"What?"

"You've got feelings for her."

The blush was instant. "I'm going through a separation, I'm obviously just confused."

"This separation won't change your life, apart from the fact that you won't have to cook Karl his tea in the evenings. It's not that. You knew this was coming. You're prepared. You know it's for the best." He nodded. "This thing with Maria's totally separate."

"There is no thing with Maria."

"She feels it too."

"She does not." Connie lifted her eyes and looked at him properly. "How can you tell?"

"Gaydar, darling. The chemistry is visibly fizzing off the pair of you."

"I'm not a lesbian."

"Labels do much more damage than good. You like her."

She took a slow sip of her drink. "Maybe I'm just a bit in awe of her."

"Her looks? Her house? Her business?"

"No, just her."

"Oh bless you, darling, I knew this was coming."

"Since when?"

"Year Eleven prom. I know for a fact you wanted to dance with Joanne Stephens."

Connie batted his chest. "Not everyone's a gaybo like you."

"A gaybo?"

She laughed. "Meant in the kindest possible way."

"There's always been something missing with you. This is it."

"What? Some new found lesbianism?"

"No, Maria."

Ryan shrugged. "It doesn't matter what sex she is. You've been missing someone like her. She brings out a lovely side in you, Connie."

"You bring out a lovely side in me, Ryan."

He laughed. "Never, ever again."

"Agreed. But you're wrong. I'm not gay. I've never even kissed a woman before."

"Some people have never tried wine… till they do."

"I think I'm just a bit intrigued, that's all."

"That's where it always begins, my love."

She sipped on her wine and grinned. "Maybe there's a slight crush there."

"Slight? You were practically humping her on the doorstep."

"Oh, Ryan, stop it. You're so mean."

"That's why you love me, darling." He smiled. "Do you need some company this weekend? That's when he's moving out isn't it?"

Connie nodded. "I want to distract Noah. He won't notice when Karl's not around in the week, but he might notice this weekend."

"Karl's having him next weekend though? And every weekend after that?"

"Yes."

Ryan sniffed. "How long do you think that will last?"

"I've got hope."

"You're a better woman than I am. And the house? You're sure he's going to pay for everything? Bills? Council tax?"

"Karl does all the finances. He promises me that everything will stay the same."

"Until he finds out you're fucking Amal Clooney."

"He won't."

"Why not? Because you're planning on keeping it quiet?"

"No, because I'd have no clue where to even begin."

"It's pretty much what you were doing on the doorstep, but without clothes."

She laughed. "Can you imagine what she'd be thinking if she could hear us right now?"

"She'd be thrilled."

"Ryan, she's a kind woman. She's taken pity on me, that's all. I'm just fascinated to be in the company of someone so different."

"You keep telling yourself that, darling." He suddenly sat up taller and gasped at a sound from outside. "Shit, the door."

Connie banged her wine glass onto the table and stood up. "Hi," she said as Karl entered the house.

Karl didn't smile. "I didn't know we had company tonight."

Ryan waved at Karl. "I was just passing through. Thought I'd pop in. Would you like a glass? It's been a while since we've all caught up."

Connie saw straight through Ryan's killing-with-kindness act and stared at him sternly. "You were just heading off, weren't you?"

Karl cut in. "It's fine. You two stay in here. I'll set myself up in the kitchen. I've got a bit of work to do anyway." He managed a half smile at Ryan. "But I will take a glass of that wine with me, if that's okay?"

The friends watched in disbelief as Karl made his way into the kitchen, returned with a wine glass and allowed Ryan to fill it. He lifted the glass in a salute to Connie and Ryan.

"Cheers," he said, managing a smile before leaving the room. It was one of the nicest interactions the two men had ever achieved.

"*Wow*," mouthed Ryan to Connie, "*progress.*"

Connie nodded with wide eyes, went into the kitchen and pulled the door to. "Thank you," she whispered.

Karl yanked off his tie and spoke quietly. "If you have to have a man in the house when I'm not here, then I'd rather it was him."

Connie nodded. "Got it."

CHAPTER NINETEEN

Walking into the Bounce-a-rama building, Connie quickly spotted Maria taking off her shoes in the centre of the room and setting up her stuff on a table. The place was as empty as it always was during the midweek toddler time with only Alice and a couple of other little ones running around. She looked at the tables, unable to see the kids' accompanying adults.

"Hi," she said, approaching Maria. "Who do they belong to?"

Maria followed Connie's eyes to the princess bouncy castle. "Don't you recognise them?" She turned back around and bent down to cuddle Noah. "Hey big man. How are you? Alice is over there on the pirate ship."

Noah kicked off his shoes, sending both flying in different directions.

"Lisssssssssssssss!"

Maria retrieved the discarded footwear and greeted Connie with a warm hug and big kiss on the cheek. "You look lovely," she said with a smile.

Connie shifted herself awkwardly out of the embrace, craning her neck over Maria's shoulder as if recognising the children was the most important thing in the world.

"They're bouncing too much."

Maria smiled at the stiff greeting. "It's the boy from playgroup. The one who's always breastfeeding."

"Lucas? Oh yes it is, and his friend as well, Crusty's son." She turned back around and scanned the large room. "So where are Earth Mother and Crusty then?"

Maria laughed. "No clue, but you really ought to find out their names. What's Crusty's son called?"

Connie shrugged. "Crusty's son." She smiled. "Or sometimes we call him Crusty's son with the bumper helmet."

"You and Ryan are so dreadful. I think I saw them going into the dark tunnel when I arrived."

"Crusty and Earth Mother? When?"

"Two minutes ago."

"You did not."

"I did." She lifted her hands to the room. "Where are they then?"

Connie turned around and looked towards the dark tunnel, which led, via an enclosed mini maze, towards the ball pit. "What would they be doing in there?"

Maria wiggled her eyebrows.

"Stop it."

"Come on, let's go and have a look."

"No!"

"Please?" The giggle was contagious. "Come on, we can do a silent reconnaissance mission. We'll sneak down the dark tunnel and see if we spot them."

"No."

"I'll take your hand."

"It's scary in there."

"I know. I'll look after you. Come on, take off your shoes." Maria offered her hand and nodded enthusiastically.

Connie kicked off her slip-ons and accepted the offer, feeling Maria's smooth fingers lock between hers, drawing her towards the tunnel's entrance. She laughed and squeezed the hand in return. "We're here, you can let go now."

"Shush! We're meant to be silent. Follow me." Maria maintained her grip and walked forward, plunging them into a quite successful blackout.

Connie paused. "Ooo, you really can't see anything at all, can you?"

Maria held her hand even tighter. "Stay close," she whispered.

Connie giggled. "Stop being dramatic."

"You never know what we might find." With her free hand out in front, Maria felt her way around a corner. "It's getting darker."

"It's already pitch black!"

She stopped their walk and turned, lowering her mouth towards where she thought Connie's ear might be. "Shush!"

"You just shushed up my nose."

Maria giggled. "Sorry, where's your ear? I can never gauge how low you are."

"Here," said Connie, stretching up in the darkness.

"Your ear's on my chest!"

Connie laughed. "Will you stop it!"

"You're the one listening to my heartbeat." She reached out and found Connie's waist, turning her around and resuming their walk. "Stay quiet," she whispered once more.

Connie's giggles turned to nervous shudders as they crept side by side in the pitch darkness. "Your perfume smells lovely," she said, unable to ignore that her working senses now appeared to be on high alert.

"So does your hair," whispered Maria.

Connie laughed. "My hair?"

"Yes, I swallowed some last time I shushed you."

"You did not."

"I did, and I can't tell you what your perfume smells like because your neck's always impregnable."

Connie laughed. "Do you want to impregnate my neck?"

"Sometimes."

The whisper was flirtatious. "I could always hold back my hair for you?"

"Now?"

"If you want?" Connie stood still, listening to the dark. "Or we could just keep walking?"

"No I..." Maria reached out and found Connie's shoulders, walking her hands down her arms until she was grasping Connie's wrists. "I want to."

Connie gasped as she was gently pushed back, her body against the hard foam wall of the tunnel. She moaned as she felt Maria's lips against her ear.

"It's lovely," came the whispered conclusion.

"So's yours," managed Connie, willing Maria closer, wanting to feel her body, desperate for more.

Maria released Connie's wrists, keeping her lips against her ear. "You need to lead this," she said.

"Lead what?"

"This. Pull me closer."

Connie closed her eyes, her body screaming out for Maria's, but her hands were unable to move.

"What do you mean?"

"Moments are missed when we take time to think." Maria stepped away from her.

"Wait, no."

"Come on." She took hold of Connie's hand and pulled her round the next corner. "Oh my good god!" she gasped, her eyes drawn to the light at the end of the tunnel.

"What?"

Maria drew Connie forward so she could get a view of the ball pit. "That!"

Connie swallowed a squeal and pulled back into the shadows. "I think I'm going to be sick."

Maria peeped out once more. "How the hell is that possible?"

"They obviously don't miss moments, do they?" Connie couldn't help but look once more at Crusty and Earth Mother, squashed into the multi-coloured ball pit, sharing a passionate embrace.

Maria flinched. "I love women kissing, but that could turn me straight."

Connie peeped out with one eye. "Oh god, they're really going for it."

"Don't look." She pulled Connie back into the tunnel. "It'll put you off."

"Off what?"

"Kissing women."

"I'm straight."

"You're straight-ish."

Connie frowned. "What do you—"

"Muuuuuuuuuuuuuuumeeeeeeeeeeeeeeee!"

"That's Noah!" Connie pointed at the ball pit. "I can get out through there. IT'S OKAY, NOAH, I'M HERE!" she shouted, racing out of the darkness and into the balls, wading as best she could through the pit. "Hi, sorry, hello," she said, stepping over the legs of the women. Then Maria appeared, following Connie with the same words of apology.

"Hi, sorry, can I just step over you there, sorry."

Crusty and Earth Mother stayed seated amid the balls in stunned silence.

"I'M IN THE BALL PIT, NOAH!"

Noah and Alice appeared at the side entrance before Connie had time to traverse the cargo net and pull herself free.

"Lucas bit Liss!" gasped Noah, face against the netting.

Alice rubbed her arm. "Lucas bit me."

Connie tried to haul herself up, slipping and falling into the balls. "Hold on," she said, trying once more.

"Let me give you a hand," said Maria, trying to push Connie up by the legs.

Alice nodded. "I'm okay. Come on, Noah. Pirates!"

"Piraaaaaaaaaaaaaates!" shouted Noah, racing away from his struggling mother.

Maria tried to keep a straight face as Connie slipped once more. "We can crawl out there if it's easier," she said, pointing to another exit.

Connie laughed at her own helplessness. "The tunnel's probably easier." She turned back around, stepping once more over the still tangled legs. "Hi, sorry, just coming through again."

"Me too, sorry," said Maria, trying to ignore the white faces of Earth Mother and Crusty.

"It's... It's that little girl." Earth Mother was using the netting to pull herself into an upright position. "Tabitha."

Connie paused, sure that someone had spoken.

"From playgroup," continued Earth Mother. "Lucas got bitten and now he's started to bite." She nodded. "I'll speak to him now."

Connie caught the last bit. "Thank you."

Crusty, whose nervous giggle was getting louder and louder, stood up. "Are we all going out through the tunnel?"

Maria nodded and led the awkward procession of women. "Looks that way."

"I'm Clare, by the way," giggled the voice in the darkness.

"And I'm Bertha."

Connie made a mental note, pairing each voice to its owner. Crusty Clare and breastfeeding Bertha. "I'm Connie, Noah's mum."

"And I'm Maria, Alice's mum," said Maria as she felt her way along the tunnel walls, leading them out into the light. "Are you two sisters?" she asked.

Connie couldn't hide her horrified expression and mouthed her disgust at Maria. "*You weirdo!*"

But Bertha nodded. "Yes, yes, sorry, right, I'll have a word."

"Why would you ask if they're sisters?" gasped Connie as the two women scuttled away. "Sisters who snog? Is that what you're in to?"

"They're wearing matching wedding rings."

"Sisters can't get married!"

"Exactly. They're obviously ashamed."

"Of being sisters who snog? Wouldn't you be?!"

"No, of being together. Lesbians are always asked if they're sisters, and sometimes it's just easier to say yes."

"And have people thinking you snog your own sister? No it's not. There's no way they're married."

"They are. I need to give them a pep talk. It's fine to say yes to a stranger just to brush them away sometimes, but to say yes to someone who knows you," Maria shook her head, "that's not okay."

"Maybe they're worried that you'll judge them."

She smiled. "So I'll show them they're wrong. I'll out myself first. I'll encourage their confidence."

"How will you do that?"

Maria grinned and wiggled her eyebrows.

"You're not getting me involved."

"I almost got you involved in the tunnel."

Connie cleared her throat and nodded towards the snack bar. "Can I get you a coffee? We need to sit down and discuss the playgroup plan. Phoebe said she'd bring Tabitha back next week."

"I'd better warn Bertha."

"Bertha sounds wrong. Let's call her Earth Mother."

"We can't. We're going to befriend them. We need to use their first names."

Connie laughed. "I feel like I'm in the playground plotting different missions with my very best friend."

Maria threw her arm over Connie's shoulder and squeezed. "I'm your best friend? I knew I could do it!"

Connie shook her off. "I have another word for you. You're childish."

"Good. At least there's no talk of an age gap."

"I'm not childish."

"I know, but I'm working on it." She pointed towards the pirate ship. "I'm just going to check Alice's arm."

Connie watched as Maria danced away, unable to ignore the skipping of her own heartbeat.

****

Shaking the hand of the final businessman to leave the room, Louise turned back around and made a fist pump in the air.

"We did it," she thundered.

"Well done, you were great." Karl spoke listlessly from his seat at the head of the large conference table.

Louise closed the door with her red soled heel and marched towards him. The meeting had been a huge success with Collis &

Killshaw landing two new corporate clients and she wasn't going to let anything dampen her mood. "You could sound more enthusiastic and you could have stood up to see them off."

"You were doing that. I didn't want to crowd them."

Louise dropped onto a padded chair and twirled herself round, unbuttoning the neck of her shirt as she went.

"Who cares, we bagged them!"

"Yep."

"Oh Karl, will you just smile?"

Karl smiled.

"Properly!"

Karl smiled again.

"You look like you're shitting."

"Oi! What's got into you?"

"Take me out for a drink. I think we should celebrate."

"Really?"

"Yes, but no funny ideas. I'm seeing someone lovely."

"Oh."

"Tall, dark," she smiled, "no nasty stubble."

"It's designer." He self-consciously scratched his chin and frowned. "You never talk about partners."

"Well I might just start."

"Must be special then?"

She paused. "I'm not sure they know it yet, but yes, they are." Using the table to start her spin once more she whooped loudly into the air. "And just so you know, your stubble's not designer, it's a sign of stress."

"I'm moving to Manchester. There's so much to stress about."

"Manchester's not a start-up, it's a roll out. It'll be easy."

"So why aren't you doing it?"

"Because I'm needed here."

"And I'm not?"

Louise stopped spinning and looked at him sternly. "Not with that face on you, no."

He checked his watch and shook his head. "It's too early for drinks."

"I'm done for the day. Someone will take me."

"Your new fancy man?"

The teeth smiled widely. "Something like that."

"Won't you miss this?" He lifted his hands to the plush conference room. "Teasing me in here?"

"Manchester's two hours away by train. I'll be coming up at least once a week. This isn't some life changing relocation where you've left London for good."

"It might be."

"Only if you choose to stay there." She stood up and tucked the chair back into the table. "We've already got the staff infrastructure in place. You're just adding some gravitas to the opening."

He rubbed his face. "You're sure the flat's nice?"

"It's gorgeous. Overlooking the canals. Have you ever known me to spare expense? It's another asset to add to Collis & Killshaw." Louise found her bag and reached for her phone. "You're taking your stuff up tomorrow?"

Karl nodded. "I'm travelling after work. I'll spend the weekend settling in, but I'm back on Friday for that meeting."

"My point exactly. We won't even notice you're gone." She smiled. "And you never know…distance could make the heart grow fonder."

He watched his colleague tapping away on her phone. "Looks like you're already distracted."

Louise tutted and rolled her eyes. "Connie, Karl. Not me. Connie."

****

Maria put down her coffee and picked up her phone. "Sorry, it might be work."

Connie laughed. "I love how you call it work."

"I do work," she typed quickly, "from a distance."

"Anything interesting?" she asked as the phone beeped once again.

Maria scanned the new message, unable to stifle her laughter. "No, sorry, it's..."

"You have to tell me now!"

Maria tried to straighten her face. "No, someone just sent me a joke."

Connie stayed patiently silent. "Come on then."

"Sorry no, it's..."

"A private joke?"

"No, a..."

Blowing on her drink Connie lifted her eyes to the warehouse ceiling. "We might need to readdress this best friends thing."

"It's nothing."

"Okay." She looked over at the bouncy slides where Alice and Noah were demonstrating the different positions they could whizz down in with Noah's knee skid leading the trials. "I'm going to see if they want any company."

Maria laughed. "They don't. Fine. Someone just messaged me asking me if I had any raisins."

Connie frowned. "Raisins?"

"Exactly. So I obviously replied saying: What? No. Why? And they just put: How about a date then?"

Connie's face stayed straight. "I've heard that one before."

Maria laughed. "I haven't."

"Well they say humour's a way to the heart."

She put down her phone. "Do they?"

"Yes, and it looks like she's almost there."

"Who's she?"

Connie raised her eyebrows. "Louise I'm guessing?"

Maria smiled, taking her time with her next question. "You're not jealous, are you?"

"No, but you said the date went badly. You said you wouldn't see her again."

"I'm not seeing her again."

"But you message each other?"

Leaning forward and placing her elbow on the table, Maria propped her chin on her fist. "Well *this* is interesting."

"No, I'm just too nosey."

"Is that all?"

"It's Louise. I've got issues with her."

"Nothing else?"

"No."

With a sigh Maria returned to her original position. "Oh, that's a shame."

"What do you mean?"

"Nothing, I'm playing with you."

Connie stared hard across the table. "Don't play with me. Ever."

"Sorry, I meant I was flirting with you."

"No, flirting's supposed to be fun."

"Sorry I…" Maria paused, taken aback by Connie's reaction. "Seriously, I'm sorry. I wasn't thinking. I know how you feel about Louise. I was trying to be funny."

Connie huffed as her lips twitched, a slight smile betrayed her mood. "Maybe I am a bit jealous."

"Says the straight girl." Maria sipped on her coffee and smiled.

"Straight-ish."

She swallowed quickly and gasped. "You *cannot* go from bitch slapping me with that death stare of yours to dropping in news of your gayness."

"I'm not gay."

"Just straight-ish?"

Connie smiled. "No. I don't know what I'm talking about. I've never even kissed a girl. Our teasing just seems to veer off on crazy not quite straight trajectories. I need to calm down."

"As long as you know it's just teasing and I wasn't being mean about Louise."

Connie glanced down at the floor. "I know. But you're the one who called me straight-ish first."

"Yes, in the tunnel after you made the choice not to kiss me."

The snake eyes were back. "I did not!"

Maria nodded. "You chose not to. It crossed your mind. Just like it did in the doorway, remember, when we were watching them sleep?"

Connie's pitch got even higher. "I did not!"

Maria nodded again. "I'm a pro. I spot these things."

"Well I'm a novice and I'm obviously getting things wrong."

"Yes, you're making the wrong choices. You should have kissed me."

Connie laughed. "Oh stop it. You're not interested in me. You're playing with me. You said it yourself. Plus I'm going through some issues. I'm clearly confused."

Placing her mug on the table, Maria spoke seriously. "You never mention your issues."

"Not when I'm with you, no."

"Why not?"

"I don't know." She smiled. "They just don't seem important. But I have to keep reminding myself that this isn't my real world."

"Yes it is."

"No it's not. I can't spend every day fooling around at Bounce-a-rama."

"Yes you can."

Connie laughed. "It's not open tomorrow. Karl's leaving tomorrow. It's an issue. I need to address it."

"So we'll do something else."

"And Saturday?"

"We'll do something Saturday too."

"Oh Maria, you're so kind."

"No I'm not. Two minutes ago you tried to gouge out my eyes."

Connie laughed. "How many times are you going to bring up the death stare?"

"Lots, I might be a bit older than you but at least I've learnt not to cross you." She nodded towards the table in the corner where Earth Mother and Crusty were gathering their things. "Oh no, it looks like they're leaving. I'll have to save my pep talk for playgroup."

"And you want me to take Alice?"

She nodded. "Yes, just for the first bit. Let Phoebe meet her, show her off for me."

"Alice shows herself off." Connie looked back over at the slides. "She's an incredible girl."

"You know what I mean, and I don't want you thinking I'm using her, I just want Phoebe to see her objectively for who she is." She smiled. "The happiest, most talented little lady in the world."

"Then you show up and claim all the glory?"

"That sounds awful. But yes."

"It's a plan."

"Right, now for this weekend."

"It's fine. Ryan says he'll keep me company."

Maria lifted her phone and clicked on the browser. "I was thinking the Eagleton in Brighton. It's five star, right on the seafront. There's a Sealife Centre close by for the little ones and a nice spa in the hotel for us."

"I couldn't."

"You could."

"I couldn't."

"Too late."

CHAPTER TWENTY

"You can't," gasped Ryan.

"I can," nodded Connie.

"Tomorrow?"

"We're leaving in the afternoon. Karl's going to Manchester straight from work."

Ryan adjusted his position on Connie's small sofa. "I knew you had an ulterior motive for asking me round. You want me to come and play chaperone, don't you?"

"No! Definitely not!" Connie coughed and lowered her voice. "No. I just want your blessing."

"What, to embark on an illicit lesbian affair?"

"I'm not married and I'm not planning on having an affair." She shrugged. "You offered to look after me this weekend. I didn't want you feeling put out, that's all."

"Darling, she trumps me. God, she even trumps Trump."

"What?"

"Donald Trump."

"She's not that rich."

"But she's paying for everything?"

Hiding behind her hair Connie nodded.

"You can't let her."

"She insists, but I'll make sure I pay for all of the meals and day trips and everything else."

"She won't let you, and what is this now? Some sort of mini-break?"

"She'll have to, and yes, we're coming back Sunday."

"Two nights? Darling, ladies like her get what they want." He pouted. "And she clearly wants you."

"She's my friend."

"Mmm-hmm. So why can't you look at me when you say that?"

"She is!"

"Tell me that on Monday when she's sucked on your tits."

Connie grimaced. "No one's sucking on my tits!" She stretched and caught sight of the clock, halting her outrage. "You should make tracks. Karl's coming home soon."

"For one final suck on your tits?"

"Enough! Out!" She shooed him off the sofa, pausing before she also stood. "Is tit sucking a thing?"

"For lesbians? Yes, a big thing, darling."

"No, for anyone?"

Ryan looked at his friend with confusion. "Darling, where have you been?"

"Clearly not getting my tits sucked."

"So bring on the weekend."

Connie batted him on the shoulder. "Out!"

He nodded. "Yes, you will be."

"Shush, you'll wake Noah."

"You're the one who's been wailing like a banshee!" Connie whacked him again. "Fine. I'm going, I'm going." He smiled. "Be good, and if you can't be good have fun."

Opening the front door, Connie kissed him quickly. "Text me, I'll keep you informed."

"As if I'd intrude on the romance." He waved camply as he danced down the path. "Toodle-pip."

Connie laughed. "Gaybo."

"Makes two of us love," came the pointed reply.

Connie smiled as she shut the door, sweet relief washing through her. Ryan's reaction had been better than expected. He was one of those friends who would tell things as they were, not in a mean or vindictive way, but with compassion and kindness of heart. He didn't want her going out in trousers that made her bottom look big, just like he didn't want her eating all the biscuits. He'd always tell it straight with on-point observations, often accompanied by good-natured teasing. Was Maria going to suck on her tits this weekend? No. But was he correct in assuming the planned road trip might lead them towards something new? Quite possibly. She checked the clock once more and turned towards her under-stair cupboard. She had time, one quick chapter.

'Sometimes in life you just know. You get that feeling. That knowledge. You're on the right path. You don't need to look back. Your loneliness is replaced with completion and your confusion's dispersed by three words. I love you. *He says he loves me.* Me. Bonnie Blythe. The lost girl who's always looking for something. Searching for what can never be found. Love's not a prize you compete for. Love's a gift that can only be given. I've touched it. I've felt it. Now I'm consumed by it. My doubts have all disappeared and my questions have all ebbed away. Nothing else matters but here. Now. What we have. What we feel. This is life. This is life at its greatest.'

On hearing the front door creak she quickly pressed save and shuffled out of her space just in time to see Karl walking into the house. "Hey, you're home early," she said with a smile.

"I thought I'd try and break the habit on my final night here."

She whispered quietly. "Oh Karl, this won't be your final night here."

He nodded and took off his jacket. "Mum's happy for me to stay at hers for the first few weekends, but she insists I free up the room for Deborah and the kids."

Ushering him towards the sofa Connie frowned. "But Deborah never stays there."

"Mum said she needs it as an option."

Connie couldn't hold her tongue; Evelyn had been the definition of difficult from the moment she realised her son had settled for someone other than Marcie Green, the vicar's daughter, or that nice lady from the vets who was always so gentle with Malcolm. "Your mother really needs to sort her—"

"Please, Connie, not tonight."

"Sorry, no." She smiled and lowered her voice once more. "I've cooked your favourite."

"Thai?"

"No lasagne. Since when's Thai been your favourite?"

"Since always." He loosened his tie and unbuttoned his collar, collapsing on the cushions. "God we're so crap at this."

"We're not. We've got this far." She sat next to him and smiled. "And we've got here without any huge rows, without infidelity."

Kicking off his shoes, Karl shrugged. "I guess."

"Haven't we?"

"Yeah. But look at us, we've failed."

Connie shook her head. "No, I think we've got lots to be proud of, and this is *your* home, Karl, you're welcome here whenever you want." She tapped the pocket of his trousers, trying to lighten the mood. "You are paying for it after all."

"Just part of my maintenance for Noah. It's the least I can do." He looked at Connie properly for the first time. "And I should have done more."

"You're providing for him. That's better than a lot of men do."

"Yeah but it sucks if that's all I'm good at."

Connie stayed silent, not sure what positive parenting traits she could add. "You're a great businessman, Karl," she said eventually.

He sat up straighter, forcing himself out of his despondency. "Anyway, like I was saying, I can't stay at Mum's for long, so I've started to look at other places. They've got some new apartments up for grabs next to the park. I'm going to take a look on the way to work tomorrow."

"The Shoreditch park?"

He nodded.

"They're really expensive."

"It's fine, business is booming. I'll be close. Noah can stay. Places like that aren't on the market for long. Things will work themselves out."

She smiled gently. "I know."

"I want you to be happy, Connie." Looking towards the under-stair cupboard he spoke with apprehension. "Your book. I think you should do something with it. The computer was left on last night and I had a read. It looks like you're almost finished."

"Oh Karl!"

"What? It's good. It's like you, Connie. Unique. Quirky."

She blushed. "I'm not finished and it's just a hobby."

"It's making you happy, and Bonnie seems really happy too. I'm just sorry I couldn't give you that." He reached out and took hold of her hands. "But I know there's someone out there for you, and believe it or not I do want you to find them." He smiled but then he winced. "I can't promise I'll handle it well, but I'll handle it, and we'll survive. We'll survive, together, for Noah."

"But last night—"

"Last night I was being the same pig-headed caveman I've been for the past four years." He shrugged and looked away. "You say in your book that true love lets you blossom. Well I've not done that." He looked at her with sincerity. "Someone else will."

"I'm not looking for anyone else."

"You won't have to. They'll come to you." He sighed, dropping his head into his hands. "I've not been good to you, or Noah, but I will be, and I'm sorry."

Connie touched his fingers and waited for his repentant gaze. "Thank you," she whispered.

"For what?"

"For everything." She stood up and walked away, hiding the emotion that was swelling from her chest and threatening to spill from her eyes.

CHAPTER TWENTY ONE

Connie spent the entire journey from London to Brighton with her heated seat on full blast. The car wasn't cold, in fact they actually had the air conditioning on to combat the heat of the summer sun that penetrated the car's tinted windows, but Connie felt she had to indulge in the luxury because ignoring such a treat would simply be wrong. Noah was doing the same with the inbuilt DVD player, his eyes mesmerised by the exciting technology. Who knew cars could be so much fun?

"And we're here," said Maria, finally steering the Porsche Cayenne between two white marble pillars.

Connie glanced around uncomfortably. "You've pulled onto the porch!"

"It's the entrance."

"You can't leave the car here! I open my door and I'll be on the red carpet!"

Maria released her seatbelt. "That's the point."

Connie glanced around again. "Look, that man's coming over to tell us off. What is he? A bell boy? Or a porter? I've never stayed anywhere with staff on the door."

"He's the valet. He'll park the car."

"You're joking?"

"No, come on." Maria got out and opened the back door, unclasping Alice from her booster seat. "Do you want to get Noah?"

Connie took hold of herself and slid out of the car, nodding apologetically to the valet as she stepped onto the red carpet.

"Greetings ma'am. Welcome to the Eagleton."

She spun around. It wasn't the valet talking, but another statuesque gentleman wearing top hat and tails, who was bowing in greeting.

"H-Hi," she managed.

"Jasper will see to the car, ma'am. May I welcome you to the Eagleton? Edward will take your bags."

Connie turned again to see another man, in a red bellboy outfit, already burrowing in the boot of the car.

"I..."

"May I help you with your precious package?" The doorman was smiling at Noah who had become visible with his face pressed up against the tinted glass.

"No I..." Connie was flustered by the buzz of activity around her and was momentarily distracted by the hotel's huge flags, flapping gently in the sea breeze.

"Albert, it's me." Maria appeared from the other side of the car, carrying Alice on her hip.

"Oh hello, Maria! How are you? So glad to see you back here, and with such beautiful company as well." He nodded at Connie's blushing cheeks before offering his gloved hand to Alice who shook it heartily. He bowed and tipped his top hat in greeting.

"Albert's funny," said Alice giggling.

"You said that last time, little lady." The old man offered his hand again and repeated the greeting. "You shake my hand and I bow. I can't help it."

Alice giggled even harder. "Show Noah, show Noah!"

Connie snapped out of her trance and opened the door, shocked when Noah came tumbling out of the seat having already unbuckled himself.

"Noah do it, Noah do it!" He shouted excitedly.

Connie gasped. "Okay, Noah, okay."

"Yes, it's okay." The doorman crouched and offered his hand. "Hello, young man."

Noah shook the fingers and watched as the funny person in the funny outfit suddenly stood up and started marching like a robot. He screamed with laughter shouting, "Again, again!"

The doorman repeated the spectacle.

"Albert walks funny for you!" said Alice. "He takes his hat off for me!"

"I wonder what he does for Connie?" said Maria with a grin.

Connie fanned away the words. "Shouldn't we be checking in?"

Albert offered his hand. "All part of the service, ma'am."

Connie shook it gently, pausing with apprehension as the doorman tapped out a shuffle ball change. She couldn't help but smile. "Wonderful. That's just wonderful."

"He only does it for the tips," said Maria with a wink.

Albert nodded. "And you're still the Eagleton's best tipper, Miss Mariano."

"I bet you say that to all the girls."

"That I do. May I have you shown to your rooms?" He tapped along the red carpet to imposing doors that magically opened via the gloved hands of another red-suited bellboy. Albert lifted his hat as the two little ones giggled and trundled past him.

Connie walked through the grand opening, taken aback by the elegance of the lobby. It was like something from Pretty Woman. Marble everywhere. Nests of ebony tables. Low lighting. Soft music. She looked towards the bar in the corner and imagined herself as Julia Roberts, sitting on a tall stool, wearing the off-the-shoulder red evening gown and long white gloves, waiting for her Prince Charming to take her to the opera. She looked at Maria and smiled.

"What?" she quizzed.

Connie whispered. "This is amazing."

"Wait until you see the rooms."

"Are we sharing?"

"No, did you want to share?"

"I just thought." She paused. "It's cheaper to share, isn't it? My friends and I used to see how many of us we could squeeze into a single Travelodge room."

Maria smiled. "I think we'll be okay for space. I've asked for two family rooms; they'll probably be interconnecting."

Albert reappeared next to them with a porter. "This is José. He'll take you to your suites. Enjoy your stay, ladies. I'm sure I'll see lots of you."

Connie tried to pay attention to the fourth uniform she'd seen in as many minutes. Stepping closer to Maria she frowned. "Don't we have to check in or something? They've not seen our paperwork. And what does he mean, suites?"

"Relax, this isn't a Travelodge."

"I know," said Connie, "there are no vending machines."

Maria laughed. "Do you like vending machines?"

Connie nodded and encouraged Noah to follow the porter to the lift. "They can be handy if you've forgotten your toothpaste, or if you need a drink or something."

Maria laughed again. "Just you wait."

****

Connie stood open-mouthed in the centre of what she could only describe as a palatial marble swimming suite. It wasn't a bathroom, it wasn't even a bath suite, it was colossal, and Maria was right, there was absolutely no need to worry about forgotten toothpaste as the shelves were filled with every product she could imagine or need. She returned to the lounge, opening a large wooden cabinet and gazed into what couldn't be labelled a mini bar, or even a maxi bar; it was a complete corner shop hidden away in the cupboard.

"I have *never* stayed anywhere like this," she said, turning to Maria who was busy pouring them both a gin and tonic. "You must let me contribute."

"No, you're contributing just by being here. Alice never usually gets this excited by the room."

"Maria, this isn't a room, it's like a penthouse suite or something."

"No, we'll save the penthouse for a special occasion."

Savouring Maria's cheeky tone she smiled. "Am I here as your bitch?"

"Only if you want to be."

Connie laughed. "Perks like this make it a pretty tempting offer." She accepted the offered drink. "Will there be tit sucking involved?"

Maria squeaked. "What?!"

"It's fine." Connie smiled. "They're in the other room, or one of the other rooms. How many rooms do we have exactly with your suite and my suite combined?"

"No, I meant what are you talking about tit sucking for?!"

Connie took a slow sip of her drink, letting an ice cube drop from her lips back into the glass. She sucked it back in again and used her tongue to swirl it around her mouth. "Just something Ryan said."

"Hmm, I see. Now you're more confident you're going to start teasing me, aren't you?"

"Confident? I'm just acting the part until someone realises I'm not supposed to be here and comes to turf me out."

"Right here, right now, you are perfect." Maria smiled. "You fit. You're standing there in your chic little summer outfit with your gin and tonic like you've done this a thousand times before."

"Ha, I wish. This is your lifestyle, not mine."

"You make my lifestyle better."

Connie waited, unsure whether to reply with another tease, or absorb the charged moment. She smiled. "This is nice, isn't it?"

Maria nodded. "It really is."

CHAPTER TWENTY TWO

Connie's first full day in Brighton had been perfect: like something in any number of classic rom-coms. The children had crashed out quickly soon after their arrival the previous evening. It prompted the closure of the interconnecting doors between the suites, even though both women would have preferred to have at least one more gin and tonic, but neither wanted to suggest the idea first. So they'd all said their goodnights and gone to sleep early, waking up with bags of energy for the adventures ahead.

They started with a beautiful joint breakfast on the veranda of their family suite, followed by an exciting morning at the Sealife Centre where the hammerhead sharks were declared the *best ever fishes* according to a suddenly very knowledgeable Noah and Alice. They stopped for lunch at a friendly beachside bistro and spent the afternoon riding donkeys on the beach. The children had announced they were definitely not napping, so their planned trip back to the hotel was replaced with fun at the fair, the helter-skelter being a particular highlight.

Connie smiled as the perfectness of the day swelled with happiness inside her, their final adventure now underway. She took a deep breath and enjoyed the warm evening breeze across her cheeks and through her hair. The suggestion of a peaceful ride along the promenade in a pedal-cart proved just splendid. Her hands were on the steering wheel but she wasn't driving. Neither were Noah or Alice who were sitting in the basket seats at the front holding steering wheels of their own. Theirs had the additional bonus of two tooting horns, which they could squeeze every time they saw anything living or stationary. The only person who had any real control over their vehicle was Maria. She was in the driver's seat playing it cool as she tried to adapt to the heavy steering and sudden leg strain in a vain attempt at making the ride as smooth as possible. They'd only been travelling for one minute and that had been with the assistance of the small ramp from the shop and a preliminary push from the owner.

Maria suddenly shrieked. The pedal-cart had a mind of its own and the pretty yellow canopy and shiny red frame did not hide the fact that they were about to be a menace on the seafront, noisily hogging the wide path as Maria desperately tried to gain some control.

"Watch the bin!" shouted Connie, suddenly catapulted from her daydream.

"I'm not near the bin!" gasped Maria, pulling down on the heavy steering wheel.

"Bin!" screeched Noah and Alice in unison, tooting their horns as loudly as possible, thrilled to have finally twisted their mummies' arms after the day had been spent with Connie and Maria saying "Maybe later" each time either of the children spotted what they had decided were "choo choo carts".

Connie breathed deeply as her head spun with the unusual exertion. Pedalling this choo choo cart was starting to take its chuff chuff-ing toll.

"We need a man," she gasped.

Maria turned her head and lifted her sunglasses. "Excuse me?"

"We need a man to drive this thing."

"You know that's like a red rag to a lesbian, don't you?"

"No, I'm just…" Connie gulped as she was thrust back into her seat, Maria's sudden surge of pedal power propelling their vehicle forward. The children started to beep their horns once more.

"Faster, Mummy, faster!"

Connie held on tight, trying her steering wheel as if it had miraculously become the one in charge of their direction. It hadn't. She stopped pedalling only to find her feet still moving around in time with Maria's.

"I can feel you've stopped pedalling," said Maria through clenched teeth. "Come on, Connie, let's show the kids what we've got. I hate the idea of Alice thinking she's missing out because she's not got a big strong father here to pedal us faster."

Noah tooted his horn and banged on his steering wheel. "Faster, Mummy, faster!"

Connie pushed down on the pedals, trying to catch up with the rotations. "Fine," she said, feeling her thigh muscles tensing, "as long as you've got control of the steering."

"I have." Maria tried to turn the wheel gently to display how in control she was but the cart continued to move in a straight line. Alarmed, she tugged on it harder, lurching them towards the seawall.

"Wall!" screeched Connie.

"Wall!" beeped Noah and Alice.

Maria tugged left, jerking them back onto a collision course with rows of parked cars that were lining the wide promenade on the landward side.

"Cars!" beeped Noah and Alice, shrieking at the tops of voices as if this was the most exciting adventure they'd ever been on.

Connie clutched her steering wheel even tighter as a particularly large people carrier appeared in her line of vision.

"Could you straighten us up a bit?"

"I'm straightening!"

Connie threw her body to the right.

"What are you doing?" gasped Maria, feeling Connie pushing into her shoulder.

"Every little helps! We're getting too close to the cars!"

"Big red car!" squealed Noah, reaching out and beeping Alice's horn as well as his own.

"I've got it. We're turning." Maria's voice sounded almost as strained as the tension she was putting on the stubborn steering wheel.

Connie allowed her bottom to momentarily relax onto her seat as they began to pass the parked people carrier at a safe distance.

"Shit! The door!" She yelled as the owner of the big vehicle decided to get out at the exact moment they passed.

"Hello!" called Noah and Alice, waving politely to the shocked driver who was about to get his door ripped off.

"Watch out!" yelped Connie, as the driver closed himself back into the car, saving them all with millimetres to spare. "Shitting hell, Maria!"

"Sorry." Maria couldn't help but laugh. "Crikey, I know it's not funny. But he should have been looking anyway and I've got it now, we're fine." She nonchalantly straightened the steering, pedalling along as if nothing had happened. "Isn't this lovely, everyone?"

Alice turned around in her seat. "Mummy, Connie said shitting. What does shitting mean?"

Connie shook her head, trying to think quickly. "No, I was singing."

Alice frowned up at her. "Shitting's a silly song."

"No, I should have sung it like this," Connie took a deep breath and tried to replicate a slightly alternative early morning chaffinch call, "shhhhh-iiiiiiiii-tttt!"

The little girl shook her head. "That's shit."

Connie continued the sing-along. "Yes, like shhhhh-iiiiii-hhhhh-iiiii-ttttt! I'm having so much fun on this pedal-cart that I can't help singing. Oh look, there's an ice cream van. Do you think you could pull us up alongside it, Maria?"

Alice spun back around to check out what lay ahead. "Ice creams!" she shouted, beeping her horn in approval.

Maria turned to Connie. "Well that was a beautiful bit of birdsong."

"I didn't know what to say! I panicked."

"And you thought impersonating a foul-mouthed chaffinch would help?"

"Oh stop it." Connie nodded at the ice cream van. "Do you think you can park us up there?"

Maria heaved on the steering wheel, finally feeling as if she had some control over the contraption. "I'll pull us so close that you won't even have to get off."

"I don't mind getting off. We'll have to stop to eat them anyway."

Maria steered them closer to the van. "You can eat as we ride. I don't fancy one." She smiled and nodded at herself in approval. "A man couldn't park us this close." She made one final fine adjustment to the wheel and pulled on the brakes, parking Connie right in front of the ice cream van's hatch.

"Excuse me love, there's a queue."

So busy with their wayward machine, neither had noticed the line of people snaking around the end of the van.

"Oh hang on, let me see if I can reverse." Maria tried to pedal backwards but the chain went slack. "Ooops, sorry, I don't think I can go back."

Some of the line of people started to tut as Maria tried to work out the best thing to do.

"Hello there, what can I get you?" asked the jolly ice cream man, poking his head out the hatch, unaware of their illegal position. "Are you young uns having a fun day?"

Alice put her hand up to answer the question. "It's," she started to sing, "shhhhh-iiiiiiiii-tttt."

Noah joined in. "Shhhhh-iiiiii-hhhhh-iiiii-ttttt!"

Connie tried to ignore the offended gasps and rumblings of the waiting queue. "Three ninety-nines please."

"Sauce, sauce, sauce!" giggled Noah.

"Shhhhh-iiiiii-ttttty sauce," sang Alice.

"And sauce please," said Connie in a whisper, handing over the money.

Maria hauled on the steering wheel as hard as she could, willing the front wheels to twist into position on the warm concrete. She flicked the right pedal back around into a high starting position, ready to make a speedy exit.

"There you go, love," said the ice cream man in a tone that Connie couldn't quite place, unsure if it was condemnation or condolence.

"And pedal," barked Maria, pushing down hard with her legs.

Connie couldn't contribute much, what with juggling three already dripping cornets, so their getaway wasn't quite as speedy as Maria had hoped. It gave the disgruntled queue members time to shake their heads and mutter under their breath as the awkward contraption squeaked slowly away along the prom.

"Well that was embarrassing," said Maria as the muttering from the ice cream queue finally disappeared behind them.

"At least we didn't have to queue," said Connie brightly. "Did you see the size of it? All the way round the back of the van." She smiled and offered her ice cream. "Would you like a lick?"

"No."

Connie smiled again. "Go on."

Maria glanced back over her shoulder. "You realise we'll have to pedal all the way down to the end before we can turn back around to make sure everyone in that queue's moved on."

"There are loads of these buggies," Connie reassured her as she licked a run of ice cream from her cone. "They won't recognise us again."

"Oh really? We're the only buggy with two kids in front singing the shit song."

Connie laughed. "I think they've got it down nicely. Go on, have a lick of mine." She waggled her eyebrows and winked at her friend.

Maria rolled her eyes and was unable to stop herself laughing. "You're going to get me into lots of trouble, aren't you, Miss Parker?"

"That's the plan. Come on, have a lick." She held out the ninety-nine once more, but fumbled as the cart hit a bump. She was unable to stop the ice cream spilling and landing on Maria's seat, directly between her two pedalling legs.

Connie instinctively bent to use the cone to try and scrape the melting mush back in.

"What are you doing?" gasped Maria, trying to keep her eyes on the route but unable to avoid the prodding and poking between her thighs.

"My ice cream's fallen off!"

"But why are you jabbing me with the cone?"

"I'm trying to scoop it back up."

"Shall we save the finger jabbing till later?"

"Queue jumping lesbians!" The sharp shout was accompanied by a tringing bell and tooting klaxon.

Connie and Maria were suddenly brought face to face with a sun-wrinkly old woman riding alongside their pedal-cart on a red mobility scooter, complete with front mounted shopping basket containing a fiercely yapping and equally elderly chihuahua. The woman was dressed entirely in mauve velour leisurewear, except for her tan double-velcro sandals.

"Excuse me?" called Maria.

The old woman revved her handlebars and snarled. "You 'eard me." She sneered at Connie's position with her hand between Maria's legs. "And ya can't even wait till ya get 'ome." She revved once more and started to pull ahead of them rapidly, weaving in and out of bemused pedestrians. "Poor kids," she called at the two women as she belted along.

Maria snapped her thighs shut, crushing the ice cream cone in two. "Pedal, Connie, pedal. We're not having this," she growled.

Connie flicked the ice cream off her fingers and took hold of her steering wheel. "Hold on, kids, we're in a chase."

"Chase, chase, chase," came the chant from the front.

Maria lifted herself off her seat, forcing more pressure and speed onto the pedals. The pedal-cart began to rumble along briskly and the children's ninety-nines started to waggle from side to side as their mouths kept missing the ice cream.

"She's up there near the seawall," said Connie, taking her role as seek-and-destroy sniper very seriously, and realising the mauve tracksuit was harder to miss than the red scooter.

"We'll pull alongside her and have a quiet word."

"Agreed," said Connie, pedalling her hardest as they steadily reeled in their quarry.

Maria turned the wheel, bringing them level with the mobility scooter and trapping the old woman between their cart and the seawall.

"Excuse me," she shouted.

The old woman turned around and snarled, "Feck off."

Maria continued to pedal, keeping up with the mobility scooter's top pace. "And you dare to criticise how we are with our children?"

"I said, feck off!" The old woman lifted her elbows like wings and stuck out her chin, driving her scooter as fast as it would go.

Maria continued to pound on the pedals. "Our cart can match your scooter for speed any day," she yelled furiously.

"Yeah we're lesbians you know," added Connie. "Faster than most men."

Maria looked at her friend, impressed, but suddenly remembering she had to steer as the cart lurched to the right, leaving no space between them and the scooter as they barreled along neck and neck.

"Hello!" giggled Alice and Noah sweetly, waving at the old woman as they licked on their ice creams.

"We'd just like an apology please," Maria continued, trying to sound reasonable and not pant. "You can't go around shouting obscenities at people or using derogatory labels like that. I hope you understand we didn't mean to queue jum—"

"Maria!" shouted Connie, spotting the fork in their path up ahead.

It was like a scene out of *Grease*: both vehicles on the same track but only one would survive.

"I'm going left!" she gasped, but it was too late. The little old lady was forced down a concrete ramp that led straight onto the beach.

Connie watched mesmerised as the red scooter and scowling face careered from view like someone doing a funny disappearing walk past a window.

"Brakes," she shouted.

"The sand will stop her," Maria shouted back.

"Not her, us! She might be thrown off when her wheels hit the beach. We're in Brighton, it's pebbles not sand!"

Maria hauled on the brakes, shuddering their cart to a halt and allowing Connie to jump off and race to the seawall. Connie peered down onto the beach. There was no sign of the red scooter. Spotting movement, she looked across at the ramp.

"Shit!" she cried, "she's reversing up! Go, go, go, Maria!"

"Shhhhh-iiiiiiiii-tttt," sang Noah and Alice in unison.

Now expert in getting the thing underway, Maria started to pedal, forcing Connie to perform a stunt-woman jump onto the moving cart.

"Is she okay?" Maria gasped.

"She's fine, but she's clearly out for blood! Get us somewhere we can hide."

Maria looked at the long wide stretch of open promenade. "Where?"

"There! To the left! That circus tent. Pull us in there!"

"No! They might be doing a show."

"I'd rather be eaten by lions than face the wrath of that nasty old bat."

Maria didn't need more encouragement. She swerved the cart off the concrete and across the grass into the big top's entrance. In the tent it was silent and quite dark and there definitely wasn't a show happening. She stepped down from her seat and ran to the entrance on shaky legs. She peeped out as the old woman went haring past on the red scooter. She sighed with relief and turned to Connie.

"Shall we just hide in here for a bit?"

Connie joined her in the entrance. "Suits me," she said with a smile. "You're one mighty fine driver, Miss Mariano."

Maria laughed and pulled Connie in tight, locking her arms around Connie's warm waist. "We survived."

Noah beeped his horn loudly and Alice copied him before singing at the top of her voice. "This ride has been shhhhh-iiiiiiiii-tttt. Shhhhh-iiiiii-hhhhh-iiiii-ttttt! Shhhhh-iiiiiiiii-tttt!"

CHAPTER TWENTY THREE

Connie moved the paddle brush through the final section of her hair, following it carefully with the straighteners. She tied the long, now smooth, blonde layers into a loose ponytail and studied herself in the huge table top mirror. She looked so small in comparison to her surroundings, sitting on the stool like a child on their first day of school with everything so grand and imposing. She stared at her reflection and decided to button her red checked pyjama top right up at the neck. She took one final look at herself and nodded, making her way back into the suite's main living area.

"Mummy, look, den!" Noah was banging his hands on top of the duvet that had been tucked into the sides of the two chaise longues, securing both him and Alice in their makeshift double bed.

Maria spoke from the bar in the corner. "Shush, shush. You two promised to stay quiet." She continued to pour the drinks without turning around. "They wanted me to push the chaise longues together to make a den so they could watch the film all snuggled up, but I've seen their eyes drooping already." She picked up the glasses and turned to face Connie. "Oh wow," she said, unable to hide her surprise.

Connie self-consciously lifted her hand to the neck of her pyjamas. "What?" she asked.

The stare continued with an open mouth. "You look incredible."

"I do not."

"You do. Your hair."

Connie shied her shoulders into herself, uncomfortable with the inspection. "I always straighten my hair before bed. But I still wake up looking like Worzel Gummidge."

"I bet you don't."

"I do."

Maria handed over the glass of wine.

"And I'm loving the tight top button look. It's very on-trend."

"They're pyjamas."

"You could wear that on a night out, like you would a shirt."

"Can we just sit down in that nice dark corner over there, please?" She pointed toward the leather sofa beside the bar.

"You don't want to snuggle up with them in their den and watch *Frozen?*"

Connie laughed. "Hmm, let me think about that. No. We've got the film, the CD, the book, the Kristoff doll, the jumper, the backpack, the alarm clock, the pencil case, Sven the singing reindeer, and I think Noah's even wearing the pyjamas."

Maria smiled. "He is. Let me jump in the shower so I can put on the Elsa nightie that Alice bought me."

"Ha. She did not."

Maria nodded. "Just you wait. But why don't you go out instead? Make the most of me babysitting since you're looking so gorgeous with your straight hair and funky checked shirt."

"It's just in a pony," she looked back at the den, "and even if the film wasn't *Frozen* there's still not enough room for all of us."

"We'll just have to have our own pyjama party in the other suite then." She smiled. "I won't be long. Just off to slip into my nightie."

Connie watched as Maria walked out of the room, unsure of the appropriate course of action. They had successfully managed to return the pedal-cart to its owner without being caught by the scootering menace in mauve: a feat that had taken time, effort and even more hiding. But they'd managed, and their giggles had continued throughout the evening as they ate delicious burgers at the Five Guys restaurant on the seafront and then as they'd walked back to the hotel with lots of child hand holding and one-two-three swings.

Maria had offered to watch the children so Connie could make the most of the hotel's spa facilities, but Connie couldn't accept her kindness. It was late and Noah was flagging so they decided to bath the children together, which only served to give both little ones a new lease of life, hence Connie's quick jump in the shower. She was sure she'd emerge to a sleepy Noah who'd be begging for bed, but instead she was faced with a gorgeous little boy and a gorgeous little girl tucked up together watching their all-time favourite film.

She crouched next to her son and whispered into his ear. "Shall we go to bed now, Noah?"

Noah shook his head.

"I've got our *Frozen* DVD in my bag. We could watch it in our room?"

"No. Noah happy here." He yawned. "Noah sleep with Liss."

Connie kept her voice low. "This is just a den, Noah. You'll need your own bed soon."

Her son shook his head once more and moaned quietly. "Noah comfy."

Connie went to lift him from out of the covers. "Come on, big man, you're falling asleep. Let's get ourselves to bed."

The piercing squeal was one of the loudest she'd ever heard emerge from his little lungs. She dropped him back into the den and hushed him quickly. "Okay, okay. But we'll have to go back to our room soon."

The answer was short and sweet. "No."

Connie had no option but to take her wine and retire to the leather sofa in the corner. What was the harm in letting them snuggle down there? Sleep there even? It was their adventure. Their final piece of excitement. Why should she be the killjoy? She peeped between the closed curtains at the dying evening sun. She knew why. Smuggling him away would serve as the perfect excuse. The excuse to hide. The excuse to ignore. She wouldn't have to confront the growing chemistry. The tension that was fizzing under the surface every time she found herself close to Maria. She'd done it last night and praised her decision, albeit after a long period of lying awake and questioning that decision, wondering why she even felt the need to make it in the first place.

She took a long sip of the chilled white wine and closed her eyes, enjoying the delicate flavour. Everything tasted better. All weekend her senses had been in overdrive. The taste of the food and the wine.

The warm glow of the sun on her cheeks. The sound of the seagulls. The touch of Maria's arm each time it brushed her own. How wonderful to be with someone who makes life taste better, she thought. Connie blinked and sat up straight. She found her phone lying on the bar and opened up the notes app.

'**Be with someone who makes life taste better. Someone who strengthens your senses. You'll see more. You'll feel deeper. You'll hear the truth ... and the truth is love. Taste love and you'll taste life, in all its glorious splendour. I've found the one who's opened my eyes and I'm never letting her go.**'

"Hey, would you like a refill?"

Connie looked up to see Maria crossing the room in a pair of low slung pyjama bottoms and tight white vest top. She couldn't help but stare; Maria wasn't wearing a bra.

"Umm..."

"You're almost empty," Maria said, leaning over the small table in front of the sofa and reaching for Connie's glass. "We have to make the most of our last night here."

"I..." Connie couldn't ignore the effect the perfect body was having on her own. "Where's your Elsa nightie?"

"Would you prefer me in an Elsa nightie?"

"No, you look..."

Maria returned the bottle of wine to the fridge and placed both glasses on the table. She moved the single leather chairs out of her way so she could sit next to Connie on the sofa. She smiled. "So do you."

"No, I..."

"Was that Karl checking in?"

"Hmm?"

"On the phone?"

"The phone?" Connie still couldn't find the words. Maria's tanned skin was so close and her smell so intoxicating.

"Sorry, I wasn't prying."

"No I..."

"It's fine. I had this girlfriend once who insisted on checking my phone every evening and I always swore that I'd never make anyone surrender their right to privacy."

"I… I was typing. My notes app. A paragraph popped into my head for my book."

Maria snuggled in closer. "Ooo, well that's different. I'll definitely be nosey with that."

Connie handed over the phone on automatic pilot, unable to regain control of her movements. She should be shifting herself upright, moving further away, yet here she was with the world's most gorgeous lesbian snuggled into her side like it was the most normal thing in the world.

"Am I okay to read it?"

"Sure." Connie swallowed on a dry mouth.

Maria scrolled up and studied the words carefully. "You wrote this? Just now?" She took a deep breath and raised her eyebrows. "It's lovely."

Connie hid herself behind her wine glass.

"Is the novel in the first person?"

"Yes, she's called Bonnie Blythe."

"Oh."

"What? You're going to laugh at the name and tell me how similar it is to Connie? Then you're going to question whether the novel's all about me?"

"No."

"What then?"

"Not many non-lesbians write lesbian fiction."

Connie grabbed the phone. "What? What have you just read? You've not been on my search history have you? I had to Google lesbian sex because Ryan was teasing me. He said—"

Maria laughed. "I wasn't reading your search history. But I LOVE the fact you've Googled lesbian sex. You cannot, however, believe what you see on the internet. Lesbians do not have long nails. They do not enjoy giving blow jobs to dildos. And they do not perform for the pleasure of men. Lesbian sex is slow and intimate. It's one of the most nerve tingling sensations you'll ever experience. You're taken to a place of complete fulfilment where you can't quite believe what's happening to you. What you feel. How it moves you." She smiled. "How you come."

Connie realised she was staring and that her mouth had dropped open. "I..." she gave up.

"So in your book it's Bonnie who's thinking these thoughts? Feeling these emotions? The ones you just wrote down."

She nodded.

"You've confused me then. Why does she say: I've found the one who's opened my eyes and I'm never letting *her* go?"

Connie fumbled with her phone, quickly looking at the screen. "Her? That should say him."

Maria paused. "But it says her."

"It's about Mark. A him. A boyfriend."

"What's Mark like?"

The wine glass was once more serving as her hiding place. "He's perfect."

"And does Mark feel the same way about Bonnie?"

"I think so."

Maria waited for the averted eyes to return to her. "I think he does. All good stories have that happily ever after." She turned her attention to the makeshift bed. "Oh bless, they're fast asleep. Let me switch off the film. Shall we make the most of our adult time and watch something in the other room? We'll keep the doors open so we'll hear them if they wake."

Connie's eyes tracked Maria's body as she turned off the TV, and again as she bent to find more wine in the fridge, then once more as she turned with a smile to beckon her out of the room.

Connie suddenly found her own body following without hesitation.

CHAPTER TWENTY FOUR

From her position in the bedroom doorway, Connie could see the two little ones snuggled up in their homemade den in the suite's main living area. She looked back at the super-king sized bed behind her, double checking the distance between her and her son. It was only a matter of metres and she'd definitely hear him if he stirred.

"They're fine," whispered Maria over her shoulder. "Come and help me choose a film."

"I should have brought my monitor."

Maria laughed. "They're just there! You'd never be one of those parents to leave them with the hotel's nanny-cam, would you?"

"God no."

Maria tapped her on the shoulder. "Actually..." She walked to one of the large cupboards and pulled out the boxed piece of technology. "Here. We can use this." Creeping back into the living area Maria plugged one monitor into the wall and faced it towards the den. She sidestepped Connie and held up the other, placing it on their bedside table. "You can give this one to the hotel's nannies and they'll keep an eye on your children for you."

"Is it a video monitor?"

"Come onto the bed and have a look." She smiled as Connie edged onto the plush quilt. "Video, audio, temperature, CO_2 emissions. You name it, it's got it. So you should be okay to relax knowing your son, who is in actuality only two metres away, is fine."

Connie studied the full colour monitor and smiled at Noah who she could now hear snoring softly. "Is there anything this hotel doesn't have?"

"Good lesbian films - the adult channel's full of those fake ones I was talking about earlier."

"You do not watch the adult channel," she said, laughing and pulling her legs up onto the bed, relaxing against the headboard but unable to resist one final glance towards the monitor.

"Don't you?" asked Maria.

"I'm lucky if I get a TV in the hotels I stay in."

Maria reached out and squeezed Connie's thigh. "You're so sweet, and I know it's wrong, but I have this overwhelming urge to mother you and shower you with all of the gifts you've never received and all of the experiences you've never experienced."

"Mother me?"

"No, maybe that's the wrong word. In fact it's *totally* the wrong word." She laughed at herself. "Yes, it's not a motherly feeling at all."

Connie picked up her glass of wine and angled herself towards the beautiful body that was now stretched out next to her own. "So what kind of feeling is it?"

"I've finally got you into my bedroom, I'm not scaring you off now."

"You couldn't." She held her breath, wondering where on earth her bravery was coming from.

"I think I could."

"Well yes, maybe if you make me watch those lesbian films of yours."

"They're not mine. Mine would be realistic. Mine would be sensuous and romantic, but still really steamy."

Connie coughed and picked up the remote. "How about *Pretty Woman*? This hotel reminds me of the Regent Beverly Wilshire."

Maria nodded. "Ooo, go on then, I bet they've got it."

"You know that bit where Richard Gere snaps the necklace box down on Julia Roberts' fingers and she bursts out laughing? That wasn't in the script and was totally improvised but the producers loved it so much they kept it in."

"Really?"

"Yes, Richard Gere did it as a joke. I think her reaction shows what a totally wonderful woman she must be. I love it when women laugh so spontaneously like that."

"It sounds like you might love Julia Roberts a little bit too. Do you want me to be your Richard Gere?"

"Well you are tall, dark and handsome and seemingly rather well off."

"No, I saved up some coupons for this stay."

"You did not!" Connie nodded at the TV. "Here it is. Do we have to buy it? No, of course we don't, silly question. In fact I'm surprised they don't bring the entire cast up to our suite and act out the whole show for us here and now."

"I told you, I'll play Gere. What was he called? Edward?"

"Yes. Come on then, Ed, top up my wine and let's get comfy."

Maria lifted the bottle and smiled. "I like you relaxed. But there's just one other thing." She straddled Connie's legs and switched positions on the bed. "You're right handed and I'm left handed."

"So?"

"So, you get to hold your wine glass in your right hand, I get to hold mine in my left hand, and hey presto, we can do this."

Connie felt a surge of electricity fire up her arm as Maria entwined their fingers together.

"Okay?" asked Maria.

Connie nodded. "Okay."

****

Dropping her phone into the old-fashioned handbag that was resting in the crook of her arm, Evelyn turned on the loudspeaker and started to shout. "I've had to turn you onto loudspeaker, Karl. I can't unlock the door with the telephone on my shoulder."

"Stop shouting, Mum, I can hear you. Why are you unlocking the door?"

"Because she's not answering. Ah, here we go." Evelyn raised her voice even louder. "Connie, are you home, dear?" She paused. "All the lights are off."

The voice on the other end of the line exhaled heavily. "We really don't like you letting yourself in when we're not there."

Evelyn waltzed herself into the kitchen. "Connie said that did she? Well that young lady lost her right to demands the minute she drove you from house and home."

"Mother, we've separated amicably. That's Connie's home now."

"No, son, you paid for it, it's yours. Where is she? It's nine-thirty p.m. on a Saturday night. She has a small child. How irresponsible of her. Where is she, Karl? Where is my grandson?"

"I don't know. I'm in Manchester."

"But it's nine-thirty at night and she wasn't answering the door when I knocked at ten a.m. this morning either."

"Why were you there at ten a.m. this morning? Why are you even there now?"

Evelyn moved from the kitchen to the stairs, sniffing her nose in disapproval. "I was on my way to Joyce's this morning so I didn't come in, but I'll be damned if I'll walk away twice."

"Walk away from what?"

"Whatever it is she's up to. She's got another man, hasn't she? That's why she kicked you out."

"I decided to leave. You know about Manchester. You know how important this is for the business."

"Don't be so naive. She's got another man and *he's* got your son. Call her, Karl. Find out where she is."

"Mother, stop it. I didn't call Connie when I was away on business before, so why would I start calling her now?"

"Because she's got my grandson and I have no idea where he is. Poor little Noah being pulled from pillar to post like this."

"He's been around for three years and you've never been bothered before."

"Don't you dare say that…" Evelyn gasped as she pushed open the doors on the landing. "The beds haven't been slept in!"

"She'll have made them this morning. Please Mum, go back downstairs and lock up."

Evelyn continued her march into the bathroom. "The toothbrushes!"

"What about the toothbrushes?"

"They're gone! She's left you, Karl!"

"We're already separated."

"Oh no, no, no, no, this is no good. I'm staying here until she comes home. Someone needs to talk sense into her. She won't win you back acting like this."

"She might be with Ryan, or staying with her mum. And no one's planning on winning anyone back."

"She stays away and doesn't tell you where she's going? Heaven knows what she's been getting up to all these years then."

Leaving the upstairs doors wide open, Evelyn returned to the lounge and planted her handbag on the coffee table. She picked up her phone and sat down straight-backed on the sofa, crossing her feet at the ankles and dipping her legs at the knee. She cleared her throat and spoke sternly into the receiver. "I'm waiting here. Are you calling her or shall I?"

****

The lights had been dimmed and the glasses refilled on at least two separate occasions already, leaving the occupants of the room in a seductive haze of enchantment. The television was glowing out of the darkness and Connie could feel her heart glowing into her soul. The film was at that critical point where Richard Gere was about to scale the fire escape and overcome his fear of heights to save his damsel in distress.

Connie squeezed Maria's hand in anticipation. "Look at her hair!" She took a gulp of wine and squeezed again. "Look, look, look. Here it comes!"

Maria laughed. "What am I looking at?"

"Her hair! THERE! Bobble out, pony gone, and her hair's down like she's just stepped out of a salon. THERE!"

"Shush!"

Connie grabbed Maria's leg in a failed attempt to pull herself into a more upright position but she missed, plunging her hand between Maria's thighs instead. "Ooo, sorry, that wasn't deliberate; I was trying to lean over you to show you that they're sleeping. Look. No reason to shush me."

Maria followed Connie's eyes to the monitor. "I know, but we want them to *stay* sleeping."

"Do we?"

Maria smiled at the cheeky tone. "Yes. This is great. Relaxing. Laughing. Enjoying a film."

"Having some slightly tipsy woman plunge her hand between your legs."

"You're not tipsy."

"I might be getting there."

"And what are you like when you're tipsy?"

Connie returned to her original position and took hold of Maria's fingers, pulling on a different one with each point that she made. "Well I don't get aggressive, or lairy. I'm not one of those drunks who cry. I don't suddenly think I'm gorgeous, or the best dancer, or want all the attention. I think I might become slightly more open. More natural. More me."

"Right, more wine."

"Ha, no honestly. I'm fine. I'm actually that boring tipsy girl who takes a breath and slows down."

Maria took control of Connie's hand and stroked down each finger with each point she made in return. "You're right, you're not aggressive or lairy, you're more confident. You don't cry, but you're sensitive. You might not think you're gorgeous, but you are ... before drinks, after drinks, during drinks."

Connie felt a shudder run through her body. The gentle fingers were expertly conjuring an uncontrollable sensation across all of her skin. "And?"

"And you're right. You are more natural. This is more like the real you."

"What is?"

"This woman lying next to me. Relaxed, happy, no cares in the world."

"Because of you."

The smile was soft. "I like that, and you make me feel that way too."

"How? You're so much better than me at everything. I squeeze your fingertips each time I make a point and here you are doing some sort of deep tissue hand massage that makes the hairs on the back of my head stick up in arousal."

"Arousal?"

"You know what I mean. When you get all shuddery and you're trying to hide it, which then makes you look like you've got a twitchy eye."

Maria laughed. "You're funnier than me."

"We work. We just work. You taught me that." Connie broke the contact, distracted by Julia Roberts who was now sticking out of the white limousine's sunroof and whooping with happiness. "That's what I want."

"Hair that looks great when it's pulled out of a pony?"

"Ha, see, you can be funny too. But yes, that would be lovely."

Maria turned her eyes to the screen. "Searching for fairytales stops you finding your story."

"Oh I like that. Let me add it to my phone."

"It's true. The best stories have endings you could never predict. Fairytales are easy. Love never is."

"That too. Say that again." Bringing her phone to life, Connie spotted the message box flashing in the corner and let out a groan of instant annoyance. "And here's the wicked step mother-in-law ready to spoil all of the fun."

****

Evelyn prickled on the small sofa as her phone started to sing Jimmy Nail's *Crocodile Shoes*. She let the crooning continue as she brushed some imaginary dust from the sleeves of her jacket, finally answering in her curtest possible tone. "Connie."

"Hello Evelyn, you asked me to call."

"Yes I did. It's ten-thirty p.m."

"Right."

"And you're not home."

"No."

"Where are you?"

"Why?"

"I'm in your lounge."

"Right."

"And you're not."

"I'm working in the cupboard under the stairs."

Evelyn yanked herself off the sofa and raced to the small door, pulling sharply on the handle.

Connie's voice echoed out from the phone that was now at hip-replacement height. "Gotcha."

"You're not..." Evelyn slammed the phone back against her ear. "Where are you? Have you been drinking? What's going on, Connie?" She paused. "Who's there? Someone's giggling. I can hear someone giggling. Who's giggling, Connie?" Evelyn closed her eyes, trying to make out all the noises on the other end of the line, pulling back as Connie's voice became clearer.

"Sorry. How can I help you, Evelyn?"

"Karl doesn't know where you are. You have his son. My grandson. You've worried him. You've worried me. You've worried us all."

"Karl's in Manchester. I told him I'd do something to distract Noah this weekend. I'm sure he's not worried."

"Well I am. Where are you?"

"In Brighton."

"Who with?"

"Noah."

"And? Who else?" She listened carefully to the silence. "Someone like you doesn't go to Brighton all by yourself. You don't have it in you."

"I might."

"You haven't. Who are you with?"

"A friend."

"Which friend? Karl always said you didn't have any friends."

"I do."

"So, who are you with?"

"Evelyn, thank you for your concern, but I'm fine. Noah's fine. Karl's fine. We're all fine."

"Give me a name."

"No."

"Why not?"

"Evelyn, I'm going now. I'll be home tomorrow afternoon if you want to pop round and see Noah then?"

"I've been round twice today. I'll be damned if I'm making a third trip tomorrow."

"Right, well I'll see you soon then."

"It'll come out."

"What will?"

"Whatever it is you're hiding. Or should I say whoever it is that you're hiding. Goodbye, Connie."

****

Connie stared at her phone in disbelief. "That woman. She hung up."

"I'm sorry, I shouldn't have laughed."

"I shouldn't have had it on loud speaker at the start."

Maria lay back down on the bed, running her fingers through her loose dark hair and as a consequence flashing Connie a glimpse of her toned stomach. "Maybe I'm better off single. The idea of a mother-in-law is just too horrendous."

"My mother's nice," said Connie, trying not to stare at Maria's midriff.

Maria patted the quilt. "Come back."

"No, I'm all uptight. I need to pace."

"I'll give you a massage. We'll talk."

"About what?"

"About why you didn't give up my name. About why you're offering *your* mother as a potential mother-in-law for *me*."

"I didn't... Oh right, yes, I see what you mean."

"Come on." Maria shuffled herself up against the headboard and parted her legs, bending them at the knees. "Sit yourself in here. We'll have a debrief under the influence of my magic fingers."

"Is that wise?"

"It is if you want the truth. You can't lie mid-massage. It's been scientifically proven."

"It has not."

"It has. Come here and I'll show you."

CHAPTER TWENTY FIVE

Connie found the lights in the bedroom completely switched off as she left the en-suite. The television was playing tracks from a late-night-love music channel but the glow from the open bedroom doorway was enough to make the atmosphere between two female friends, who were simply enjoying a night of gossip and giggles, just about acceptable. That's what Connie told herself anyway, completely ignoring the fact that every red flag would be flying had Maria been a man.

"So, where do you want me?" she said with a smile.

Maria patted the space between her legs. "Right here."

"Okay." Connie clambered onto the bed, positioning herself with her back at Maria's mercy.

"You'll have to undo your top button."

"Really?"

"And maybe the second one too. I need to access your shoulders without strangling you."

Connie laughed. "Maybe I should call Evelyn back. Tell her I have a lesbian wanting to access my shoulders."

"Lesbians *can* access other women's shoulders without there being an ulterior motive involved."

"Access away. I'm past the point of analysing our *thing*."

"And what is our thing?"

Connie moaned involuntarily as the strong fingers made their first deep knead into her shoulders. "It's our...our..."

"This works better if I ask the questions and you just give yes or no answers."

Connie's mouth dropped open, responding to the divine sensations spreading down her spine. "Okay," she managed.

Maria expertly worked her fingers under the shoulder blades and up and over past the collar bones. "Have you really stopped analysing our thing?"

Connie was aware that she might possibly be dribbling and was relieved that no one could see her face. She moaned again. "No. Constant. Analysing."

"I told you you wouldn't be able to lie during a massage. Does it worry you when you analyse our thing?"

Connie gasped, feeling her muscles manipulated like never before. Ryan was a professional masseur and she had served as his guinea pig on numerous occasions and also been treated to the real deal at his salon many times before, but it was never like this, never as deep or electrifying.

"No," she finally replied.

"Is this thing more than a friendship?"

Connie arched her back, responding to the penetrative movements of Maria's hands. "Special. Friendship. Thing."

"You could have told Evelyn you were here with a friend called Maria. Was it a guilty conscience that stopped you?"

"Y-yeah. Maybe." She gasped. "This is so good."

"Shush." Maria used her palms to pull up the muscles around the back of Connie's ribcage making Connie moan in gratification. "Do you want this to be more than a special friendship thing?"

Connie's staccato words were punctuated with pauses of pure unadulterated pleasure. "I'm. Not. Lesbian."

"That's why I hate labels. Never label yourself."

"You're. A lesbian. Label."

"But I don't go round introducing myself as Maria the lesbian. Never be scared of your feelings, Connie. Feelings don't make labels. Labels make labels. Feelings make experiences."

Connie groaned as Maria's thumbs pushed deeper into her muscles. "This is. The best. Experience."

"Just this?"

She couldn't reply. She'd lost the power of speech. Maria's hands were everywhere. Across her shoulders, down her spine, kneading her muscles into a splendid stupor.

"Let me move to the bottom of your back. Lean forward a bit."

Connie didn't hesitate in following the instruction, shifting herself down the bed and letting her own head drop towards her knees. Maria's thumbs were now working their way up either side of her spine.

"Can I unstrap your bra?"

"Mmm-hmm." Connie managed a small laugh as she strung a half-sentence together. "This works with the women?"

"Every. Single. Time."

"You're... taking... the mickey... out of my... ahhh... my... moaning voice. Ahhhhhhhh."

"Too hard?"

The blonde head shook. "No, perfect." Maria's hands were now spread out either side of her back with the thumbs working up her backbone and the little fingers brushing both sides of her body. "So... good."

"Shush, enjoy."

Connie closed her eyes and let herself succumb to the structured movements. Up, down, in and out. She gasped as Maria's palms kneaded the skin near the top of her back, forcing it towards her spine, causing her chest to widen as it was pulled apart, her nipples moving roughly against her top. She moaned. Maria's fingers were so close, stroking the sides of her body, one movement and she'd be there, touching her nipples, kneading them like she was the rest of her skin. She opened her eyes, trying to erase her previous thought, but Maria's hands were there once more, close to her sides, working her muscles. Connie lifted herself into a more upright position, freeing her breasts, feeling her chest forced apart once more by the movements.

"So good," she managed, pausing as Maria's thumbs moved away from her spine and back onto her shoulders. Connie cursed herself. What did she think was going to happen? Of course Maria wasn't going to slide her hands forwards and start cupping her breasts. She'd obviously been scared by her moaning and retreated to the safety of her shoulders. Connie moaned once more, she couldn't help it. Maria's fingers were now on her collar bone, working the muscles at the top of her chest. Two inches lower and she'd have her nipples, clasped between her fingers. Connie leaned further back, needing the contact, wanting the line to be crossed.

"You have to lead this," whispered Maria.

Connie tilted her head back and opened her eyes, locking their gaze in an intimate connection. "I want this," she said. "I want all of this."

Maria moved herself beside Connie's body and took her face in her hands, slowly placing the tiniest, most delicate kiss on her lips. Connie could feel the emotion welling up inside her. The touch of Maria's lips against her own was all the evidence she needed. This wasn't infatuation or intrigue. It wasn't even lust. This was love, in all its glorious splendour. She leaned forwards, wanting to taste it once more.

"Kiss me," she pleaded.

Maria repeated the gentle embrace, pulling away slowly but maintaining the contact with her fingers. "Next weekend," she said. "We'll make this so special."

Connie gasped, left wanting more, but nodding as she remembered the monitor in the corner. Maria continued. "You're perfect, Connie. Everything has to be perfect."

Connie shuffled down the bed and spoke over her shoulder. "Hold me?" she asked. "Let me sleep in your arms?"

Maria slotted herself into the body's contours, fitting instantly into the curves. "Just like a jigsaw," she said with a smile.

CHAPTER TWENTY SIX

"What the hell's going on?" demanded Ryan once Noah and Alice were safely out of earshot and away on the pedal-karts. "It's Wednesday! You've kept me waiting till Wednesday and you call yourself a friend?!"

Connie walked towards the chairs in the corner of the community hall. "I've been busy."

"With Maria?"

"Maybe."

"Look at you! Sashaying in here like the cat who's got the cream! Where is she anyway? Have you adopted Alice already? Oooo look at you sitting down and crossing your legs like that. Why are you acting so sexy?"

"Oh stop it."

"Tell me everything. Start to finish. I can't believe you've left me in the dark for so long. Actually scratch that, I just want the juicy bits."

Connie stood up. "Let me get us a coffee from the hatch first."

"Sod the coffee!" Ryan banged on the empty chair. "Get yourself back down here."

Connie giggled.

"Look at you lording all the attention! Something's definitely gone on."

She sat back down and pulled the chair as close to her friend's as possible. "I didn't want to tell you over the phone."

"You fucked her didn't you?"

"No! Don't be so crude." She lowered her voice. "Maria held me. She held me all night."

The face Ryan pulled was one of sheer revulsion. "You lesbians. It's true what they say. Gay men fuck, lesbians hire a truck."

"What?"

"A removals truck, because it's always about emotions, falling in love so quickly and declaring they've found their life partner within a matter of minutes. Gay men get it right. We fuck and fuck off. Life's about enjoying the physical, Connie, not getting wrapped up in some emotional bullshit."

"Trust me I enjoyed the physical."

Ryan gasped. "So you did fuck her?"

"No, she gave me a massage."

"Oh good god, this gets worse. I'm not sure I want to hear any more, darling."

"Shush, you can't anyway, here comes Phoebe. Remember I told you the plan. She's Maria's old friend. We've got to show off Alice."

Ryan groaned. "I like soap operas, but this is getting too much."

"She's anti gay parents. She'll see how amazing Alice is compared to her exorcist kid then Maria can waltz in and take all of the glory."

"So she *is* coming today?"

"Yes, and we can all go for coffee afterwards."

"Me, you, your lesbian lover and her anti-gay best friend. Can't wait. Oh look there's Earth Mother and Crusty, should I invite them as well?"

"Might work. They're married, but ashamed, so our other mission involves bringing them out of their shells." She nodded. "But Maria said she'd take charge of that one."

"What? Who are you? One brush with the dark side and you're camper than me."

"Not possible. Quiet, here she is." Connie stood up and reached for another chair. "Hi Phoebe, I'm glad you came back." She knelt next to Tabitha. "Hello little lady, how are you?"

Tabitha furrowed her brow before lurching at Connie and gnashing her teeth. Connie held her ground.

"Very nice and shiny. You must be good at brushing? Why don't me and Mummy take you to do some reading over there with Alice and Noah? They'll get off the pedal-karts if I ask them nicely."

The little girl paused, unsure how to handle the reaction. She tried a growl instead. Connie took hold of her hand. "Come on then, we can play doggies. You lead the way."

"No!"

Sharp teeth suddenly sank themselves into the back of Connie's hand.

"Oww!" she gasped, releasing her grip and watching the wild child run off to the blocks.

Phoebe slumped down onto the seat. "This happens wherever we go."

"Aren't you going to call her back?" questioned Connie, shaking away the pain in her hand and checking for broken skin.

"I find it best if I leave her."

****

"How long you keep secret?" snapped Maddalena, crossing her arms and furrowing her brow. "You let no one have Alice but me. Good job Tony sick or I no see this… this… this Connie girl come take away my Alice."

Maria tried to move her elderly aunt from behind the counter of the Shoreditch branch of Mariano's. "The crew say they're fine."

"One manager in every store. I work here today. Where she take her?"

"It's fine, I can cover this morning and they've got Gail coming in this afternoon."

"I organise Gail and I organise me. We not need you. You go get Alice back."

"No, they've just gone to the playgroup. I'm heading over there in a bit. We'll be back for drinks afterwards. I can introduce you properly then."

Maddalena's brow softened slightly. "I officially meet?"

"Yes, she's a good friend."

"Friend friend or," the elderly woman puckered up and kissed her fingertips, "*innamorata* friend?"

Maria smiled. "Maybe you could have Alice for one night this weekend so I could find out?"

"*Sì, sì, sì, sì, sì!*" Maddalena shuffled back to the counter and reached for a reserved sign, taking it to the best table and placing it with a bang. "I save this for you and the beautiful *bella bella* Connie."

"We'll be a couple of hours at least."

"No, no, no, no, no. This saved. You let Aunt Maddalena spoil you when you return. And I take Alice whole weekend."

"No—"

"*Sì.* Whole weekend."

****

"Right, isn't this lovely," said Connie, relieved to have finally gathered all three children into the playgroup's reading area and successfully coaxed Phoebe to join them.

"Big booby!" said Tabitha, scrunching up her nose and pointing straight across the piles of beanbags and books towards Earth Mother's loose udder. Lucas popped off the nipple and turned around.

"Urgh!" continued Tabitha. "Big booby dripping!"

Crusty appeared at Earth Mother's side with a hanky, trying to dab away the wet milk.

"Stop it," hushed Earth Mother, turning her shoulder on the help, flustered by the intimate gesture.

Connie watched with interest, trying to catch Crusty's eye and give a reassuring smile. She failed.

"Connie stare at big wet booby," said Tabitha continuing her tell-tale-ing.

Phoebe wagged a finger at her daughter. "No. Ladies do not stare at other ladies' boobies."

"Daddy stare at boobies on iPad."

"That's different, Tabitha. Daddy's a man."

Connie coughed lightly and lowered her voice, unsure if Phoebe was joking. "Let's all just agree that staring's not good in any situation."

"Especially when it's women staring at other women's boobies," added Phoebe once more, relishing the opportunity to discipline her daughter who was sitting still for once in her life.

Connie turned her attention to Phoebe. "But men can?"

"Oh it's in their nature isn't it? You're fighting a losing battle if you're trying to teach Noah to look at the eyes."

Connie knew it was now or never. Pin her down and flush her out. She might play the "poor me" card, but if homophobia was present then she deserved everything she got. She nodded to herself, pleased with her plan of attack.

"Well then, Alice and Tabitha should be free to stare away too."

"Why in heaven's name would they want to do that?"

"Some women marry women. The lady breastfeeding is married to the lady who's hovering around behind her."

Phoebe moved uncomfortably on her beanbag. "Really? Well they do say that same-sex parents delay child development and that boy's clearly behind, still on the breast at that age. I don't think that's right." Phoebe gasped. "And is that other child theirs too? That one with the bumper helmet? Does he have some sort of brain damage?"

"No. I don't know. I don't think so. I don't know them that well." Connie took hold of herself. This wasn't going quite as she'd planned. "Right, who's reading a book?" she said, desperately trying to get the task back on track.

Phoebe continued her assessment. "I know Tabitha's no saint, but she doesn't have *issue* issues."

Connie paused. "I try really hard not to judge."

"Be confident. On the whole I think we're getting it right." The woman smiled, overlooking the fact that her daughter was ripping out the hide-and-peep flaps in the latest *Spot the Dog* book.

Connie was unsure how she'd been grouped together in the Good Parent category just because she was apparently straight.

"Having the ability to produce children doesn't automatically make you a perfect parent," she said.

Phoebe ignored her point. "But I do think Tabitha's too young to be exposed to relationships like that."

Connie couldn't let it lie. "And I don't think anyone says same-sex marriage delays child development."

"Don't get me wrong. I'm not against people like that. Ryan seems lovely and my best friend used to be a," she mouthed the word, "*lesbian.*"

"And she's not anymore?"

"Not what?"

"A lesbian?"

Phoebe nodded. "Oh she probably is, but I don't see her. She used one of those *procedures* to get herself pregnant. I couldn't stand by and watch."

"Maybe she wanted you to stand by and hold her hand?"

"Oh I couldn't." She glanced towards Earth Mother and Lucas. "And it looks like I did the right thing."

"Can I read this to you?" asked Alice, shuffling up to their feet with a large wooden version of *The Very Hungry Caterpillar.*

"Of course you can, sweetheart," said Connie, relieved for a break in the sermon. "Noah, Tabitha, pull up a bean bag. Let's hear Alice reading."

"Liss good at stories," said Noah, nodding with pride.

Tabitha didn't turn around.

The blonde-haired girl opened the book and started to read.

"She's remembering!" screamed Tabitha, spinning herself into the circle.

Her mother wagged her finger once more. "It doesn't matter if she is, we can still listen quietly."

Alice continued her story, pointing at the words and using big biting actions whenever the caterpillar ate something.

"Remembering, remembering, remembering!" screamed Tabitha. "Playing caterpillar by myself!"

Phoebe sighed as her daughter stomped away. "I'm sorry, Alice, please carry on. Tabitha's just having a funny five minutes."

Connie nodded, encouraging Phoebe to re-engage. "Can you see how she's pointing at the right words as she reads? It may well be remembering, but it's a really great first step."

"She's definitely ahead. Let's hope some of this rubs off on Tabitha. I think social engineering's really important when it comes to your children. Make sure they have friends who'll advance them."

"So you approve of Alice?"

"Of course! She's so well behaved and very polite. I saw her on the pedal-karts earlier. A real all-rounder. Your friend must be very proud. And Noah's wonderful too. A real cutie. I appreciate this branch of friendship you've extended to me, Connie. It's never happened before. I'm usually asked to leave each playgroup before I get the chance to meet people properly."

Connie felt a momentary pang of guilt. Had it not been for Maria's connection she would have steered well clear of exorcist girl and her head-down ignorant mother.

"JOSHHHHHHUA!" Top Dog was on her feet yelling into the centre of the room. "LET GO OF HER HAIR!"

Connie and Phoebe turned towards the action just as Ryan arrived at their station.

"SHE BIT ME!" screamed the little boy.

Ryan knelt beside Connie and hushed his voice. "Sorry, I saw it. Tabitha's bitten him. I thought I'd better come over. You don't want to get on the wrong side of Top Dog."

"YOU KEEP PULLING THEN, MY SON!" shouted the mother with the slicked back hair and array of tattoos.

"MUMMY!" cried Tabitha.

"What do I do?" gasped Phoebe.

"You go over there!" Connie was now on her feet. "You tell him to let go."

"It always ends like this, with a huge confrontation."

"MUMMY, SHE BIT ME AGAIN!"

Top Dog was now scanning the perimeter. "WHOSE IS SHE? THE WILD GIRL. WHOSE IS SHE?"

"Hello, everyone. What have I missed?" Maria was standing in the middle of the bean bags, smiling at the gathering.

"Mummy!" giggled Alice, dropping her book and throwing herself into the outstretched arms.

Phoebe paled. "Maria?"

"Oh, hi Phoebe. What a nice surprise. It's good to see you. Have you met Alice?"

"I... I..."

"And which one's yours?" Maria looked to the clusters of children who were now all staring at the spectacle unfolding in the centre of the room.

"NO ONE WANTS HER? I DON'T BLAME YOU. FILTHY LITTLE ANIMAL BITING OTHER KIDS LIKE THAT."

"It's a phase," cried Connie, racing to her rescue. "You were just pretending to be *The Very Hungry Caterpillar*, weren't you?"

"I want my mummy," sniffed Tabitha.

Phoebe got up from her beanbag. "I guess that one's mine."

CHAPTER TWENTY SEVEN

"How dramatic," giggled Ryan, sipping on his mocha.

"It's not dramatic, it's heart breaking," corrected Connie.

Maria pushed the plate of pastries into the centre of the table and propped herself on her elbow. "I shouldn't have encouraged you. I shouldn't have suggested it at all."

Ryan reached out to stroke her back. "Don't worry about it. She says it happens at every playgroup she goes to."

"But Phoebe's my friend."

"She *was* your friend," corrected Connie, "until she got on her high horse about same-sex parenting."

Maria sighed. "Weren't you the same? Full of ideas about how you'd mother your child. What you'd be strict on. How great you'd be. It changes. You never know how you're going to cope in each situation."

Ryan sniffed. "Well she's not coping now, is she? Don't mind if I do," he said, biting into one of the muffins.

"So we should help her," said Connie and Maria at the same time.

"Oh darlings, look at you both." He swallowed quickly. "Like two peas in a pod. But Connie, sweetheart, I know you. Be honest. Phoebe's a knob."

"Okay, she might be a knob, but only because of the strange things she says. She just doesn't seem to have the awareness that she, of all people, shouldn't be judging how others bring up their children. She's naive. Maybe just misguided. Mis—"

"…understood," added Maria.

"And you're even finishing off each other's sentences. How adorable."

Maria ignored the teasing and lifted her mug. "She was one of those girls at school who thought she had lots of friends." She took a breath and blew gently on the coffee. "When really she didn't have any at all."

Connie smiled. "Except for you."

"I felt sorry for her," said Maria, managing to take her first sip.

"I don't think you should feel sorry for her anymore." Connie paused. "I'm not sure she's good for you."

With an eyebrow raised Maria looked teasingly across the table. "And you are?"

Connie's smile was huge. "Very."

"Err, ladies, I *am* here!" gasped Ryan, leaning forward and trying to get back in the mix. "So, I hear you do massages, Maria?"

Maria gasped. "You told him?"

"No!" hushed Connie.

"There's more to tell?" He was open mouthed. "You're right, I can't compete with that, but I *am* the professional masseur and Connie *won't* find anyone better than me."

"She's better than you," confessed Connie.

"Touché," he gasped, laughing. "Maria, my darling, *whatever* it is that you're doing to my friend, please keep on doing it. I've not seen her this happy in years."

Connie tutted. "Yes you have, Ryan."

"No, I haven't." He paused and looked at Maria. "But I'm worried you might have some competition. That little old lady's been staring at Connie ever since we arrived. The one behind the counter. Doing your bit for help the aged, I see?"

Maria laughed. "That's my aunt Maddalena. I've told her about Connie. She's desperate for an introduction, and she's desperate to impress, hence the reason why this table was reserved and laden with cakes and pastries. Let me go and get her so I can introduce you properly." She made her way to the counter and leaned over to speak to her aunt.

Ryan hushed his voice. "She's told her aunt about you? What's she told her? Introductions to the family, Connie? This is moving so fast!"

"Stop it. She saw me picking Alice up this morning. That's all."

"And the rest," gasped Ryan. "This chemistry is electric!"

"No, you're just on a high from the drama of playgroup."

"I'm not! There's a real energy between you. It's sparky. We're all sparky. I think she likes me as well."

Connie smiled. "Of course she likes you. You're my best friend."

"And she's your soon to be lover. Unless that's happened already, missy?"

"No!" Connie smiled. "The children were there."

"People with children do still have sex you know."

"We might not even—"

"Oh don't you dare start with the *I don't know where this is heading* card. You two are on a collision course with passion."

"Stop it."

"No, I'm your best friend. I'm allowed." He smiled. "Karl's having Noah this weekend isn't he?"

"Yes, why?"

Ryan lifted his fingers to his bald head and stuck out his elbows bursting into his best version of *Dirty Dancing's Hungry Eyes*.

"Stop, they're coming, and she's old and Italian so lay off the campness."

"God no, darling. Italians love the gays. Hello, Maddalena," he said, jumping out of his seat and kissing the little woman on both cheeks. "We've heard so much about you."

Connie stood up to join them. "Hi, I'm Connie."

Maddalena ignored Ryan completely, choosing to throw her arms around Connie's waist instead. "*Bella, bella bella*. I watch from counter. Maria smiling. You make Maria be smiling."

"Aunt Maddalena, this is Connie."

"We already meet. *Bella, bella bella*."

"And this is Ryan, Connie's best friend."

Maddalena turned around. "Pastries are good, no? I see you eating from counter. You like my spread. *Buono*. This need to grow." She stepped forwards and hit him in the gut. "Too skinny."

"Aunt Maddalena!"

"It's fine," said Ryan, bending down and sparring like a boxer, "your aunt's a feisty one. I like feisty Italian women, especially ones who feed me up."

Maddalena nodded. "I like him too." She turned back to Connie. "Your son good boy. He play lovely in playpen. I watch from counter. I take him this weekend? Like Alice?"

Maria coughed. "Connie and I haven't really spoken about the weekend yet."

Ryan cut in. "Noah's father's got him this weekend, so Connie's a free agent."

"Ahhh, Maria too. *Perfetto, perfetto, perfetto.*"

Maria took her aunt's shoulders and moved her to the playpen. "Let me introduce you to Noah."

Connie and Ryan watched the little old lady reach over the white picket fence and ruffle Noah's hair into a frenzy. "Connie, darling," he whispered, "we need to go shopping."

"For what?" she asked.

"For sex."

"What?"

"It's happening. This weekend. The sex. And it's my duty, as your very best also-gay friend, to get you prepared."

"No."

"You'll need—"

"No."

"But if she's—"

"No."

"Not even—"

"No."

Ryan picked up another muffin. "She might want—"

"No, and you can't call me gay." She lifted her drink and took a long sip, finally letting her smile show around the sides of her mug. "You really think there's chemistry?"

"Darling, fine, ignore the labels, but you can't ignore what you feel when you're with her. Or what you feel when you're *about* to be with her. I can see it. It's bursting out of you, and I've always known it was in you."

"I'll admit I might get a little bit excited, but that's just because I can feel my life coming back to me. Noah's easier now. I've got more free time."

"Bollocks. You get excited because of her. Because you're into her. Tell me then, when you're not with her... and you're not due to be with her... what are you thinking about?"

Connie scrunched up her eyes and smiled. "The times I *have* been with her and the times I *might* be with her again."

"This isn't a friendship, Connie. This is something much much deeper."

"I know." She looked towards the playpen at Maria who was sitting with both children on her knee, talked into reading a story. "She's just perfect."

"Connie!" The gush was false. "I thought it was you."

Connie looked up at the big tits and big teeth. "Louise!"

"How are you?"

"Good thank you. You?"

"How are you holding up?"

Connie watched the dark ponytail swinging from side to side, sure that the look of concern was entirely bogus. "Great thanks. Have you met Ryan?"

"Maybe briefly. At a Christmas party. I think he raced in and—"

"Long time ago," he said, cutting her short.

Connie flushed. "Yes. Anyway. How's work?"

"Oh it's fantastic! I was up in Manchester yesterday with Karl. He's doing such a brilliant job. Working so damn hard. He said you'd been holidaying in Brighton?"

"Just distracting Noah."

"Poor little mite. How's he holding up?"

"He's not even noticed Karl's gone. Are you here for Maria?"

Louise reddened. "How do you...? Did she...?"

"Louise. Hi." Maria appeared next to the woman.

"I've... I just popped in to..." She straightened her suit jacket around her ample bust. "Connie, Ryan, nice to see you both again. Maria, could we grab a quick drink?"

Connie watched as the two women retreated to the stools by the door, unable to judge Maria's reaction. She had looked down at her and their eyes had connected, but Connie wasn't sure if it was a look of apology or guilt? Or was she trying to convey her innocence? Or—

"Your mind's in overdrive," whispered Ryan, "I can hear it whirring."

Connie barked back. "Two things: Evelyn's told Karl about Brighton, and *she* wants a piece of Maria."

Ryan followed Connie's glare. "Which bothers you the most?"

"I don't care about Brighton. I'm free to do as I please."

"So why didn't you tell him?"

"Karl? He knew I'd be doing something."

"But you weren't specific?"

Connie shrugged. "He never likes my friends. Why should I mention Maria? I'll just say I went with you."

"He doesn't like me!"

"He tolerates you."

"A clear conscience has nothing to hide, Connie Parker."

"Exactly, so why's Maria hiding that?" she said, narrowing her eyes to slits.

Ryan joined in the gawking. "What? What is it?"

"I don't know. She's hiding it. Look, she's trying to use her back as a shield so we can't see."

"No she's not. There! It's a picture. Is that from Louise?"

Connie nodded. "I saw her pull it out of her bag."

"Why would Louise give her a picture?" Ryan continued to stare. "It looks like some arty-farty sort of thing. Nice frame though."

"That's obviously what lesbians do. They don't do flowers or chocolates. They do pieces of art and surprise visits. I'm *so* out of my league. Clearly they've got a connection. That's what Maria wants, she doesn't want... let me think..." Connie paused. "See, there's actually *nothing* I could offer her anyway."

"You like art."

"But not enough to know what to buy the lesbian whose coffee shop's already overflowing with the stuff."

"Offer her great sex then. I'll take you shopping. We'll—"

Connie stood up. "No. The only place you can take me is home."

****

Maria looked at the print once more. "It's lovely. But I can't accept it."

"I want you to. It's my way of apologising. You see how the woman's holding her daughter? It symbolises how wrong I was to not ask you about Alice. You two come as a pair. I understand that now. I just want one more chance. Please, Maria? My raisin joke was funny, right?"

"The baby's a boy."

"What baby?"

"In the picture."

Louise shook her blunt fringe and frowned. "It's just called *Mother and Child*. It looks like a girl to me." She pointed at the Klimt prints on the wall. "It's the same artist though, isn't it?"

"No, this one's by B.K Lusk."

"Oh damn it. I popped in at the weekend, hoping to bump into you, but you weren't here. I saw all the pictures and thought it would be nice to get one to add to your collection."

"It was a lovely thought. Thank you, but..." she paused, distracted by the movement at the playpen. "Give me a second." Maria moved towards the doorway to block Connie's exit. "You're not going are you?"

Connie nodded. "We'll leave you two in peace."

Maria took her arm. "Wait."

"Have fun," she said, not able to control the crispness of her tone.

Maddalena used the broom that was resting at the end of the counter like a walking stick to increase the speed of her shuffle. "You not go! You stay longer. Tell her, Maria. *Bella, bella* Connie not go."

Connie smiled at the old woman. "Sorry, Maddalena, Noah needs his nap."

"Big boy not tired. Look!" She squeezed on Noah's cheeks. "Alice miss big boy. Maria finish with customer in no time."

Louise piped up from her stool. "I'm not a customer."

Maddalena glared at her niece. "Why you with her and not Connie then?"

"Hi, I'm Louise." The dazzling teeth were out on display as she joined them in the doorway, offering out her hand to Maddalena. "You must be a relative? I've always been told there's some Italian in me."

Maddalena ignored the outstretched fingers and glanced at the blue-eyed lady's breasts, unable to see anything higher. "No Italian in you."

Maria tried to turn her aunt back to the counter. "Louise is a friend."

Maddalena spun back around. "Lady friend from date?"

Louise pretended to blush. "I'm usually a very private person but it seems Maria here's been telling everyone about our little liaison."

"Shoo." Maddalena lifted up the broom and tried to brush the woman out of the shop. "Shoo, lady. You no good for my girl. My girl want nice lady like Connie."

"Oww!" Louise bent down to rub her ankles, knocked off balance by the broom.

"Shoo, lady. Shoo."

"Stop it!" Maria took the weapon away from her elderly aunt. "Sorry, Louise."

Louise straightened her suit and stood upright, realisation hitting her harder than the broom. "Someone nice like Connie? So that's where you were this weekend." She turned to her rival. "Karl was wondering about Brighton."

CHAPTER TWENTY EIGHT

It was one-thirty p.m. and nothing was different, yet the house seemed quieter than usual. Noah was halfway through his midday nap and Connie was tucked under the stairs trying to step into Bonnie and Mark's perfect world, but it just wasn't happening. Usually she'd be sucked in the minute she sat down, an outpouring of words flowing from her fingers, advancing their story with all of the thoughts and visions that had consumed her since she'd last been able to write. Not today though. Today she was sitting in silence, just listening to the loneliness that seemed to be lingering around her. Connie closed her eyes. What was so different? Karl was never usually around at this time, and neither was Ryan, so why did it feel so quiet, so empty? She squeezed her eyes tighter, hoping the small tear welling behind her lashes wouldn't find its way onto her cheek. It did, and she let it run freely, following its downward journey towards her keyboard, flattened into a thin film, broken by the impact. She lifted her fingers, she knew the answer. Bonnie's story was too saccharine. People wanted the happy ending, but only after the struggle. Life wasn't easy. People made mistakes. Mark would have his moment of madness.

'Trust is to believe, then accept, and have faith in, without knowing or seeing the truth. I know I've never cheated, I've seen how I behave, so I trust that I'll be loyal. I love him. I won't hurt him. But how can I trust him when I don't see his proof? When I don't know his truth? We're strangers brought together after years of living apart. What do we ever truly know about that person? Do we trust what they say? Or wait until we see what they do? Only then accepting their truth for what it actually is: honesty or lies.'

She paused her typing, sure that she'd heard a quiet tapping. She listened again. Noah would usually shout out the minute he woke, calling her upstairs for a cuddle. She checked the time. He probably had at least another hour in him yet. Her ears pricked up at the quiet noise. Yes, something was definitely tapping. She pushed herself backwards out of the cupboard and spotted the shape in the window. Someone was standing on the tiny strip of gravel outside her lounge. She abandoned the chair and knelt on the sofa to pull up the net curtains, an essential for every main road London property where the pavement was only metres away. She smiled, her heart swelling as she saw Maria standing there, waving.

"What are you doing?" she mouthed, unable to stop her grin.

Maria shrugged. "Just waving," she mouthed back.

Connie pointed right. "Do you want to come in?"

Maria's response was an adorable, yet meaningful, nod.

Connie tiptoed to the door and opened it quietly.

"Ryan came back," she whispered, standing still on the doorstep. "He told me to come."

"Did you want to come?"

"I've wanted to come here every day since I met you, but you've never let me."

Connie lifted her hands to the pitiful porch and kept her voice low. "Now you know why."

"He told me to tap on the door so I didn't wake Noah, but I knew you'd be writing so I thought I'd try the window instead."

"Door, window, it's all the same in my metre wide house."

"I'm not here to see your house."

Connie lost herself in the brooding brown eyes. "No?"

"I'm here to see you." Maria took Connie by the waist, holding the back of her head and kissing her with passion.

Connie felt her knees buckle, overwhelmed with emotion, terrified by her lack of control but too intoxicated by the intensity to end the connection. They were kissing, so deeply, on her doorstep. She pulled back, drawing Maria into the house and shutting the door, returning the kiss with as much force as had been given, touching Maria's skin, tasting her sweetness. "Here," she gasped, pulling her down onto the sofa.

"He's sleeping?" managed Maria, her lips back on Connie's, their bodies pushed roughly together.

"Mmm hm." Connie was breathless. "Alice?"

"Maddalena."

"Good," she gasped, unable to hold herself back from the smooth skin and supple lips, feeling the heat from their flushed cheeks as they kissed with such fervour, igniting every sense in her body. Connie felt Maria's fingers on the back of her neck, trailing down her top until they reached her spine, finding their way onto her skin. She moaned deeply, wanting the contact, encouraging the exploration, needing the experience. "Touch me," she urged.

Maria shifted her position, straddling Connie on the sofa, forcing her back into the cushions with each powerful embrace as she trailed her thumbs up her body.

Connie succumbed to the sensation, her skin sending shivers of anticipation with each inch Maria continued to climb, strong fingers now at the edge of her bra. Connie gasped, desperate for them to slide beneath and touch her. Desperate for them to feel her properly. Desperate for them to own her. Desperate for them to—

Both jumped at the groan that sounded from the monitor, with Maria diving off the sofa in shock. "Noah," she gasped.

Connie tried to straighten her hair, aware that it would be pointless, but feeling it was the appropriate thing to do. "He's just stirring."

Maria stood up and tucked herself in. "So…"

"So."

"So I just came round to say hi," she said with a smile.

Connie laughed quietly. "Can all of our hellos be like that from now on, please?"

"I'm not sure a polite cheek kiss would suffice anymore." Maria crouched in front of the sofa and stared at Connie with sincerity shining in her dark eyes. "Louise is a no one. I saw the look in your eye, Connie. You have to trust me. It's exactly as I said. We had a date, it was awful, she texted a couple of times trying to entice me back but it didn't work, so she showed up today with her final play."

"That picture?"

Maria nodded. "And it was sweet, but I'm not interested."

"Why not?"

"Because she's not you."

"Really?"

"Really. She won't be back." Both heard Noah's second groan. "Bounce-a-rama tomorrow? We can plan out our weekend?"

Connie smiled. "Just try and stop me."

"I'll let myself out," said Maria. "You're looking rather incapacitated down there."

Connie laughed as Maria sneaked out the door. As it shut she closed her eyes and let out a silent wail of pure exhilaration. She jumped up and raced to her keyboard, typing as fast as she could.

'He said: "Marry me." Mark wants to marry me! That's all the proof I need.'

"Coming, Noah."

CHAPTER TWENTY NINE

"Well hello, lady," said Connie, walking up to Maria's table at Bounce-a-rama.

"Hello to you too, pretty miss." Maria stepped forwards and kissed Connie on the lips, lingering slightly too long for mere friendship.

Connie could feel herself floating with giddiness, as if it were just her and the dark-haired seductress in the room. She pulled away quickly and glanced around, spotting Earth Mother and Crusty in the corner. "Maria!"

"What? You said you wanted every hello to be special."

Connie looked again. "They saw."

"Good, maybe they'll come out of the closet."

"They might just be friends who happen to have the same wedding rings."

Maria frowned. "And engagement rings? And they snog in the ball pit?"

"Ooo, can we snog in the ball pit?"

"After I bounce you on the princess castle."

"You're on," giggled Connie, kicking off her shoes and running towards the big pink inflatable.

"I've already got my shoes off!" sang Maria, catching up with her quickly and lifting her by the waist, throwing her straight onto the cushions.

"Make me fly!" squealed Alice, sliding herself off the pirate ship to join the whoops and the laughter.

"Noah fly too!" giggled the small boy, bounding towards them and diving straight onto Maria's back.

Maria rolled over and scooped him up, bouncing around as she flew him in her arms.

"Me, me, me!" pleaded Alice, leaping about in utter excitement.

"I'm coming for you, little lady," said Connie, chasing her and swinging her round by the hands.

"Me swing, me swing!" yelled Noah, wriggling free from his position as pilot and charging straight at his mother.

Connie lost her balance, letting go of Alice like Fatima Whitbread throwing the hammer.

"Again!" shouted Alice, peeling herself off the pink castle wall.

"Let's do a group one," said Maria, forming a circle and encouraging both of the children to take hold of her hands. "Come on, Mummy Connie, you've got to go opposite me."

"On my way, Mummy Maria," said Connie, trying to pull herself up and wade across the bouncy pillows as quickly as possible, a difficult feat given her short legs and the sheer size of the castle. "I'm here." She joined up the hands. "What are we doing?"

"This!" said Maria, jumping them all round in a circle.

"Whirlpool!" giggled Alice.

"Faster!" shouted Noah, his feet not touching the floor.

"Whirlpool?" said Connie, finding it more difficult to breathe with each swinging bounce. "Good word for a three-year-old."

"We play this in the pool when we're swimming, don't we, Alice?"

"And we let go!" giggled the little girl, freeing her fingers and launching herself into the air, causing Connie to fall backwards once more, this time dragging Maria and Noah down with her.

"Alice!" Maria laughed. "We'll keep going round when we let go in the water, but not in the air!"

"Again, again, again!" said the little girl, desperate to fly up to the turret.

"Do you mind if we join you?" Earth Mother and Crusty were standing barefoot at the base of the castle.

"Umm sure," said Maria, trying to remember their real names. "Bertha wasn't it?"

"And Clare," added Connie.

Earth Mother's voice was louder and more confident than ever before. "Yes. It looks like so much fun, and please forgive us, we didn't realise you were a rainbow family. We'd have approached you sooner had we known."

"In the club." Crusty giggled, still as nervous as ever.

"Slides!" shouted Alice, pulling her friend away by the hand.

"I thought you wanted to do the circle again?" said Maria, aware that the family of four were already clambering onto the pillows.

"No," said her daughter, bouncing onto another inflatable.

"Slides," agreed Noah, more than happy to be taken charge of.

"Come on, Noah, once more?" asked Connie, trying not to sound too desperate as he disappeared behind a wobbling wall. "Obviously not," she said to the group now all standing rather awkwardly as if they were about to embark on some sort of old-fashioned circle dance. She couldn't look at Maria knowing she'd laugh if she did; the toe-curlingly cringe-worthy nature of the situation too much to address.

"So," said Maria, clearly struggling to keep hold of her own composure, "let's all hold hands."

The family of four joined up, leaving one of Crusty's hands and one of Earth Mother's hands free for Connie and Maria to complete the circle. Maria grabbed hold of Connie, squeezing their fingers together in amusement, before taking Earth Mother's hand too, so Connie would pair up with Crusty.

"Right," said Connie.

"You've got soft hands," giggled Crusty, looking more excited than both of the little boys.

"And go!" said Maria, starting the bouncing.

"Bounce round!" added Connie as she jumped straight into Crusty's side.

"Oh we see, we see, we see," said Earth Mother, getting into the rhythm.

Connie couldn't bear to look. The huge udders were flying free, totally braless under the thin fabric tie-dye dress. She felt her fingers being squeezed even tighter and lifted her eyes to Maria, letting out an involuntary snort as she saw the sheer amusement on Maria's face.

"Faster!" said Maria, deliberately encouraging the chaos.

Connie couldn't stop laughing. Crusty was leaving a snowstorm with each bounce and Earth Mother was lucky to be conscious as her breasts hit her face with such force. "And let go!" she shouted, needing to be out of the mix, unable to catch her breath with her giggles.

The group fell backwards with the little boys the only ones not to laugh, both simply sliding off the pink pillows and marching towards the pirate ship.

"Oh, was it that much fun?" asked Maria.

"Yes," giggled Crusty, pulling herself back up onto her feet and offering out her hands once more.

Connie looked at her, then back at Maria, laughing at the idea that the four women would play bounce. "I'm okay thanks, I think I'm a bit too giddy. I need to sit down."

Earth Mother rolled herself off the pillows of air, hauling herself back onto her feet at the base of the castle. "I think I need a sit down too."

"Looks like it's me and you then, Cru— Clare," said Maria, quickly correcting herself, taking hold of the woman's hands and swinging her round.

Connie watched in amusement as Maria swung Crusty like a child, seemingly not bothered by the showering of white stuff flying free from the woman's hair. "I'll get us the coffees," she said, relieved to be walking away.

Earth Mother rushed up behind her. "May we join you?"

"Of course. You've not hurt yourself have you?" asked Connie, noticing the woman was rubbing her chin.

"Maybe a little. But it was worth it."

Connie nodded, unsure of quite what to say next.

****

"So," Maria took a sip of her coffee and addressed both women with her words, "how long have you two been together?"

Crusty giggled. "Since school."

"And how long have you been married?"

Earth Mother leaned forward, sending her breasts a good distance over the table. She hushed her voice. "We civil partnered in 2006 and signed the papers to upgrade it to marriage last year."

"Wow, that's a long time. Why are you whispering?"

Earth Mother nodded in the direction of a group of new comers. "People can be funny."

Crusty continued to giggle. "Hence why we were thrilled when we saw you kissing." She turned to Connie. "We always knew that man of yours was," she lowered her voice as well, "gay." The nervous giggles continued. "I don't think any of the other women at that playgroup realise, but we spotted it, didn't we, Bertha?"

"We did indeed," said Earth Mother, tapping the side of her nose.

Maria continued her inquisition. "Who carried the children?"

"We used the London Women's Clinic."

"Ah, so did I."

"We both started treatment and decided whoever caught first would carry first, and we both caught at the same time."

Maria frowned. "But they don't both call you Mum? I've heard Lucas calling you Clare, and I'm sorry, what's your other little boy called?"

Connie stayed silent. She knew what Maria was doing - getting as much information out of them as possible before they realised there was a straight imposter present, causing them to clam up.

"Leeroy."

"Lucas and Leeroy, that's nice. Why does Leeroy wear the bumper helmet if you don't mind me asking?"

"I was such a klutz as a child," said Crusty, unable to talk without giggling, "I thought it best."

Maria turned to Earth Mother. "So why doesn't Leeroy call you Mum too?"

"I didn't carry him."

"But you all live together?"

"Of course."

"So you're his mum?"

"Not biologically."

"But they're from the same donor?"

Crusty giggled. "Can you imagine if yours were from the same donor too? We'd be one big rainbow family."

"Umm," Maria paused, not wanting to show her distaste for the suggestion. "Well I used the same clinic, but my donor only donated for a very short period of time. Only one pregnancy was reported and that was mine."

Connie cut in, unable to let this titbit pass by. "How come?"

"I don't know. The donors never find out when a child is born, who they're born to or anything like that, but they *are* notified when a pregnancy is reported. A bit like being told their donation has been successful. Anyway, after I had Alice I called the clinic to reserve some more vials just in case I ever wanted another child and they told me he'd stopped donating after my pregnancy was reported."

"Why?"

"They can't tell you."

"Sorry," said Earth Mother, her breasts pushing further across the table, "but how don't you know this?"

Connie coughed. "I'm actually a single mum. I had Noah with an ex-partner."

"Female?"

"No, male."

Crusty glanced nervously across at her wife.

"And you?" said Earth Mother to Maria, drawing her breasts back onto her lap.

"Single. I had Alice on my own."

"Clare, I think we should leave."

Crusty giggled. "Right."

"Wait. We never said we were a rainbow family, you did."

"You kissed, and you were calling each other Mummy Maria and Mummy Connie."

Maria nodded. "And how did that make you feel?"

The flaking woman ignored her wife's glare and spoke quickly. "It made us want to rush over and join in."

"Exactly. Visibility's the only route to acceptance. You two should be proud of each other. Your children should be shouting from the rooftops that they have two mothers who love them. You shouldn't hush your voice because you think people might judge. Hold hands. Be brave. Show the world that you're equal."

Earth Mother stood up and tucked her chair under the table. "And be ridiculed by straight women like you. No thank you. Clare, we're leaving."

"We're not straight." All eyes were suddenly on Connie. "Well Maria's definitely not, and I don't think I am either."

Maria took hold of Connie's cheeks, planting tiny kisses all over her small button nose. "You're so brave, you're so brave, you're so brave!"

Connie laughed. "Not brave, just honest." She looked at the two women. "Maria's right. Visibility's the key to acceptance. People need to see families like yours. They need to see same-sex relationships like yours. That's the only way to tackle prejudice, by hitting it head on."

"Good luck with that," said Earth Mother, pulling her wife up by the hand.

"Right. Bye," giggled Crusty.

Maria watched the women return to their table and pack up their things before turning to Connie and smiling. "Soooo," she said, "now you're not straight?"

Connie grinned as their eyes locked together. "Let's take a turn down the tunnel and see."

CHAPTER THIRTY

"Ryan, I need you," gasped Connie, stepping out of the store and into the sunlight as she turned up the volume on her phone. "Mum's got Noah; I've got about an hour."

The voice on the other end of the line sounded concerned. "For what?"

"For shopping."

"*Shopping* shopping?"

"Yes, Ryan, *shopping* shopping. Can you get to Ann Summers?"

"I'll cancel my client. I'll be there in five. Let's walk and talk. What's going on?"

Connie found a bench and sat down as she heard Ryan instruct his receptionist to reschedule. "Are you out?" she asked.

"Out of the building and en route."

"I don't want you getting in trouble."

"I'm the boss. You're more important. Philippe's on cover. Go. Talk. What's happening?"

She lifted her face to the sun and took a deep breath. "I came on my own."

"During sex? And now you need toys to pleasure her?"

"No! To Ann Summers!" Connie paused. "Oh god, could that happen?"

"It could, darling, but I'll get you kitted out. Why the hell did you go there alone? I told you I'd help you."

"I needed to get something, but then I went in and there were so many of them that I got all flustered and had to come out."

"What something are you talking about, darling?"

"I don't know. Maria's made comments."

"Ooo, I knew she was a devil. What sort of comments? I'm passing by Greggs."

"Good, you're close." She closed her eyes, remembering the connection. "In the tunnel yesterday."

"What tunnel?"

"At Bounce-a-rama."

"The dark one?"

Connie smiled. "That's the one."

"You dirty bitches."

"No! We just kissed." She paused, feeling a shiver of memory run through her body, re-living the sensation of Maria's lips against her own. "Lots of kissing."

"And? Darling, I'm flat out running now!"

"And it got heated."

"She touched you?"

"No. She's only ever stroked the skin on my back and maybe a bit of my stomach."

"So?"

"Well she said something."

"God, Connie, hurry up! I'll be there before you tell me."

"Okay, well it was getting heated, and we were kissing, and I kind of pushed her backwards against the wall."

"You go girl."

"Well she…"

"She what?"

"She groaned."

"Good, and?"

Connie sat up straighter on the bench. "And she told me she couldn't wait for me to be inside her."

Ryan hooted. "What?! Oh darling, she needs you!"

"But I haven't got anything to put inside her!"

"Oh bless you, you don't have a clue, do you? Look at you sitting on that bench like a little lost soldier."

Connie scanned the pedestrianised street, spotting him trotting towards her. She ended the call and stood up to hug her very best friend. "Bastard," she said with a smile.

"Yes, but you love me. Come on, let's get you lesbianised."

Connie followed his lead into the pink-fronted shop, bumping straight into him as he stopped suddenly at the tiny-waisted mannequins. "No, they're at the back," she whispered.

"I know, but we're doing this properly. We've got an hour, right?"

Connie nodded. "But I only want one thing."

"No. This is *your* weekend. We need to set the scene. Maria's a *real* lesbian. She's been with other *real* lesbians. Her memory bank will be full of wonderful women with hot bodies and beautiful faces. You need to set yourself apart and rise above the rest of them with something just that little bit different." He reached out and lifted a hanger from the rail. "How about this? Good girl gone bad."

Connie looked up and down at the sheer, tight-fitting erotic jail jumpsuit complete with stripes and matching prison-issue hat and handcuffs.

He tapped the label. "Prisoner 69. Could work? And look, it's reduced to nine pounds."

Connie pointed at the mannequin behind him. "Why don't I just go all out and turn up as a naughty nurse?"

"Oh no, darling, you're not a slut."

"Exactly! As if I'd wear a see-though jail jumpsuit. What am I meant to do? Knock on the door and just stand on the doorstep looking like a convict?"

"No, you wear a mac."

"So I look like a stripper and then a convict?"

"Oh Connie, you have to get in the right frame of mind. If you don't feel sexy, you won't appear sexy." He paused. "What pants are you wearing?"

Connie self-consciously stepped backwards. "Why?"

"Fine, forget the dress up, but the underwear must be perfect. Half the fun's in the unwrapping anyway. Give her a last layer to remember."

She nodded. "My underwear's fine."

"I'm not just talking about knickers that aren't fraying. I'm talking about lingerie."

"It's fine. I've got a nice set from M&S."

"What do you mean *a* nice set? You need more than one. What are you wearing right now?"

She shrugged. "My comfies."

"From where?"

"Tesco."

"Oh god, darling, you've bought one of those awful packs of supermarket knickers, haven't you?"

"They're practical and you get five for five pounds."

"Right, that's it." He marched over to the hangers and started to flick through the two-piece sets. "I'll pick you out a selection. You're definitely trying something on."

Connie followed him sheepishly, daring to finger some of the labels. "Why have they all got such scary names? Look: Savage Beauty, Pummelling Plunge, Extreme Brazilian Boost."

"It's better than: Five Pack White Cotton Full-Briefs." He tutted. "And your bra won't be matching will it?"

"It's a black minimiser. I like it. It takes attention away from my chest."

"Well this weekend your chest will be the star of the show. Come on, changing rooms." He pulled open one of the pink curtains and hung the selection next to the mirror. "Now. This is important. Show me how you undress."

"What?"

"For Maria. Show me. Start with your top, that's the sexiest part."

"No!"

"I've known you for how long? And I've seen you in far more compromising situations than this. Come on, Connie, this could be your make or break."

"Fine, but I'd step back if I was you." She held onto the sleeve of her jumper and pulled her arm free.

"No! Put it back in! Think fifty shades. The way he takes his top off. One smooth action every single time. You reach up with your hand, grab your jumper at the back of your neck and just pull the whole thing free."

Connie looked at the gay man standing in front of her. "That may well do it for you, Ryan, but I think women like to tease a bit more."

"Ooo, okay, improv, I like it. Show me what you've got."

Connie took hold of the sides of her jumper and started to wiggle them upwards, adding in a slight knee bend in as well.

"Darling, I'm stopping you. You look like a chicken taking a shit."

"Oh for god's sake, can I just take this bloody top off? I'm getting all hot and bothered."

"Maria's the one who'll be hot and bothered if you take it off right."

"Fine," said Connie, just wanting to move on. "Like this?" She reached up and grabbed her jumper at the back of her neck, pulling it off with one movement.

"Shit!" they both gasped.

Connie looked at herself in the mirror. "The static! I look like I've stuck my fingers in the sockets."

"No, I'm shitting about the two wind socks you've got strapped to your chest. Connie, you have zero visible flesh from your stomach to your neck. It's all covered with that boulder-holder bra!"

Connie batted him out of the changing rooms with her jumper. "You're so bloody mean, just get out and leave me to it." She swiped the curtains closed and looked at herself in the mirror. Ryan was right. It was like she was wearing a binder or a full body bandage. She unbuckled her jeans and looked down at her white cotton briefs. A body bandage and a nappy. Maria wouldn't be interested in someone sporting a body bandage and nappy. She unhooked her bra and moaned with instant relief as her breasts dropped free.

"Oh, darling, try pushing them out a bit and lean back so they're upright."

Connie gasped, seeing the face in the curtains. "Ryan!"

"Why are you covering your boobs?" He stepped back into the changing room. "I'd be more concerned about your super-sized knickers. You could smuggle me out of the shop in those." He picked up the Sweet Treats lingerie set instead. "Get this on before the wind picks you up and blows you away."

Connie used two fingers to hold up the hanger, slightly anxious about the lack of visible fabric.

"It's a thong, darling, you'll be fine. Just slip it on."

The idea of just slipping it on proved much easier said than done with Connie needing Ryan's shoulders for support as she clambered into the thin thing. "And we're up," she said, finally snapping the material into place and looking at her reflection in the mirror, unable to ignore the fact that the thong was digging in and puffing out her white pants even more than usual. She paused for a moment, before daring to look over her shoulder. Her bottom looked like a piece of pork trussed up with string, ready for a roasting.

Ryan nodded. "Without that white double duvet under there, those pants could look hot."

"They're hardly pants!" She reached for the bra. "And this won't fit either."

"Yes it will," he said, helping her arms through the straps. "We'll just hoik up these bad boys and then… Ooo, can you breathe in a bit? And just a little bit more? And… Wait… There, we've got it." Ryan forced the clasps together and looked over Connie's shoulder into the mirror. "Oh yes," he said, making a camera shape out of his fingers, "nice set. Imagine it without those billowing knickers and *that's* what I'm talking about."

Connie couldn't help but smile. "It does look kind of cute."

Ryan pulled her shoulders backwards. "Now, just work on your pose. Try sticking out your chest a bit more."

Connie transferred her weight onto one hip and forced her breasts forwards. "What the hell?" she gasped as her nipples popped through the fabric at the front.

Ryan jumped backwards. "Good god, woman, you could take someone's eyes out with those."

Connie fumbled with the material, desperately trying to push her nipples back into place. "I can't close it up!"

"Peepo," said Ryan.

"Oh stop it! What the hell have you brought me?"

He lifted the hanger and re-read the label. "Sweet Treats peephole bra and crotchless thong. I'm sorry, I honestly didn't know."

"Crotchless thong? There's no material there as it is! How is it crotchless?"

"Spread your legs and bend over."

"No! My nipples are still sticking out!"

"Oh just do it, Connie, we're well past any embarrassment here!" He pushed on her back and crouched down behind her. "Just a little bit lower. Argh, and there you have it."

"What?" Connie side-stepped in her upside down position towards the mirror, conscious that her nipples were well past the point of peeping and were now giving their audience a full-on waving hello. She pulled her breasts under her armpits and looked through her legs. The thong string had split into two like a wishbone, leaving a flap of white cotton poking out of position.

"And that's where she'd enter," said Ryan with authority.

Connie pulled herself upright, adding a flushed face to her already static hair. "Sweet treats, my arse. No one wants to see that and it would be more like loose juice."

The gay man screwed up his face. "Loose juice?"

"It's true. You'd be dribbling all over the place."

"And on that note, I'm going."

"Good, please bring me something that's sensible." She smiled, glancing back at herself in the mirror. "And maybe a little bit sexy."

****

Half an hour had passed and they had a basket in which were three sets of more appropriate lingerie. Ryan had resumed his role as Gok Wan and was clapping his hands as they approached the rows of DVDs. "Right, the scene has been set. She's seen you, you're sexy, so now for the spice."

"That's why we're here," she lowered her voice, "to buy something from the back."

"Wait, wait, wait. We work through the shop like you'd work through your date. That's how it's designed. Dress up by the door, lingerie next, now the DVDs."

"I'm not going to stop the snogging so I can ask for the remote and load up a movie."

"No, the DVD's the foreplay, darling." He scanned the shelves. "Ignore all that. That's straight stuff. Here's the girl-on-girl."

Connie looked at the small selection, unsure if it were the titles or the pictures that were putting her off the most. "*The milf and her kitten?*"

"Just like you and Maria."

"She's not that much older than me!" She peered at the cover more closely. "And I won't be wearing a tail."

"Okay, how about this one? *Muff Bumpers.*"

"I'm not buying a DVD called *Muff Bumpers.*"

"Fine. *Pussy Party.*"

"No."

"*The Tribe of Wet Panties.*"

"No!"

"Fine, go for *Piss Pals.*"

"Ryan, I am not buying one of these!"

"You need experience, Connie. Just buy it and watch it for yourself before you go. Here. *First Time Lesbian.*"

She snatched the film from his hands and dropped it into the basket. "Fine, as long as we can move on. Right, at the back they've got—"

"Wait, last aisle. The final piece of the puzzle when assisting arousal."

"What?"

"Poppers."

"I'm not buying party poppers!"

Ryan laughed. "Oh bless you."

"What?"

"Well you don't put them in her punani, pull the string and – wayhay."

Connie frowned.

"You..." he paused. "Fine, forget the poppers, but I would buy one of these." He signalled to a shelf of small bottles.

Connie scanned the names and lifted the strawberry spray, squirting some onto her wrists and rubbing them together.

"Darling!" shrieked Ryan.

"What?" Connie felt the tackiness start to form on her skin.

"You're spraying lube like it's perfume!"

"It says strawberry spray to excite her."

"Yes, but not in an aphrodisiac kind of way. She's not going to smell the strawberry spray perfume on your skin made by loo-bay, and go weak at the knees." He pointed between her legs. "You use it down there."

She pulled her wrists apart, staring at the shiny snail-trail like shimmer. "Why would I need this?"

Ryan mouthed his words. "The more mature lady can sometimes suffer with dryness."

"She's thirty-five!"

"So use it to widen your path."

"What path?"

He took Connie's hand and pulled her to the back of the shop, pointing up at the wide variety of objects. "This path. We've got bullets, rabbits, wands, dildos, cocks, cocks with balls, cocks with veins, cocks with foreskins, cocks that are snipped." He paused. "A big black cock, and a fist."

"Oh god, I'm right back where I started."

"Okay," he said, nodding at the shelves, "she wants you inside her. You've got the loo-bay spray, so let's start with something simple." He picked up one of the flesh-coloured dildos.

Connie gasped. "That wouldn't fit in a fucking horse!"

"It's a double-ender. You both hop on and ride it like you're at the rodeo."

"What?"

He put it back on the shelf. "Okay darling, we're going to have to go back to basics." Walking down the aisle he shook his head at each implement. "So that's a no to the clit clamps, a no to the doggy strap, a no to the chain flogger, a definite no to the nipple enlargers - I've already seen the size of your babies, peepo!"

Connie hit him on the shoulder. "Just find me something simple. What's this? This looks okay."

"Darling, that's a butt plug." He reached up to the shelf. "And look, you *could* be the kitten, this one's got a tail."

"A butt plug with tail? Why would anyone want to use that?"

"Anal toys are great." He winked. "Pain in the arse when you can't find the right size though."

"Oh Ryan, I'd have been better off without you."

"No you wouldn't, you'd have ended up with a muzzle and a crop flogger."

"A what? I just need something I can put inside her. Anything."

"Fine then. I'd go for the love eggs and if you get the remote control ones you can pop them in, head home and switch them on from the safety of your sofa."

"Why would I do that? And what are love eggs anyway?"

"They're vagina balls, darling. And I'm saying that because you're not really feeling this." He started to thrust his hips. "You should be wanting to pump yourself into her, deeper, harder." His eyes lit up. "We'll get you a strap-on!"

****

Connie was standing in the changing rooms with the same white nappy on display, this time bound up by black leather. She stared at her reflection. "I look like a tit."

Ryan grabbed hold of the hard erection that was sticking out from between her legs. "No, you look like a cock, on lesbian legs, and she'll love it."

Connie held her hair back and looked down at the huge protrusion of plastic. "Am I meant to wear this under my clothes?"

"No of course not. You turn on the DVD, slip out to the bathroom, pop it on, lube it up, and away you go."

"It all sounds rather segmented. Maria said lesbian sex was the most sensuous act I'd ever experience."

"She'll probably be giving you poppers."

"What?"

"Nothing, you're fine, just buy it." He pushed his way out of the curtains, dramatically wiping the non-existent sweat from his brow. "And we are done."

Connie looked at herself in the mirror, turning side on and attempting to thrust. "Oh god," she gasped, too embarrassed to watch her reflection. She reached down for the buckle on the side of her hip and tugged on the hard leather. "Ryan, wait. I'm struggling." She tried again, but the buckle was locked. "Ryan!" She stuck her head out between the curtains, pulling them taut round her neck as she looked left and right.

"Connie, is that you?" Maria appeared. "I thought I saw Ryan. Hey, it is you." She smiled. "What a pleasant surprise."

Connie's face flushed to what she knew would be beetroot colour. "I'm... I've got... There's a hen party next month, fancy dress." She stared helplessly at Maria, conscious that her shopping basket was on the floor.

Maria smiled. "Oh great. I love this shop."

Connie kept the curtains tight around her neck. "Really?"

"Yes, for one reason, and one reason only. The batteries. They're the cheapest on the high street. You know what it's like having a three-year-old with electronic toys. You need a constant supply." She lowered her voice. "The rest of this stuff's a bit dodgy though. Fine for hen weekends," she added quickly.

Connie nodded, shifting her weight from foot to foot as she spoke. "She wants us to dress up."

"Ooo, can I see?" asked Maria, glancing down at the curtain.

Connie lost her attention. "Maria!"

"Well *hello* there!"

"Ignore the basket. It's Ryan. He's messing around."

"What basket?"

Connie looked around outside the cubicle, confused; there was no basket. "Oh, he must have taken it to pay. What were you..."

Suddenly she felt the straps around her bottom begin to shake and a definite tightening occurring at her crotch. She scrunched up her face, finally daring to peep down. Her strap-on was sticking out between the curtains and was in Maria's hand.

"Just shaking hands with your hard-on," said Maria with a wicked smile.

"It's not mine."

Maria looked disbelieving and began to tug, pulling Connie's hips forwards.

Connie remembered her nappy. "Okay! It's mine, let go! Please. I'm embarrassed."

Maria stepped back quickly. "Sorry, I was just..." She paused. "Connie, this isn't for me, is it?"

Without further pretence, Connie pulled her bottom back into the cubicle, hiding the strap-on from view. "No, it's for Ryan."

"But he's already got a..."

Ryan rounded the corner reading from the receipt. "So the sexy sets, luscious lube and dirty DVDs are on me, but you can pay for that bad boy."

Connie closed the curtains completely and buried her face in them. "Oh hi Maria," she heard Ryan say.

CHAPTER THIRTY ONE

Maria pulled sharply on the strap around Connie's thigh. "This has to be secure."

Connie nodded nervously. "You're sure it's on right?"

"I've fastened thousands of these things. Trust me, it's on right."

"Okay, where do I start?"

Maria nodded. "Just take it slowly, and don't be scared. It's all about trust. You can do this, Connie, I know you can."

"So I make the first move?"

"Of course you do. I just respond to your rhythm."

Connie looked up at the colourful climbing wall in front of her. "Right," she said, tugging her harness once more. "You promise you'll keep that rope taut?"

"I told you, I'll respond to your rhythm, and when you get to the top you lean backwards so I can lower you."

Connie took a deep breath and reached out for the first red bump, hauling herself up with her fingertips. "When you told me to bring three different outfits I never imagined the shorts and t-shirt were for traversing Mount Everest."

"This is wall one. The basic boulder climb. Up next we have slabs, cracks, overhangs, and arêtes."

"Great."

"Trust me, it's a buzz. I used to come here most weekends before Alice. It's the best indoor climbing centre in London." She paused. "What were you hoping the shorts and t-shirt were for?"

"Oh I don't know, a spot of leisurely tennis, or maybe some pool-side attire at a beautiful spa." Connie reached up for the second coloured hold and slipped, dropping back down onto the mat. "You said you'd save me!"

"You weren't even a foot off the floor." Maria pulled on her rope, tugging Connie back towards the wall. "Let's get you started."

Connie felt the harness tighten around her bottom as her body started to rise. "Ooo, this is more like it." She reached for the holds, securing her trainers onto a ridge in the wall. "What now?"

"Now you climb."

"Where?"

"To the top."

"Can't you just pull me up?"

Maria laughed. "Come on, you'll feel a real sense of achievement when you reach the red button."

"Is that a euphemism for something?" Connie made a play for the bump above her, straining as she made contact with her fingertips. "I know what this is. You've brought me here to strengthen the tendons in my fingers."

"No need. Your strap-on can do all the work."

Connie laughed out loud, losing her grip and falling away from the wall. "Maria!"

"What? Grab back on." She kept the rope taut until Connie had regained her position. "You're the one who bought it."

"I *nearly* bought it, and only because Ryan told me to."

"And what does Ryan know about lesbian sex?"

"Lots apparently, but I'm a bit concerned about these party poppers going off in my..." She wiggled her bottom in her harness.

Maria laughed. "The view I have from down here. Sorry! No, don't look down! Concentrate!" She waited for Connie to get back into her rhythm. "Gay men and gay sex are a totally different entity. Now, when it comes to us lesbians..." She raised her voice as Connie continued to climb. "Don't get me wrong, one day I might ask you to go back and buy that bad boy, but for the moment I'd prefer to keep things simple."

"Stop it, you're putting me off."

"And poppers are things people sniff to relax."

"Maria!"

"What? Once I've finished with you, you won't need any relaxing."

Connie felt the harness tighten around her crotch, imagining what it must feel like to have Maria finish with her. "Pull me up a bit more?" she asked.

"No, you're almost there."

Connie discarded her daydream and focused back on the wall. "Ooo yes, I'm quite high, aren't I?"

"I told you this would be fun. Go on. Go for that pink hold. That's it. Now the yellow one. And reach."

The buzzer sounded out and Connie grinned from ear to ear, looking down at Maria on the mat below. "I did it!"

"Well done! That's amazing. Now hold on to your rope and lean back. That's it. Use your feet to step back down the wall."

"I'm abseiling!"

"You're abseiling brilliantly!"

Connie dropped back onto the mat, turning herself into Maria's arms. "You're so sweet to me."

"No, that was brilliant," said Maria, hugging her tightly.

"It was all of ten metres."

"That wall's three actually, but it's a start, and a great one at that."

Connie reached out and flicked the dark ponytail. "You look cute with your hair up. It really shows off your eyes."

Maria smiled. "Can I kiss you?"

"Where did that come from?"

"The moment. So can I?"

"I'm..." Connie glanced around at the indoor centre and clusters of climbers making their way up a variety of brightly coloured boulders. "I'm not sure if we..."

"Life's short," she said, taking hold of Connie's neck and bringing their lips close together.

Connie moved into the embrace, closing her eyes, getting lost in the soft skin and warm breath. "And stop," she finally managed.

Maria smiled. "I love this."

"What?"

"The fact you're so open."

Connie rolled her eyes at herself. "God, imagine what I'd be like if I wasn't fresh out of a relationship? If I wasn't still wary of people seeing me." She laughed. "I'd probably be taking you up against that boulder in full view of everyone here."

"I look forward to that day."

"It's true! I'm usually so shy and self-conscious, but I seem to lose everything around you."

"Would you walk down the street holding my hand?"

"Right now? Yes probably."

"Ha, no I mean if we are ever a couple."

"Of course! I'd be proud to show you off." She smiled and unhooked her carabiner, freeing herself from the rope. "I've never felt like that before."

"I think this is the most full-on first date I've ever been on," said Maria, repeating the action and walking them both away from the wall.

"Am I full-on? Is this too much? You've told me to always be honest."

"Sorry, not full-on, maybe fast-moving."

"Too fast?"

Maria pulled a face. "We've not even got past first base. Come on, let's try this wall next."

"We have children. We might never get past first base."

"That's why I planned the day like this. I thought we'd do everything we can't do when they're here. Dangerous sports in the morning. Spa in the afternoon."

"We're going to a spa?"

"There's one next door. It's only small but we're booked in for massages and facials."

"Together?"

"Of course."

"Oh Maria, you're so good."

"I just wanted to arrange a fun day-date. Then after the spa you'll change into your second outfit for tonight's meal."

"But you won't tell me where we're going?"

"Nope, and your third outfit's for tomorrow."

"Surely I'll be at home tomorrow morning to get myself changed?"

Maria responded to Connie's sarcasm with a look of scepticism. "You think?"

****

"Just call Connie," said Evelyn, chastising her son for the umpteenth time that morning.

Karl knee-shuffled along the old-fashioned maroon-coloured carpet. "No, I have to prove I can do this. Come on, Noah, tell me what's wrong."

"You can't do this. He's crying. He's been crying since you brought him round here this morning. What did she say when you picked him up? Is he ill? Has he been under the weather? And who's this Liss he keeps shouting about?"

"I was late, she had to dash off."

"Where?"

Karl moved the cat out of his way. "I don't know."

"Watch Malcolm! And why don't you know?"

"We're not together anymore, Mum. She can do what she wants."

"In your house? With your money? Your father would never hear of such things."

"Good job I'm not my father then." He knelt down in front of his son. "Let's go out, Noah. Where shall we go?"

The little boy suddenly stopped crying. "Narnos."

"Where's Narnos? Is it a play centre?"

"No, Narnos and Liss."

Evelyn picked up her cat and paced around her living room. "Liss, Liss, that's all he's been saying."

"Mum, I'll be in my new place in a couple of weeks. Could you please just try and help me out while I'm here?"

The woman peered down at the boy. "What's Narnos?"

"Muh Narnos."

"Bananas? You want a banana?"

The tears were back. "Narnos!"

Karl stroked his cheeks. "What do you do at Narnos?"

"See Liss."

"What does Mummy do at Narnos?"

"Drink juice."

"Juice?"

"Hot juice."

Karl reached under the little boy's shoulders and threw him into the air. "Mariano's! You want to go to Mariano's!"

"Narnos! Narnos! Narnos!" squealed the little boy.

"Okay then, let's do it. And then afterwards shall we go to the zoo?"

"Yay! With Liss."

Evelyn tutted. "I'll get my mac. The zoo's always windy."

"Mum, you're fine. Stay here and enjoy your day."

"And surrender my already restricted hours with my grandson. I don't think so."

****

The air in the small massage room was warm and infused with the delicate aroma of sweet spices and the sound of soft music. Incense sticks burned in a corner and pan pipes poured from speakers in the ceiling, creating an atmosphere of real relaxation, which somehow managed to put Connie on edge. "What are we waiting for?" she whispered, lifting her head up from her table's face hole.

Maria propped herself onto her elbows on the nearby bed, their heads only inches apart. "They give us time to get ready."

"We only came in in towels!"

"You should have taken it off under your sheet."

"What? I'm wrapped up tighter than a mummy. I thought they'd loosen me up."

"It's fine. Lie down, relax. They'll do it. Don't worry."

"Wait, you're naked under that sheet?" She grinned naughtily. "Prop yourself up a bit?"

Maria did as instructed.

"And a little bit more."

"What are you hoping to see?"

Connie smiled as Maria's cleavage came into view. "You're *so* incredible. So..." she struggled with the word, "...so hot."

"I'm a woman; this is what women look like."

"I don't look like that, like some Agent Provocateur model; I'm more the BHS bird with big boobs and big bras."

"You couldn't put me off you even if you tried. And anyway I saw the sets from Ann Summers. Ryan showed me while you were wrestling that huge strap-on of yours."

"It wasn't my strap-on and I made him take the bras back."

"I hope you didn't?"

"I did, and that DVD. And what was the other thing he made me buy? Oh yes, lube. He took that back too."

"Why buy lube in the first place?"

"He said I'd need it to open you up."

"What are you? Some sort of surgeon?"

Connie laughed. "Stop it. I was confused and flustered and he was the only help I had."

"Why did you need help in the first place?"

Connie glanced towards the door. "Because I'm a novice. I've got no clue what to do." She lowered her voice. "What you like." She smiled. "How to pleasure you."

"This is pleasuring me. This morning pleasured me. Last week pleasured me. Simply spending time with you pleasures me, Connie."

"Okay."

Maria propped herself up even further, inadvertently lifting her breasts into full view. "I don't mean to be dismissive, but it's like I said, we just see where this takes us and if it takes us to bed then we do the same thing and just see where that takes us too."

"But I don't know any routes! At all! And I'm lying here with your tits in my face, just wanting to drive drive drive."

Maria glanced down at her chest before looking up at Connie, slowly exposing her position some more. "How?"

"How do I want to drive you? Right now? Right up the road and round the corner. But you're torturing me by keeping me active. Keeping us surrounded by people. We could have stayed at home. You could have cooked. We could have spent the whole weekend all alone, just the two of us."

Maria smiled. "But isn't the wait half the fun? Isn't the build-up what makes the moment more special? I want to wine and dine you, Connie. I want to spend time making memories of us, real memories, out and about doing regular things, not just playgroups and play-dates. I want to get to know you for who you are, not just for who you become when you're Mum. I've seen you carefree today, dangling from a precipice, clawing your way up to victory, never giving up."

"Was that the ten metre wall?"

"No, the five, but you were great, and you've been funny and endearing and so so cute in your little harness, and I like you. I really like you." She smiled. "So much."

Connie looked at the beautiful woman lying opposite her, not quite able to not stare at all the flesh still on show, but trying her best all the same. "How did this happen?"

"Fate, soul mates, a collision of destinies, you know more than I do."

"Why?"

"You write about it."

Connie smiled. "I finished my novel."

"And does Bonnie get her happy ending?"

"The happiest."

Maria reached out to Connie's bed, cupping her face in her hands. "Like ours," she said with a smile.

"Do you really think so? Do you really think we can—"

Chiiiiiiing.

Both women turned to the doorway where their ladies had marked their entry by *chinging* on their tiny finger cymbals and bowing their heads. "Serenity," they whispered. *Chiiiiiiing.* "Peace." *Chiiiiiiing.* "Calm." *Chiiiiiiing.*

Connie tried to tuck herself back into her blanket, feeling anything but calm, serene or peaceful. Maria had just declared her feelings. This was real. This was happening. This was a moment of great excitement, not a moment of tranquil reflection. She closed her eyes as the towel was pulled away and the warm oil made contact with her skin. Or maybe it was, she mused with a smile.

****

"Lissssssssssssssss!" screamed Noah, running straight towards the playpen in Mariano's, ignoring his father's request to wait in the queue.

"I'll get him," snapped Evelyn, bustling past the small tables and marching after her grandson.

"Mum, it's fine, he obviously wants to play."

"No, you've asked him to stay in the queue, so he should stay in the queue. Come here, Noah," she said, finding the boy trying to unlock the safety catch on the little white gate. She picked him up with authority. "We asked you to wait in the queue."

"Lissssssssssssssss!" he wailed, kicking his feet out in fury.

"Stop it right now, or we'll take you straight home."

"Mum! It's my job to discipline him, not yours."

"Start doing it then! Look at him, he's like a wild animal!"

"Lissssssssssssssss!"

"You put my Noah down," said the elderly Italian woman, letting herself out of the playpen and shuffling towards the screaming. "My Noah just want Alice and my Alice make me come here on day off because she hope to see Noah."

Evelyn looked the intruder up and down. "And you are?"

"Aunt Maddalena. My niece own Mariano's."

"Thank you, but this is a private matter." She paused, unable to control the thrashing any longer. "And this child is not *your* Noah." She placed him back on the floor. "He has nothing to do with you."

Maddalena watched him run straight to the playpen. "He is good boy. Son of special special lady. I tell Connie I look after him, but she say he already looked after." She scowled. "I tell her he not."

Evelyn straightened her now ruffled coat. "*I* am Noah's grandmother and *this* is Noah's father." She took her son by the arm. "Karl, this person thinks she knows Noah."

"She may well do. Connie comes here a lot." He smiled. "Hi, I'm Karl. So that's the Alice we keep hearing all about?"

"I tell Connie and Maria to keep them together, let them play. Why should they have all the fun and not the bambini?"

Evelyn frowned. "Fun? Karl, who is this *Maria?*"

"Just a friend of Connie's."

"Special special friend," added Maddalena with a look of particular triumph.

****

Karl placed the tray of coffees and cakes on the table before finding his phone in his pocket. He looked towards the counter at his mother who was still trying to pull rank. *Tell me again what you said about Connie,* he typed.

CHAPTER THIRTY TWO

The warm evening air lovingly greeted the women as they walked down the wide stone steps from the restaurant. Connie paused to look back at the grand architecture and huge clock face that stood proud from the brickwork. "Well I never thought I'd be dining at The Holly," she said with a smile. "And this evening sun is just glorious."

"Did you enjoy it?"

"Oh my goodness, Maria, it was the best meal I've ever eaten, and I'm telling you, that was Bobby Davro sitting in the corner."

"That wasn't Bobby bloody Davro." She laughed. "And even if it was I wouldn't start shouting about it."

"Why not? I've never seen a celebrity before."

Maria rubbed her nails on her shirt, blowing on them in one-upmanship. "Rick Waller was in there last time I went."

"That huge guy from the singing programmes? He hardly beats Bobby Davro."

"That wasn't Bobby Davro!"

"It was!"

"Oh come here, you cutie." She threw her arm over Connie's shoulder and tugged her in tightly. "Shall we walk for a bit before we catch a cab?"

"More delaying tactics?"

"No, just enjoying the journey. And delaying for what? I thought I was dropping you home?"

Connie looked up in mock anger. "You did not!"

"No, I didn't. I'm taking you back to mine so I can kiss you slowly, undress you carefully and touch you tenderly. Giving us the perfect end to the perfect day."

Connie fanned her face. "Shall we walk a bit faster?"

"No!" laughed Maria. "Describe this to me. You're the writer. Describe the image of two women walking along together, lost in each other's arms."

"Okay." She smiled. "I wouldn't call myself a writer, but Bonnie might say: **'Happiness isn't an illusion. It's the feeling of your true love's arms wrapped around your waist as the warm summer sun makes its final descent. Distant noises blend into the background as the soft tune of your heart is exposed.'"**

Maria smiled. "And what tune's your heart playing?"

"Right now I think my heart's dancing."

"Connie, you really are adorable." She paused. "But why does Bonnie even pose the suggestion that happiness *might* be an illusion?"

"Because it always was. The whole novel focused on Bonnie's refusal to accept the idea of fate, love, soul mates, all of those things," she paused, "and she was doing really well. But then she met Mark and the standard happy-ever-after happened and my novel sold itself out."

"I very much doubt that. You should send it off."

"Where?"

"To an agent."

"No, it's just a hobby."

"Okay, so keep writing as a hobby but let Bonnie run free. See where the wind takes her?"

"Maybe."

"At least let your two walking lovers stop for a kiss as they gaze over the river?"

Connie smiled, feeling herself guided towards the stone wall that ran the length of their walkway. "Only if the water's glimmering."

"Glimmers, ripples, look, we've got it all."

Connie succumbed to the smile and kissed the beautiful woman standing in front of her, moved by the passionate response she received in return. Looking up, Connie lifted her fingers to Maria's soft cheeks, surprised by her emotion-filled eyes. She kissed the lips once more and whispered with true meaning. "I need you in my life."

Maria pulled her even closer. "I'm here."

****

Connie gasped, feeling her shoulders forced backwards into the soft leather. "What happened to taking it slowly?"

Maria held her in position, kissing her deeply. "You happened."

"You happened first," replied Connie, pushing up and moving Maria back, responding to every advance with a reactive move of her own. "I want you so badly."

Maria slid her hand up Connie's thigh, holding it tightly. "Where?"

"Everywhere."

The knock on the plastic divider shocked them both back into their seats. "We're here, love," said the taxi driver, completely nonplussed.

Maria straightened her hair and fumbled in her handbag for her purse. "Sorry, thank you. Sorry." She handed over notes worth double the fee as she hurried Connie out of the taxi. "Bye. Thank you."

Connie stumbled, giggling as she tried to get as much distance as possible between herself and the taxi. "Oh this breeze is nice, isn't it?" she said, waving her hand in front of her face. "Quite hot in there didn't you think? Has he gone yet?"

Maria ushered her up the wide path. "Not yet," she said, finding her keys and pushing on the ornate doorknob, scooping them both inside as quickly as she could. "There," she said locking the bolt and keying in the alarm code. "I'm sure he didn't care one bit, but I'm always irrationally scared that they'll follow us in."

"You and all the women you bring back to your mansion?"

"You know what I mean."

Connie smiled in the sudden darkness, sure that her voice was echoing up the curved stairs and onto the balcony landing. "So," she said.

"So indeed."

"Do you need to make any calls?" she asked, aware that Maria was stepping into her space and closing the distance between her and the wall.

"No, I've been informed that all's well. You?"

"All's fine."

Maria stepped even closer. "So it's just us. Alone. With no curfew."

"And no sleepers insisting we're quiet," she added, taking Maria's arms and switching positions, pinning her against the cool wall instead. "I want this, Maria."

"What do you want?"

"This." Connie pressed their bodies together, lingering her lips close enough to make contact, wanting to memorise the first few magic moments where their skin danced softly together, circling back and forth before their mouths parted fully with pleasure.

"More," groaned Maria, lifting her hands to the base of Connie's head, pulling her lips even closer.

Connie responded quickly, fast absorbed by the deep heated passion, pressing their breasts together and pulling on Maria's waist so their thighs were forced into each other's. She kissed deeper, harder, unable to get enough, needing to be closer, wanting to feel more. "I need you," she gasped, sliding her fingers under Maria's top, feeling the smooth skin of her waist.

"Wait, wait," Maria breathed quickly. "This way." She took Connie's hand and raced them up the curved stairway, crossing the balcony landing before reaching the large bedroom door. She pushed on it gently, allowing Connie to enter the room first. "Horrendously cheesy, but doesn't everyone have this dream?" She opened the chest of drawers and found the matches, carefully lighting each candle in turn. "For you," she said, gesturing to their surroundings.

Connie stayed still, mesmerised as the draping white curtains and four poster bed became illuminated in the soft flicker of flames. She walked forwards and picked up a petal. "Red roses?"

"Petals and a four poster. I'm sorry, it seemed like a good idea this morning."

Connie inhaled the sweet scent, turning around slowly. "This is the nicest thing anyone's ever done for me."

"It's nothing."

"It's everything."

Maria smiled. "Would some gentle music add to the effect?"

"As long as you promise to dance."

Pressing play on the sound system Maria took hold of Connie and pulled her close. "You've done something to me, Miss Parker. You've made me want to wait."

Connie moved their bodies together. "Haven't you been giving *me* time to be sure?"

"No, it's because *I* felt sure that I needed this to be perfect."

"And not in some dark tunnel at Bounce-a-rama?"

"Exactly." She smiled. "But I did want you so much in that moment."

"And this moment?"

"In this moment I'm living the dream." She leaned forward and kissed Connie gently, moving their bodies towards the bed. "I need to show you what I feel, Connie."

Connie breathed softly. "I feel it already."

"Do you feel this?" she asked, lowering Connie onto the bed, delicately kissing her neck. "Whenever our skin touches I shiver."

Connie tilted her head further back, exposing her skin to the lips. "I feel it."

"Whenever we start I want more."

Connie gasped as Maria's teeth grazed up towards the base of her head. "I feel it."

"Whenever there's more I can't stop it." Maria forced Connie's shoulder's down onto the covers, kissing her mouth with a depth of raw intensity.

"Don't stop," moaned Connie, pulling Maria's body over her own. "Take me," she said. "Take all of me."

CHAPTER THIRTY THREE

Connie stirred as the soft light of a sunbeam glowed through the gap in the curtains, waking her naturally for the first time in over three years. She yawned, stretching her arms up, suddenly realising where she was. Turning slowly to the other side of the bed she found Maria sound asleep on the pillow with her silky brown locks cascading around her shoulders, shining in a sunbeam all of their own. Connie smiled with completion. Last night had been everything. All her doubts and inhibitions put to rest.

Pulling back the covers, she crept out of bed and padded quietly to the bathroom. The cheeks she saw reflected in the mirror were glowing with fulfilment and the hair was more than just messy, it was sex messy; stylishly sex messy. She left it as it was, remembering the moment of sheer ecstasy when Maria had tightened her grip at the base of her skull, pulling her hair as she came in her arms, legs wrapped around waists and breasts pushed together. She shuddered. She'd made Maria come. Not once, but twice, and every inch of her being had experienced it with her, the pleasure of giving the gift almost as fulfilling as receiving it in return.

Connie rinsed her face, dried it and cleaned her teeth before creeping back into bed. She curled herself into a ball and lay on her side, watching the specks of dust caused by her movement as they danced in the sunbeam. She smiled to herself. Life was good. Life was really good. Not only was she happy, she was complete; that missing element of all her previous interactions suddenly present with Maria. It wasn't simply the fact she was a woman, more possibly the fact that she was the woman she was. Captivating, kind, generous, compelling. The type of woman you wanted to want you. The type of woman you hoped to spend time with; to get to know. Connie paused her thought, feeling soft fingers finding their way around her waist. She smiled at the sunbeam. The type of woman you had to have touch you.

Connie closed her eyes, aware that Maria had moved closer; she could feel the knees fit into her body shape and the breasts push tight into her back. The fingers were moving now, slowly trailing the skin of her stomach with small circles that were edging upwards along the side of her body. Connie kept her eyes closed. What a lovely way this would have been to wake up had the sunbeam not already done its job. She lifted her arm slightly, resting her cheek on her hand, exposing her breast in the process and giving the fingers a clear path for their journey, signalling to Maria that she was awake and aware, encouraging this early morning contact.

Maria understood the movement, teasing her fingers down the side of the breast, stopping short of where she was needed the most.

Connie moaned and arched her back, wanting to be touched, wanting to be taken, wanting the fingers to continue their path. Maria circled slowly, careful not to move from the soft skin. Connie moaned again, pushing herself back into Maria's body, needing the touch on her chest.

"You're going to come," whispered Maria, her lips against the back of Connie's head, "and I'm going to take it so slowly, so softly, that you'll be begging for more." She let her little finger brush the hard nipple, causing Connie to gasp her arousal. "You'll want me tugging and squeezing, but I'm taking my time."

"I need it harder," urged Connie, spasming in pleasure as the fingers dared touch her once more.

"I know you do, but you're waiting," Maria whispered, moving her thumb in a circular motion.

"Please," moaned Connie, "take me, pull me." She gasped. "Be firm."

Maria held the nipple between her first finger and thumb, gently drawing it out. "Not yet," she said with a smile, moving her mouth to the base of Connie's throat, biting gently on the skin of her neck.

"Ahhh," Connie cried out, desperate for the roughness, moving her hand to Maria's bottom and pulling it closer to hers.

Maria released the nipple and took hold of the hand, lifting it back up above Connie's head and locking it in position with the other. "Stay," she whispered, trailing her fingers back down to their target.

Connie could feel her arousal throbbing between her legs. Maria's touch was so gentle, yet perfectly planned to elicit the desired response, her nerve endings were screaming with need.

"I want you to want me," said Maria, moving her other hand down Connie's spine, as she continued the tease of her fingers.

"I want you," said Connie, arching her bottom into Maria's curves, encouraging the path of the contact.

Maria moved her hand lower, using her thumb to stroke the soft skin of Connie's bottom, her other fingers working the nipple. "Really want me."

Connie inhaled, pushing her chest forward and her bottom out. "I *really* want you."

"How?" asked Maria, increasing the pressure, using her other hand to move lower and part Connie's thighs.

"Inside me. I need you inside me."

Maria whispered softly. "You'll take it. From behind."

The words, combined with the increased assault of the fingers brought Connie close to the edge. She threw her head sideways, finding Maria's mouth and kissing her deeply, their tongues devouring each other's as Maria's hands held her firmly in place.

Maria moaned. "This feeling... this need..." she brought her fingers into position, ready to force them in, "...this is what sex is about."

Connie cried out in ecstasy as she was entered from behind, Maria pushing up against her wall, trapped by the tightness of her closed legs.

Maria took her time with her movements. "You're perfect," she whispered, "and you're going to be pleasured, over and over again."

****

The door to the top-floor apartment flew open, causing Connie and Maria to fall into Ryan's outstretched arms.

"Get your hands off each other!" he wailed, whooping in glee at the vision in front of him. "You've got sex hair, Connie!" He stepped back and yelped. "And Maria, you just look thoroughly fucked!"

"Hello Ryan," said Connie, dancing herself into the modern living space.

"Ryan," said Maria with a shy smile.

"I've never seen you looking so dishevelled, it's utterly wonderful." He slammed the door behind them and spun around. "But it should *not* have taken me ten texts to convince you to come over. I can't remember the last time I cooked you lunch, Connie, and I know you've been busy doing whatever it is you ladies have been doing, but everyone needs to eat." He led them into the lounge, pointing at the sofa and nest of tables that held two bowls of nuts and a beer glass of breadsticks.

"Is this it?" asked Connie, laughing at the pitiful offering.

"No!" He sat down and nodded. "I've got some grapes for afters."

"Oh Ryan."

"What? We never get to gossip properly when the kids are around. Indulge me. I need to know everything."

Connie smiled, sitting on the Union Jack sofa and encouraging Maria to cuddle in closely. "We had a wonderful date yesterday. Rock climbing, followed by massage and food."

"What sort of massage? What sort of food. I need details! It took so much strength not to message you, I hope you realise that, Connie dearest."

"The massage was beautiful and we ate at The Holly."

"The Holly?! Oh good god who did you see?"

"Bobby Davro."

"You didn't?"

Connie nodded. "I did."

"Oh Maria, you don't realise the light you're bringing into our lives. Twenty years we've known each other and things have never been so good."

Maria laughed. "I bet you two were the same at primary school, weren't you? Gossiping over the play kitchen and racing around in the cosy coupes."

Ryan jumped up. "No need to imagine it. I've got it all here."

"Ryan, no," said Connie, watching as he pulled the large photo album from the bookcase.

"Ryan, yes," said Maria, laughing and patting the arm of the sofa, signalling for him to squeeze down next to them.

Flicking past the first few pages he tapped on one of the pictures. "Here we go. Connie aged five."

"Oh bless," said Maria leaning in closer and studying the photo. "Your hair looks darker there."

"I dye it."

"You do not!" Maria looked up in disbelief. "I thought you were a natural blonde?"

"You didn't discover the truth yesterday?" asked Ryan, raising his eyebrows at the pair of them. "Scratch that, I forgot you lesbians finally got with the programme and started to shave." He banged Maria's arm. "Can you remember the days when lesbians showed their status with underarm hair?"

"I thought it was thumb rings? But seriously, Connie, I can't believe you're not blonde!"

"It's sort of a dirty blonde."

Ryan tutted. "No it's not, it's mousy brown."

Maria continued. "But Noah's hair's so fair."

"My mum's blonde. Stop looking at my roots!"

"Sorry." She turned back to the album. "Come on then, Ryan, where are you?"

Ryan flicked right back to the front, needing no further encouragement. "Born bald, dying bald, but I *did* have hair once." He cooed at the pictures of himself new born and swaddled in a blue blanket, before turning the page and pointing his finger. "I'd just learnt to sit up."

Connie laughed. "You were so chubby!"

"I was not."

"You were." She flicked further into the album. "Here. Your school trousers were always flapping around in the wind because your waist was so high."

Maria edged herself off the sofa. "Sorry, Ryan, could I use your bathroom?"

"Sure, it's at the end of the hall." He turned over the page and wailed. "Oh, darling, can you remember this? Our first nativity play. You hated that I got to be the archangel Gabriel."

"Only because I was a donkey." She paused as Maria walked from the room, waiting for an extra second before grabbing Ryan's thigh and shaking it with force, letting out a wide-mouthed silent scream.

"That good?" asked Ryan, with a laugh.

"Shush!" She giggled. "It was *mind-blowing* and so intense and moving and—"

"Moving?"

"Yes! And deep and totally totally fulfilling."

"I think the word for you right now is spent."

"Oh no, I could do it all over again." She smiled. "And then again, and again, and again."

"Did you..." He whistled.

"Come?" Connie threw her head back onto the sofa and yelled. "God yes!"

Ryan laughed. "What happened to being quiet?"

"I can't keep it in. I'm so happy, Ryan. I just want to shout it from the rooftops."

"Did she..." He whistled again.

Connie smiled with pride. "She did."

"You're sure?"

"I'm sure."

"How do you know?"

"I felt it. And I shouldn't have worried about her comment," she lowered her voice, "when she said she wanted me inside her." The smile was back. "Because she made me feel exactly the same way."

"And she satisfied you?"

"Completely."

"With what?"

Connie fanned her face. "Her fingers, her tongue, her mouth, her lips."

"She got all that up there?"

"Oh stop it!"

Their giggles were cut short by Maria's reappearance in the doorway. "Maddalena's just messaged. I'm sorry I've got to dash off."

Connie stood up. "Oh no, is everything okay?"

"Fine, but I really do need to go."

"Is Alice okay? I'll come with you."

"No, you stay. She's fine. Enjoy lunch." She tried to smile at the bowls of nibbles. "Thanks, Ryan. Right, I'll get going." She stepped towards Connie, hugging her awkwardly. "Bye."

Connie looked at her carefully. "What's wrong?"

"Nothing, I just think she's missing me." She waved at Ryan. "Right, thank you. Sorry to cut this short."

"Give me a call to let me know she's okay," said Connie, taking hold of Maria's hand and slowing her exit. "And don't worry, we can be open with Ryan."

Maria nodded. "I know and will do." She kissed her quickly. "Bye."

Ryan waited for the door to close before lifting his shoulders and pulling a face. "Something I said?"

"No, she must be worried about Alice. You know what it's like when you get a text that even slightly hints at a problem."

"So it's not that she faked it with you, heard us talking about it and suddenly felt guilty?"

Connie jumped down next to him, elbowing him roughly. "Trust me she enjoyed it, and I think I may have found a new talent."

"Ha. What? Lesbian sex? I've been waiting twenty odd years for this day. Right. Start to finish. Moment by moment. You're debriefing it all."

Connie took a deep breath and smiled. "Where on earth should I begin?"

CHAPTER THIRTY FOUR

The submissions process had been complex and not quite the five minute job Connie had been expecting. Who knew a novel had to have a synopsis? Wasn't that going to spoil the ending for the reader at the agency? Condensing the whole book into 500 words meant no intrigue, no suspense, no character development. Of course they wouldn't message her back asking to read the whole thing; they already knew the ending so there'd be no point. She sighed. Her cover letter wasn't her saving grace either. The submissions page had suggested she include all previous writing experience and noteworthy literary accomplishments, which left her with a rather sparse introductory paragraph. She couldn't sugar the pill. She had no experience; and the idea that she had a long list of literary accomplishments was just laughable. Connie paused, thinking carefully, suddenly remembering that certificate in Year Ten. Wasn't that for English? She scrunched up her eyes and tapped on her teeth, before shaking her head at herself. No, that was for poster design. How to handle a bully. It was good, and a hard fought contest, but probably not one the agency would be all that interested in.

The final requirement on the complex list of instructions was to attach the first three chapters of the novel. Connie saved the document entitled *1-3*, even though she felt the end of the book was much better than the start, and linked it to her email, pressing send before she had time to change her mind. She watched as the submission disappeared, nodding to herself as it went. No amount of padding would make her book more saleable. People would either like Bonnie or they wouldn't, and Maria had been right, it *was* exciting to set her free and see where the wind might take her. She looked at her outbox; Bonnie probably wouldn't get any further than the agent's trash folder, but still, it was something.

Closing down her computer and shutting the cupboard door, Connie glanced around the lounge, looking for a further distraction. Everywhere was tidy. There was no washing to start, no ironing to do, even Noah's pyjamas, toothbrush and flannel were laid out ready for his return. Cursing herself she lifted her phone and typed out another message.

Hey, still no reply about Alice. I hope everything's okay. Not sure if you're getting my texts? Missed you this afternoon, but I've used the time wisely (after my huge gossip with Ryan) to send my book out to an agent. Thanks for the suggestion…you never know, I may become the next E.L. James.

Connie watched as the message registered as delivered. She waited for a moment hoping the grey typing cloud would appear, and was dismayed when it didn't. Maria was usually so good at replying. Something *must* have happened to Alice.

****

Maria tucked her daughter into bed, kissing her cheek and dimming the pink light further. "Night night, precious."

"She be sleeping already," whispered Maddalena, shuffling out of the room in front of Maria. "Holiday with me be good for her. You let Aunt Maddalena look after her more often. She sleep good in my house. She not need all these disco lights and mobiles."

Maria pulled her phone from her back pocket. "She's always been a great sleeper."

"No, she *really* sleep well when I be in charge." Maddalena crossed the landing and reached for the bannister, starting her slow descent of the stairs. "We do this next weekend too? I have her then bring her back Sunday?" She paused. "What you be staring at? Why you look so, so…" She studied her niece. "…sulky?"

Maria laughed. "I don't look sulky."

"That bad woman be texting you?"

"Louise? No. I think she got the message when you swung your broom and brushed her out of the shop."

"Who message you then?"

"Connie. Come on, I'm making you supper."

"No. I go. You make things good with *bella* Connie."

"They are good."

"Your face not be good."

"It's fine, everything's great. She's being funny actually. You enjoyed the *Fifty Shades of Grey* books, didn't you?"

"*Non capisco.*" Maddalena continued her descent. "You make me some supper."

****

"Mummy!" squealed Noah, racing into the house and jumping into her outstretched arms.

"Hello big man, I missed you! Have you had a nice time?"

Noah shook his head. "No."

"Yes we did," said Karl, shutting the front door and following him in. "We went to the zoo and the park, and last night we stayed up late to watch The Turtles."

"Grandma not like Turtles."

Karl leaned in and whispered into his son's ear. "Next time we'll make sure Grandma's not there."

"Yay! Turtles!"

Connie laughed. "Thank you. It's nice to see you boys getting along."

"It's been lovely. Let me change him and pop him into bed for you."

Connie smiled. "Why didn't we do this years ago?"

"We were living a lie. You know that better than I do." He took Noah out of her arms. "Put the kettle on. I'll stay for a chat."

****

From her low down position on the wooden bench, Maddalena reached up to the farmhouse style table and dipped her focaccia bread into the olive oil. "So Connie like racy racy then?" she asked.

Maria swallowed quickly. "What?"

"*Fifty Shades?*"

"No, she just texted something funny about the author."

"That woman not care what people say. She got millions."

"Connie's written a book. She was joking that hers might be as popular."

"Good! Everybody like racy racy. You read it? What's it about?"

Maria placed her bread on the table, moving her plate out of the way. "Oh, Aunt Maddalena, I think it's all about me."

****

Connie smiled as Karl crept down the stairs. "Noah the turtle who closes his eyes at bedtime to strengthen his super powers?" She handed over the mug of tea. "Nice story. You've got hidden talents, Karl."

"And what have you got hidden, Connie?"

Connie frowned.

"In the kitchen."

"What?"

"Get in the kitchen."

"I need to check him first."

The voice was raised. "Get. In. The. Kitchen."

Connie followed him quickly, not wanting to wake her sleeping son. "What?" she asked, closing the door as Karl took a seat at the table.

"It finally all makes sense. The perfect little virgin. Every man's dream." He looked up at her with loathing. "Saving yourself for someone special then blaming your son for your lack of sex drive."

"What are you talking about? What's happened? You came in so nicely. You've been so great with Noah."

"Don't turn this round on me. He's my son. I'll always be civil."

"But only when he's around?"

"You're a lesbian. What do you expect?"

"What?"

"Don't deny it, Connie. Louise has told me everything."

"Louise from work who's actually a lesbian herself?"

Karl stood up from his seat. "Louise isn't a lesbian." He smiled. "Trust me. I can vouch for that"

"Oh Karl, you're such a cock. Louise *is* a lesbian and she's clearly been spouting rubbish about me because I'm friends with the woman she wanted."

"Oh bollocks, Connie. You can't talk your way out of this one. I spoke to that old lady at the coffee shop. Your girlfriend's aunty. She told me the truth."

"Maddalena?"

"You took my son to Brighton with your lesbian lover. You've spent this whole weekend alone with your lesbian lover."

"She's not my lesbian lover."

"Isn't she? Isn't that why you never fucked a man before me? Why you waited for the right person? But you didn't realise that person was a woman so you settled for me instead?" He paused. "Or maybe you knew it all along? Maybe you just used me to get pregnant?"

"Stop it, Karl."

"Why? I'm not wrong."

"Yes you are."

"So there's nothing between you and this *Maria?*"

Connie looked down at her feet. "We're friends."

"Oh god, it's true. You've been fucking her haven't you? That woman you were slagging me off to? That brunette at Bounce-a-rama? That's Maria."

"No, I..."

"She's *so* out of your league."

"No she's not."

Karl shook his head, turning his back on the kitchen. "What a fucking waste of four fucking years."

****

Connie typed quickly. *Karl knows. Is there any chance I can call you?*
This time the reply was instantaneous.
I'll be round in an hour.

CHAPTER THIRTY FIVE

Connie heard the gentle tapping and opened the door, greeting Maria with a huge silent hug. "Thank you for coming," she whispered, deliberately brushing her cheek against Maria's neck as she inhaled the soft scent of her perfume. "How's Alice?" she asked, noticing Maria's hesitant gaze over her shoulder and up the stairs. "It's fine. He's out for the count. Karl settled him nicely."

"Karl's still here?"

"No. Relax, it's fine." She closed the door and took hold of Maria's hand, leading them both towards the sofa. "He dropped Noah back earlier and everything was going really well. He was polite and chatty. Crikey, he even put Noah to bed." She paused. "But then all hell broke loose."

"Are you okay?"

Connie smiled. "I am now. Sit down. I've poured us some wine."

"I've got the car and Maddalena's with Alice so I can't be long." She glanced around. "Wouldn't we be better off talking in the kitchen?"

"It's only one glass, and no, we can snuggle up here." She patted the sofa, lifting her own glass from the coffee table. "As long as you don't make those erotic howling noises from last night."

"Connie."

"What?"

Maria left the wine where it was and perched down on the edge of the cushions. "I should have replied to your texts."

"It's fine. I know what it's like when you're distracted by children."

"It's not that."

"What's wrong?" She looked at Maria but couldn't catch her eye. "Is Alice okay?"

"I'm fine. Alice is fine."

Connie waited patiently, studying Maria's beautiful profile, hoping for a tilt of the head or a flicker of a smile, but when they failed to come she moved closer and reached out for her thigh. "Talk to me."

"Don't."

"Don't what?"

Maria crossed her legs, sending the hand back to its owner.

"What? What's going on?"

The brown eyes were suddenly present. "We need to talk."

"You're joking? Please tell me you're joking?" Connie threw herself backwards, plunging her head into the cushions. "You're joking." She peeped back up. "Aren't you?"

The layers of brown hair shook slowly.

"What are you doing?" Connie watched as Maria removed herself from the sofa. "Why are you standing up? Sit down, talk to me."

"I can't."

"You have to," she said, jumping up to hold her tightly around the waist. "Don't try and wiggle away from me. This time yesterday we were having the time of our lives, eating, drinking, mingling with Bobby Davro." Connie felt the slightest shudder of laughter and continued. "We were! It was great! And he definitely looked at me."

Maria finally smiled. "Because you kept staring."

"This is better. I didn't. He was checking me out. Come on, sit down. Whatever this is we can sort it."

"We can't."

"Maria, I've spent my whole life looking for something, for anything, that made sense." She dared to release one hand so she could reach up and stroke the soft cheek. "When I'm with you everything makes sense. This morning was the most special morning ever."

Maria shook her head. "Please."

"Please what? I'm not letting you brush me aside because of something I've done. Whatever it is I can change. I'm a fast learner."

The brown eyes came to life properly for the first time that evening. "Oh Connie, you've not done anything wrong. It's me. I'm the one with the issues."

"No problem. Hit me with them. I'm sure I've handled worse shit before."

Maria laughed. "Stop making this difficult."

"Making what difficult? You've not come here to dump me, have you? One date in and I'm getting the boot?"

"No, it's..."

"Oh my goodness, you have. You are."

"No, I'm..." Maria shook her head. "We should sit down."

Connie did as instructed, waiting on the cushions with wide eyes. Nodding as Maria finally took her place next to her. "This is nice."

"No it's not. You need to stop being so bouncy."

"I'm just being me."

Maria turned towards Connie. "Maybe I'm not being me." She sighed. "I haven't been honest."

"You faked it, didn't you? The sex, the orgasms. I was crap."

Maria shivered. "No way, you were..."

"Really?"

The stare was intense. "You *know* what I felt. You *know* how hard I..."

"So what is this? Everything seemed great until Ryan's."

Maria took a deep breath. "I lied to you. Can you remember when I told you about my past relationships? I blamed the other women for not wanting to commit." She shrugged. "It wasn't them. It was me. I get scared whenever anything gets serious."

"I don't believe you."

"It's true, and you were so open with Ryan. You were talking like you wanted the world to know. I heard you."

"So?"

"And then you messaged me telling me Karl knows."

"He suspects."

"You didn't confirm it?"

"Not directly, but he'll find out eventually. I don't want to lie, Maria. Meeting you has been the best thing that's ever happened to me. And I know it sounds strange but I have to think of you as if you were male. Karl will just have to get over it. People will see I've moved on. I'm not going to stay single forever, and the fact you're a woman should play no part in it."

"That's easy to say, but people won't get it."

"So all your chatter to Earth Mother and Crusty? That was rubbish too, was it? I don't believe you, Maria. There's something else. What is it?"

"There isn't."

"So what do you want?"

"I don't want this."

Connie stood up, shaking her head. "What? You spend however long wooing me and coaxing me into bed, then you end it the minute we've fucked?"

"It's not like that. I'm just not ready."

"Since when?"

"Since now. I'm sorry, Connie, but the thoughts in my head couldn't be clearer. We rushed into this. You've barely been separated a week."

Connie talked down to the sofa. "People have affairs. Time scale means nothing when you meet the right person."

"You're not my right person."

"Since when?"

Maria stood up. "Since now."

"Oh god, I've never heard so much crap in all my life. What happened to the jigsaw? What happened to seeing where this went? So what? I told Ryan. So what? I didn't deny it to Karl. I'll calm it down on both counts if that's what you want."

"No."

"What then?" Connie ran her fingers though her hair, exasperated by the confusion.

"You're younger than me. You've not figured out who you really are."

Connie took hold of Maria's waist once more. "I want to be the person I am when I'm with you."

"Oh Connie."

"What?"

"I need to go."

"Don't you dare, you've only just got here."

"We'll keep going round in circles."

"Circles? I'm on a zig-zag. Look at me, Maria. I've no clue what's going on."

Maria broke away. "This is just too much too soon. We need to step away from each other so we can figure out what we both truly want."

Connie shook her head. "Too late... I love you."

CHAPTER THIRTY SIX

"She just kissed me and left."

"What do you mean she just kissed you and left?"

Connie shrugged. "Exactly that. She just kissed me and left."

"What a total bitch! You tell her you love her and she walks away?"

"It wasn't like that, Ryan."

"You feel sorry for her, don't you? You're dumped yet somehow you're the one left feeling guilty."

Connie sat unmoving on the plastic chair and stared around at play stations bustling with young children eager to explore life and have fun, but still she was left feeling empty. Usually the vision of little people completing their first paintings or clambering up the apparatus to the triumphant pinnacle of the small slide brought smiles and warmth to her being, but today she knew she was lifeless. "I must have done something wrong," she managed to say.

"Like what? Her behaviour's inexcusable."

"She got upset."

"When she kissed you? Yeah right, crocodile tears for her final goodbye. And you need to stop looking at the door. She's not replying to your texts or calls so she's hardly going to rock up at playgroup." He shook his head. "You've been played, darling."

She spoke slowly. "So have you."

"I didn't fuck her!"

"No, but you thought she was perfect, and shush, there are children about."

"Top Dog and her gang spout worse shit than that, and I'm angry; I've got every right to vent."

"Not in the community centre, you haven't," said Connie, drawn back into her surroundings.

"It's where you first met her. It's the perfect place to kick off. Get angry, she used you. She made you look like a fool."

"There's something more, there has to be."

"Connie dearest, she couldn't have been clearer. It's over. She's ended it."

"What if she just needs time?"

"For what? She was the one driving this thing. She clearly had one destination in mind and when she arrived she saw the sights and drove home." He shook his head. "Maybe if you'd bought all that kit from Ann Summers like I told you to she'd still be there, appreciating the view."

Connie hushed her voice. "The sex was amazing."

"Yes for you, a woman who's only slept with two people. She's clearly a player. She'll have high standards and expectations. You had to set yourself apart."

"Stop making me feel worse. Honestly, Ryan, you're not helping."

"The truth and tough love are always best in the long run. It's been three days and you've heard nothing. How many texts have you sent her?"

Connie hid her face behind her hair. "Maybe five."

"And calls?"

"Maybe the same." She spun back around. "But I've not left any warbling voicemails. I've just checked in, asked if she was okay and said I'm here for her whenever she needs me."

"Don't do that. You'll become her booty call."

"I love her, Ryan. I'd take anything."

"Oh darling, you don't! You can't. It's too soon, and she's clearly a player."

"Stop saying clearly. Nothing's clear. All I know is how I feel, and I feel lost without her."

"You should be angry."

"I'm not angry, I'm hurting."

Ryan nodded. "Well get ready for more pain. Phoebe and exorcist girl have just arrived."

Connie looked to the entrance at Tabitha who was bucking against the straps of her pushchair because Phoebe hadn't let her run free. "Do you think she's heard from Maria? They exchanged numbers last week. Maybe she knows something."

"Maria might be a sex-crazed player bitch, but she'd never choose that nut job over you. Hi there," he said, suddenly changing his pitch. "Good to see you again. How's things?"

Phoebe brought the pushchair and thrashing feet to a halt in front of their seats. "Tabitha, stop kicking."

Both Connie and Ryan eased their legs back out of striking distance. "Isn't she playing?" asked Connie, squeaking in pain as a toe managed to make contact.

"Tabitha, will you just sit still! I should have left her in the car really but she'd no doubt find her way out and start causing havoc on the street."

Connie frowned. "You're not staying?"

"No, but I had to pop in. I just wanted to say how much I appreciate everything you've done for me. You helped me with Tabitha. You got me back in touch with a good friend. Through you I saw the light. Alice is a wonderful little girl and I should never have been so judgemental. Anyway, four years on and we've patched things up. Life couldn't be better."

Connie straightened her back. "You've seen her?"

"Who?"

"Maria."

"Oh yes. She called me on Sunday. We did Dizzy Kids on Monday, the park yesterday and we're off to Sealife today, but I was passing through and thought I'd pop in. You really were so kind to me. Without you guys I'd never have reconnected with such a wonderful woman."

Connie yelped out in pain as a small foot made contact with her shin.

"Tabitha! Right, I'd better be off." She drew the pushchair back. "I'm in charge of the picnic and you know how fussy Maria is with her food. Only the best from the M&S express. I want to get there before the shelves clear."

Ryan pulled a face. "It's only ten past nine and just so you know, Maria's—"

"Ryan!" Connie punched him on the knee and stood up, turning to face Phoebe with a smile. "Thanks for coming in. Have a good day. Right, where's Noah? I fancy snuggling up with a book."

Ryan took hold of the top of Connie's jeans, pulling her back to her chair. "Just you sit down." He paused, staring at Phoebe. "Bye then."

"Okay, bye," she said turning the pushchair around, not noticing the tongue-out, finger-wiggling raspberry being pulled by her daughter.

Connie sat down as Phoebe wheeled her away. "Nice parting gift. Pretty much sums up how totally crapped on I feel."

"Little shit," growled Ryan.

Connie shook her head. "Since when has Maria been a fussy eater?"

"You've only known her two seconds. You've never done picnics. Phoebe was obviously a very close friend."

"So close that she dumped her? This whole thing's just rubbish, and I'm not playing along."

"You think it's a game?"

"Why else show up here, spouting off about their perfect play days?"

Ryan shook his head. "I think it was genuine. You're giving yourself too much importance."

"I *am* important. Maria liked me. We had something special."

"She saw you as a straight girl experimenting, nothing more, nothing less. What lesbian wouldn't play along?"

"I haven't been played."

"You have. Us gays are notorious for it. There's no other explanation. Alice is fine and it's not like Maria's snowed under at work. She's out and about with her new girl."

"They're just friends! She'd never go there with Phoebe."

"Wouldn't she?"

"Stop it, Ryan, you're making me angry."

"Good! Get het up! Let out your rage." He gasped. "Oh god, hold it in for a second."

"What?" Connie followed his gaze to the entrance. Earth Mother and Crusty were signing in, squeezing each other's bottoms as they giggled with flirtation.

"They're coming this way!" he wailed. "And they're holding hands!"

Top Dog and her gang wolf-whistled at the two women. "Ai ai!" they shouted, causing Crusty to halt her walk, turn to her wife and kiss her hard on the lips.

"Bout time too!" yelled one of the tattooed women.

"We all knew you were lovers," added Top Dog. "More action than my bloke gives me."

"He's busy givin' it me," laughed one of the crew.

Earth Mother smiled at the banter and continued her walk. "Go on, Lucas," she said to the little boy as he scooted up to their shins on the pedal-kart, "go and play with your brother. Mummy Clare and I will be sitting over there."

Connie smiled for the first time that day as she followed the direction of the finger. She stood up to rearrange the chairs for their arrival. "Hi," she said, welcoming them properly.

"Thank you, thank you, thank you," gushed Earth Mother, wrapping her arms around Connie and enclosing her in a huge breast-first hug.

Crusty joined in, tightening the circle. "You were right. This *is* the way forward. You and Maria talked total sense. We went home, thought things through and decided we should well and truly step out of the closet. Things have been fantastic. It's like we can finally breathe."

Earth Mother ended the embrace, scanning the immediate surroundings. "Where is she? Where's Maria?"

Ryan sneered. "She's out shopping for wardrobes."

CHAPTER THIRTY SEVEN

The atmosphere in the house was tense and not at all conducive for a smooth change over. Noah had woken up that morning complaining about Grandma Evelyn's itchy sheets and horrible tasting breakfast. He'd also said she smelt funny, and whilst Connie had to condemn his negative tone of voice, she didn't fully dispute his criticisms and may have even let a slight snigger slip from her lips. This was to be the third time he'd stayed away and the previous two Sundays she'd seen him arrive home rather subdued, with last weekend being the most horrific when it transpired that Karl hadn't seen him at all. Evelyn had been left in charge while he travelled to Manchester for a meeting that involved an overnight stay and apparently a second day of essential golfing.

Even more worrying was Karl's sudden u-turn on property, saying he was more than happy to lodge at his mother's at the weekends because he'd most likely invest up north where prices were cheaper. Connie knew he couldn't possibly be happy with Evelyn which led to her conclusion that he was barely there, choosing to spend any free time he had in Manchester instead.

She wilted on her chair, dropping her head onto the kitchen table as Karl confirmed her suspicions. "That's not okay," she said with a moan.

Karl stayed standing, checking his watch once more. "I'm giving you lots of pre-warning this time. Noah will be fine. Right, we really need to go."

Connie lowered her voice. "I want him to see *you*, not your mother."

"I have to work, and it's not for another month yet."

She propped herself back up, resting her chin in her palm. "He was complaining about her this morning."

"Mum? Saying what?"

"That she... Oh it doesn't matter." Connie sighed and shouted through to the lounge. "Come on then, Noah, let's get your bag."

"I have it here," said Evelyn entering the kitchen with the little red rucksack dangling between her two fingers. "I think I'll go upstairs and change a few things. Last weekend he looked terribly scruffy."

Karl spoke first. "Mum, it's fine."

His mother maintained her position. "No, we're meeting Audrey and Joyce at the garden centre for lunch and I want him to look smart."

Connie raised her eyebrows at Karl. "You're meeting Audrey and Joyce are you? That will be fun boy time for you and Noah."

Evelyn sniffed. "No, we're dropping Karl at the retail outlet so he can pick up some suits."

Connie's eyes flashed. "Karl!"

"I'll just nip Noah upstairs to pick out something more suitable," said Evelyn, backing out of the kitchen, totally satisfied with her meddling.

Karl shut the door behind her. "It's going really well in Manchester. I'm exposed to new clients on a daily basis. I need to keep up appearances."

"On Noah's time?"

"It's only lunch. What's with you today? You're all sulky and you've been lolling about all over the place."

"I have not and you've only been here five minutes."

"Long enough to see you're not right."

"I'm fine, and if you don't want Noah at the weekends you should tell me. He'll be in nursery soon so I'll have less time with him during the week. It might suit both of us if we change your responsibility to every other weekend."

Karl blinked quickly. "That's better for you?"

Connie smiled at his inability to hide his quiet, yet pleasant, shock. "Yes."

"Well if it's better for you then I don't see why not." He looked at her carefully. "Are you sure you're okay?"

"I'm fine."

"Listen," he lowered his voice, "I was wrong to speak to you the way I did."

"When you accused me of being a lesbian?"

"Shush!"

"No. It's not a rude word, or a word that should be silenced."

"Okay, okay."

"But once again I give you complete assurance that *absolutely nothing* is going on with me and Maria, or any other woman for that matter, but if it was then I hope you'd realise that it would be none of your business."

"I know, I know, and I was only saying shush because of Mum being so old-school."

"And you're okay exposing Noah to that, are you? Sorry, of course you are. It's the upstanding male role model of Ryan that you hate."

"No, yes, I mean..." Karl ran his fingers through his hair. "What is it with you today? And anyway it was just the shock, especially when you threw in that allegation about Louise and I felt ganged up on."

"Oh don't be so ridiculous, Karl."

"I did," he looked at the floor, "but she told me."

"Told you what?"

"Last week. She's bisexual." His eyes returned. "And she admitted she was wrong about you and Maria. So I'm sorry. I shouldn't have shouted."

"What does that woman know about me and Maria? She's always been there on the outskirts of whatever you and I have had. Why can't she just mind her own business?"

"Oh I don't know. I ignored her the first time she mentioned something but when I spoke to that old woman in the coffee shop I couldn't help texting her to find out what she'd been going on about."

"There's nothing going on."

"I know that now. I think Louise is quite smitten with Miss Mariano. It's as you said, sour grapes."

"Something's happening with Louise and Maria?"

"No, Maria's apparently got someone else who's got a daughter as well, or so says Louise who I think could be stalking her to find all this out." He paused. "It's strange really, how you think you know people, only to have them surprise you with the most unexpected things."

"And this is unexpected because you've slept with her and a declaration of her bisexuality hurts your male pride?"

"No, I…" He sighed. "I'm trying to be civil, Connie, and I don't care who you end up with, man, woman, freak of nature." He smiled. "I just want you to be happy."

"Yeah. You too."

"Do you mean that?"

She shrugged. "I guess."

"It's just that I've met someone," he quickly sat down next to her, pulling his chair as close as he could, "and it's early days, but she's wonderful, and she's in business too. She wants to travel the world and conquer the globe. She's full of sparks and ideas. The type of person who makes you want to be the best version of you."

Connie looked up at him slowly and spoke with a rolling of eyes. "Oh good god."

"It's true and I know it's quite sudden, but she's special, and I want your blessing."

"You don't need my blessing. You were just a man I shared a house with."

Karl recoiled. "Ouch."

"Sorry. I didn't mean it quite like that. I'm happy for you. Is she based in Manchester?"

"For now, but she wants to expand her business worldwide."

"Great."

Karl nodded quickly. "She's so determined. She infuses everyone with such confidence when she meets them. You can see it in their eyes. She makes them believe they're capable of anything. She's called Erin."

The monotone continued. "Wow."

"Oh Connie, you're cross."

"Honestly I'm not. I'm sure she's lovely. Does Evelyn approve?"

"No, Mum doesn't know."

Karl's mother opened the door, clutching a small pile of shirts. "What doesn't Mum know? Connie is this really all you've got? He ought to have a smart suit by now for occasions such as this."

"It's only the garden centre, Mum." Karl stood up quickly. "Come on, we should head off. I'll have him back by four tomorrow."

Connie pulled herself out of her seat and followed them both into the lounge, smiling as she saw Noah sitting on the bottom step of the stairs with his arms wrapped tightly around the bannister. "I love you, big man," she said, kneeling in front of him. "You have fun with Daddy and Grandma."

"Grandma Evelyn smell funny."

Connie shook her head. "Noah."

"Sorry," he said, his mouth turning down even more.

"We'll have none of that nonsense this week," snapped Evelyn, trying to grab hold of his hand.

"Mum, it's fine, I'll take him. Come on, Noah, let's get you an ice cream at the garden centre. We can look at the fountains again." Karl nodded with encouragement as some fingers came free from the bannister. "That's it, and the others." He smiled and lifted the little boy. "Shall we have two flavours this time?"

"What about your suits?" snapped Evelyn.

"I can do that next week. See you tomorrow, Connie."

"For goodness sake, you need to get things sorted, Karl, and I've told you about the dangers of sugar."

Connie stood still as the shrill voice tailed off, watching the three disappear out of the house. "Bye," she said in a whisper, turning to the emptiness awaiting her, nothing planned to fill the void that Noah's departure inevitably created. Last weekend she'd watched two seasons of *The Good Wife*, the weekend before that it was *Damages*, but today she knew Netflix couldn't tempt her out of her gloom. It had been over a month since Brighton and the start of what she had then believed would be a long-term rapport of friendship, possible intimacy and most definite affection. They had liked each other, she was sure of that, and no amount of recycling the days and events leading up to her dismissal gave her the answers she needed. Something had gone wrong. Something had changed, yet she had no idea what, and the only plausible explanation was that she'd been played. Used for sex, and when the sex failed to live up to standard she'd been flicked in one sitting.

Connie dropped onto the sofa. That couldn't be right. Maria had been so vocal about their need to relax and just see where this took them. *She'd* been the one reassuring them both. *She'd* been the one telling Connie to make the first move. Connie closed her eyes, feeling the tears building once more. She missed her. She loved her. Even after the silence, she still loved her. "*What am I doing?*" she gasped, wiping her cheek and looking around for any distraction. She found her phone and refreshed the screen, clicking on the three new emails in her inbox. The first was from lastminute.com asking her to escape to Gran Canaria for all year round sunshine. The second was from Sheena at Flexicover telling her to get 20% off her travel insurance, and the third was from The National Lottery stating they had news about her ticket. Connie sat up straighter, quickly clicking on the link. What if she'd won big? She could message Sheena at Flexicover and get that 20% off the insurance she'd need to travel to Gran Canaria. Connie entered her login details. No, she wouldn't go to Gran Canaria, she'd go to Australia, or America. What the hell, she'd just travel the world. The message page on her National Lottery account flashed up. **News about your ticket. You've won £2.70 on EuroMillions!**

Connie threw down her phone. £2.70. Why on earth did that require an exclamation mark? She couldn't even get a bus ticket to Hackney for that. Maybe the staff at the National Lottery threw it in to laugh at her and say: "Ha! No money, no partner, no job, no life." She paused as her inbox beeped again. What was it this time? An email from Slimming World telling her to join? Or a message from a funeral parlour reminding her it was never too soon to plan for the inevitable?

She scanned the sender's name and subject, slowing her reading as the words came into focus. It was from the literary agent. They had received her submission. She re-read the next sentence twice before daring to read it aloud. *"We loved the first three chapters of your novel and would like you to send us the whole manuscript on an exclusive basis."* She jumped up, clutching the phone and repeating the words once again. *"We loved the first three chapters of your novel and would like you to send us the whole manuscript on an exclusive basis."* The doorbell buzzed and Connie didn't care who was standing on the step, she was throwing open the door and greeting them with the very same sentence.

"My novel's a whole and they want an exclusive!" she said as the woman on the doorstep came into view.

"Your what?"

"My, my..." Connie stood still, staring at the soft brown eyes. "My novel's..."

"You have an agent?"

"I... I think so... I... What are you...?"

The voice was gentle. "Oh Connie, that's brilliant. May I come in?"

She nodded, inhaling the sweet smell of cherry blossom as it swirled into the house, following the beautiful woman with her eyes. "You... You look... You look lovely," she managed to say.

Maria smiled. "So do you." The stare was intense and the voice was earnest. "And there's so much I need to say and so much I need to apologise for but you must tell me about your book first."

Connie lifted her phone, finding it easier than speaking, watching as Maria read the words for herself.

"This is fantastic! They say you have a really unique voice. I'm so happy for you. Come here, Connie."

Connie felt the arms wrap around her shoulders and the lips press against her cheek, but she froze, unable to enjoy the connection. "You're... you're here."

"I should have been here last week, and the week before that." Maria stepped backwards. "Can we sit down? Can I try and explain?"

"I don't want your sympathy."

"Maybe I want yours?"

"What? Why would I give you that? You walked out of here and left me—"

"I know, I know, can you just listen? Can you come and sit down?" Maria made her way to the sofa, patting the space next to her.

This time it was Connie who sat on the edge of the cushions. "Where have you been?"

"I've got something so serious to tell you, something that's taken me this long to come to terms with, something that was so unexpected that it sent me into a spiral of confusion, a spiral of self-doubt, a spiral of stupidity that made me push you away."

"What? What was it?"

"Before I tell you I want to ask you something. Will you tell me again?"

"Tell you what?"

"What you said before I left."

Connie sighed. "I told you I loved you."

"Well I love you too."

"What?"

"I do, and I think I loved you from the first moment I met you when I had to apologise for my daughter hitting your son."

"She didn't hit him. She snatched a block away from him."

"Exactly, I can't remember all the details because all I could think of was you. Standing there, looking so sweet and innocent, yet intriguingly alluring."

"I'm not alluring."

"You are. You were. That's why I fell for you. I wanted you from day one."

"Then you had me and dumped me."

"No."

"What then?"

Maria reached out and took hold of Connie's hands. "I love you. I've always loved you. I want everything with you. I want the dream. I want the house, the home, the children at the same school."

"The private one? As if I could afford that."

"I don't care. I can. I want it. I want us. I want you. I want Noah. I want the dream. I love you, Connie Parker."

Connie felt the emotion swelling in her chest. "You can't do this to me."

"I know, I'm so sorry, but there's a reason."

"What reason?"

Maria wiped a small tear from her own cheek. "I need to know that you want me. I need to know that you're sure."

Connie leaned towards Maria and kissed her on the lips. "I'm sure," she said, overcome with affection, not caring what Maria had to say, not wanting to hear the full story, just content she was there, open and honest with the truth.

Maria moaned in satisfaction, an eruption of longing overtaking her, forcing Connie back into the cushions as she straddled her, kissing her deeply, unable to stop her hands from stealing under the t-shirt, frantically making up for lost time.

The bang of the door and shrill voice echoed through the lounge. "You didn't secure the lid on his beaker! He's covered in juice! We had to turn back."

Connie pushed Maria off her, wiping her mouth and trying to jump up, but it was too late. The scream was ear-splitting. "Get him out, get him out, get him out!" Evelyn was fanning Noah back out of the door. "She's with a woman!"

Karl looked towards the sofa. "Oh Connie, you lied!"

"You knew about this?" yelled Evelyn. "That's why you split up!?"

"Stop shouting, Mum, you're scaring him." Karl picked up his son. "I'll change you in the car, mate."

"Mummy!" cried Noah, throwing his hands out over Karl's shoulder.

"You've lost him now," shouted Evelyn. "I'll make sure he files for custody. I'm not having a homosexual raising my grandson!"

Connie ran past the venomous accusations, chasing Karl out of the house. "Wait!" she shouted. "I didn't lie. I..." Her attention was snapped away by the roar of the motorcycle. "Karl! There's a bike! Don't cross!"

Karl paused on the pavement. "I hear it, Connie. Go back inside."

Connie raced towards the edge of the road and rows of parked cars, stopping next to the van where Karl was currently shielding her son. "Please Karl, let me explain."

Karl waited for the motorcycle to pass. "No," he said, stepping out onto the road.

Connie couldn't remember what she saw first. Was it the wheels of the second motorcycle? Or the sight of her son, thrown from the arms, sent crashing into the windshield of the parked car on the left?

CHAPTER THIRTY EIGHT

The hospital room was light and airy, but the horrible feeling in the pit of Connie's stomach was one of total anguish and sorrow. The doctors had said Noah was fine: a couple of cuts and bruises but nothing that needed more than a dressing. Still, it was her fault. She had chased them out. She had forced Karl into the road. Her actions had sent him straight into the path of the motorcycle. *She* was the one responsible for the vision in front of her.

"He's just sleeping." Maria spoke softly from the chair next to Connie's. "I know what you're thinking, but he's fine."

Connie looked at the huge hospital bed and her little boy tucked under the covers. "He's here because of me, because of us."

"No, he's here so the doctors can keep an eye on him while he naps. They said he'd probably be home later today. And the same goes for Karl. Please, Connie, don't blame yourself."

"So who do I blame? Evelyn for threatening the custody card? Karl for bringing him back? You for kissing me on the sofa?"

"You're answering your own question. A change in any of those things might have stopped it from happening. But it was just an unfortunate chain of events where no one person's to blame."

"How come I feel so guilty?"

"Because you're his mother." Maria smiled and rubbed Connie's back. "He's fine. Karl's fine. That ghastly ex mother-in-law might never be fine though."

Connie managed a small laugh. "The look on her face when she saw us."

"She's got quite the shriek, hasn't she?"

"What if she's serious?"

"You're his mother. You'd never lose custody."

"Karl could take the house. I have no income, no security."

"You have me." Maria smiled. "And a soon to be best-selling novel."

"Why? Why do you want me?"

Maria gently stroked Connie's cheek. "Because you're perfect and these past few weeks without you reminded me of how my life was." She shrugged. "I was just living, and it was okay. I was fine. I was seeing each day through to the next, having fun with Alice, spending time with Maddalena and my fair weather friends, popping in and out of the shops and just doing what I usually do, letting the weeks run their course into months and waiting for the months to turn into years. I've been okay, good even, but when I met you, Connie, I was whole. From that very first moment I knew you were special." The brown eyes smiled. "And I know it sounds stupid but you turned my 'just fines' into fantastics and my 'just living' into loving life. Loving love. True love. Real love. The kind of love that rips you apart when you're not with it. You have an energy, Connie, and I want it, I want to be part of it. You're my missing piece and when I'm with you my picture's complete. It's beautiful. You give me hope, and I'm happy. I'm just so happy whenever I'm with you."

Connie turned to the window and looked at the metal jug sitting on a folded square of white paper. "I think I need a drink. That jug's filled with water but it could be for flowers."

"Let me go and get you a coffee."

"And then can you tell me what happened? Can you tell me what I did wrong?"

"You didn't do anything wrong."

"Your story then. Whatever it was you were going to say before Evelyn came back."

Maria shook her head. "I don't think now's the right time."

"Today's taught me that now's always the right time. Every moment counts. I *need* to know, Maria."

Maria rose from her seat. "Milk and two sugars?"

"Thank you," she said, watching the beautiful woman leaving the room. The softly sprung door clicked closed and Connie turned her attention back to her son. "I love you, Noah," she whispered. "I love you so much, and I'm sorry for causing this, but I want to be happy. I want us all to be happy." She wiped a tear from her cheek. "I've never been happy before."

Ryan lurched her out of her distress as he came crashing into the room, racing up to her chair and dramatically throwing his arms around her shoulders. "I'm so sorry, Connie!"

"Shush. He's sleeping. He's fine."

Ryan glanced at the bed before kneeling down in front of her. "Your text said he'd been hit by a bike."

"No, it said not to worry because he was fine. Karl was hit. He was carrying Noah. It was just outside our house. We're lucky it's a thirty."

"Is Karl okay?"

"He's fine. They're both fine. It was an accident. The biker didn't even come to hospital."

Ryan lifted himself up and sat down next to his friend. "God, Connie, this just shows."

"I know. I was saying the same to Maria."

"She's here? Was she there when it happened? I didn't think she'd get to yours until later."

Connie frowned. "What do you mean? When did you speak to Maria?"

The door swung open once more. This time it was Evelyn who marched into the room waving a chart about and looking flustered. "Oh no, no, no, no, no, this can't be right."

"Shush, Evelyn, he's sleeping. Why can't people walk in quietly?" She paused. "Is everything okay? Is Karl okay?"

"They're letting him out, but I've said there must be a mistake. Nursing knowledge never leaves you, despite what that foreign doctor just told me." She lifted the chart on the end of Noah's bed, carefully comparing it to the one she was holding. "Yes, a mistake, definitely a mistake."

"If the doctors say he's fine then I'd trust them."

"Just like Karl trusted you?" She sneered. "They're running the test again. This makes no sense at all."

"What doesn't?"

"These charts! It's just mind boggling. Unless…" She looked at Connie. "What's your blood group?"

Connie shrugged. "I don't know."

Ryan tapped her on the knee and nodded. "It'll be on your card. From when we donated blood together."

"Your type can't donate blood," Evelyn said to Ryan with venomous disdain.

"Actually my type, who haven't seen any action in twelve months, can. And the last boyfriend I had was over two years ago." Ryan pulled the card from his wallet. "See, some good does come out of my inability to find a date. Really, the outright ban is so irrational and—"

Evelyn interrupted Ryan's speech. "It says Noah's an O. Karl's an AB. This is just preposterous." She looked up from the charts. "What are you, Connie? Wait, no that doesn't matter. A male with blood type AB can never produce a child with blood type O. That's what they taught us." Her eyes burnt into Connie. "Noah can't be Karl's son!"

"Evelyn, I assure you that Noah is Karl's son. Will you please stop talking so loudly?"

Karl's head appeared in the doorway. "Mum, are you okay to drop me home?" He whispered quietly. "I won't come in and wake Noah."

Evelyn lifted her nose. "You might as well. All we need now is for Connie's floozy to turn up so we can have a real little get together."

Connie couldn't help herself. "She's getting a coffee."

The sneer was back. "I'll prove it. I'll prove you philandered."

"Why are you talking so loudly, Mum? Think about Noah."

"Connie wasn't thinking about Noah when she impregnated herself with someone else's child."

Karl frowned. "You're pregnant, Connie?"

"No! Of course not. And Evelyn, I've only ever slept with your son, so if you'd please stop analysing my sexual activity and leave Noah in peace."

Evelyn dropped the charts on the end of the bed. "Incorrect information. That's what you get with these foreigners running the place. Come on, Karl. I'll insist they test you again."

"I'd rather you just took me home," he said, pushing the door wider for his mother. "Kiss Noah for me, would you," he asked Connie, "and I'm sorry. I shouldn't have judged. If I hadn't raced out none of this would have happened. I understand if you hate me. Maria came in earlier to check I was okay. She seems so lovely, she really does."

"No she doesn't and yes you should judge!" snapped Evelyn, waltzing out of the room.

Karl let his mother go ahead before mouthing an apology. "I'm so sorry," he said, leaving the room and closing the door quietly.

Ryan stared down at the card he was clutching. "I'm an O."

Connie looked at her son, pleased that he was still sleeping. "So?"

The voice was low. "That night."

"Oh don't be so ridiculous. You sound worse than Evelyn."

"Think about it, Connie."

"Why? We haven't thought about it before. In fact it was you who said we should never think about it again. Let alone ever discuss it."

"What if..."

Connie turned towards the pale face. "Oh come on, you can't be serious?"

"We did enough."

"No we didn't."

Ryan moved his seat even closer. "Connie, you were upset. You'd just seen Karl kissing Louise at the Christmas party. I raced into the office, had my rant at them. How dare he be unfaithful to the woman who'd given up her virginity for him?"

"Stop saying it like it was a gift. I just got fed up of waiting."

"Yes, but I took you back to mine. You were drunk. We both were. You told me how crap the sex was with him. How you'd saved yourself for so long and couldn't understand why. I think you described it as the biggest anti-climax you'd ever experienced. You asked me if it was like that with all men."

"Ryan, I'm cringing already. Can we just stop this?"

"No! Look at Noah's hair! Look at my hair."

"You haven't got any hair!"

"I was blond. You remember me blond! Karl's got black hair. You're a muddy brown."

"Stop it, Ryan. I'd be more convinced by Evelyn's blood group conspiracy than this. You know how blonde my mum is."

"What if it's not a conspiracy? What if an O can make an O?"

"It can. I was good at science, remember? But Ryan, nothing happened. I've only ever slept with one man."

"Yes, and you said it was crap and we were drunk and I offered my services."

"You did not."

"I did. I was in such a strange place that it made sense at the time."

"It didn't make sense at all. It was the most excruciatingly embarrassing drunken fumble that two best friends should ever wish on the other."

"It was more than that."

"It was nothing. It was barely a grope and I'm so ashamed that I encouraged you. It's just too embarrassing to talk about. What gay man would ever want to get it on with his best girl friend? I must have looked so needy."

"Connie, I wanted it. I was driving it more than you were."

"Oh as if! Can we please stop talking about it?"

"I was confused."

"No you weren't!"

"I was." He hushed his words. "I'd just found out that my donation had resulted in a pregnancy."

"What donation?"

"The sperm bank."

"What are you talking about?"

"I was a donor, for a really short time. I thought I could use the expenses payment as a way of making a bit of extra cash. I'd just got my flat, remember? I was too embarrassed to tell you, or anyone else for that matter. But they phoned me to tell me they'd had news of a pregnancy and I just freaked out. I never wanted to be a father, and I know it's stupid thinking like that because donors aren't fathers and they have nothing to do with the kid, but it felt so strange thinking there'd be part of me running around somewhere, and all this when I'd never even slept with a woman."

"So you decided you'd try and sleep with me?"

"We did whatever it was that we did. I guess we kind of gave each other what we needed in that moment."

"It was less than a moment, Ryan."

Ryan looked up at the little boy sleeping soundly in the bed. "It was more than enough."

Connie rolled her eyes. "You're not Noah's father. We'd have questioned it before and the fact that this hasn't even been a passing thought for either of us tells me the truth."

"I agree, why would we consider it? But that's because he looks like you, Connie, and like you said, what we did stopped as soon as it started. Remember? One pathetic thrust and we both just looked at each other laughing in embarrassment. As if I'd give you the great male sex that Karl couldn't, and as if you'd make me a man by being my first female fuck."

"Ryan!"

"What? It was stupid at the time and we both knew it. Hence why we've never spoken about it before, but I'm O. Noah's an O."

"And Evelyn's right, they've probably got Karl's blood group wrong – or Noah's even – and you know how these doctors are with their writing, it's always illegible."

"It's obvious! He's mine! Oh god, Connie, I can't be a father. I said the same to Maria this morning. I might have donated sperm, but that's all it was. I'm Ry Ry. I'll always be Ry Ry. I don't want to be anything other than Ry Ry."

"What do you mean, Maria?" Connie's eyes widened as realisation finally dawned on her. "The baby photos... In your flat... That's when she walked out." She stood up and started to pace. "The woman got pregnant with your donation just before I got pregnant." She shook her head. "Alice is a few weeks older than Noah... No, it can't be. Maria said her donor was a physiotherapist."

Ryan shrugged apologetically. "A masseur likes to embellish. She was coming to tell you. I assumed you knew?"

"She… She…" Connie put her hand to her mouth. "They're brother and sister."

"If the blood groups are right."

"Oh Ryan, look at them! They're practically twins!"

"A real rainbow family."

"Don't, it's…. It's… No it can't be. This is just ridiculous. I was with Karl for two months. The sex was constant. Crap, but constant."

"All it takes is one swimmer."

Maria pushed opened the door, entering the room with two coffees. She looked from one stunned face to the other. "Oh sorry, should I wait outside? I didn't know you were here, Ryan." She glanced at the bed. "Is everything okay? I can come back later if you like?"

Ryan stood up, taking the cups to the safety of the windowsill before returning to Maria's side. "She knows," he said with a whisper.

Maria turned towards Connie, hands outstretched. "I was coming to tell you. Please understand I was shocked. I saw Ryan's baby photo and freaked out. It was the same one the clinic gave me and I never wanted Alice's donor to play any part in her life yet there I was suddenly faced with him in the flesh. Someone I'd have to see every day because of you." She shook her head. "I made the wrong choice. I ran away. I threw myself into other things, other people. I even hung out with Phoebe like she was my best friend."

"That bit probably hurts the most," joked Ryan.

Maria continued. "I thought it would be easier to just ignore you. Ignore what I'd discovered. But I couldn't. I love you, Connie, and I need you in my life. I knew I had a choice. Beg your forgiveness and blame my absence on a wobble, never to mention my discovery to either you or Ryan, or tell the truth and face up to the facts. Ryan's Alice's donor."

"No, I'm just Ry Ry."

Maria smiled at him. "I know, and I'm glad we've spoken." She turned back to Connie. "I needed to explain things to Ryan so I could be open with you, so things would start properly, with the truth out there for us all to explore. I don't know what this means, or how things will work—"

"I'll just be Ry Ry!" interrupted Ryan once more.

"I know, but when Alice asks, what will I tell her? When will we tell her? There's so much to discuss."

Connie shook her head in total confusion. "This may be even more complex."

"No, Ryan and I spoke this morning. We're fine. We both want the same thing. For the moment he's just an anonymous donor, like he was yesterday and like he was the day before that."

"You don't understand." Connie sat down on the end of the bed, stroking the outline of her son's little legs. "Noah might be Ryan's as well."

CHAPTER THIRTY NINE

<u>Six Months later</u>

It was the fifth day of the New Year and the frosting of snow was adding an extra crispness to the evening air. Connie and Maria left the Shoreditch townhouse, both hugging a child into their hips.

"Down please?" asked Alice.

"Down too!" shouted Noah.

"No, you've both got your posh shoes on and there's snow on the ground." Maria locked the front door and followed Connie down the path.

"Say please, Noah," shushed Alice.

The little boy nodded at the instruction. "Down please, Mummy?"

"No, the car's just..." Connie stood still, smiling at the stretch limo parked next to the curb. "This isn't for me?"

Maria's dropped her spare arm over Connie's shoulder. "Of course it is. Tonight's your big night. We're arriving in style."

The two children used the distraction to wriggle free from their arms. "Snow!" shouted Alice, bending down to touch the glistening sparkles.

"Snow!" added Noah, scraping some up and scooping it straight into his mouth."

Alice tutted at him. "Mrs Honey told you NOT to eat snow."

"Sorry Mrs Honey." He stuck his tongue out and let the melted crystals fall from his mouth. "Thorry Alith."

Connie scooped him back up. "And what would Mrs Honey think about us taking you out so late on a school night?"

Alice clapped her hands. "School tomorrow!"

Maria lifted her daughter and whispered to Connie. "We could say we forgot?"

"Inset day?" said Connie, adding to the conspiracy.

"Noah missed Mrs Honey."

Connie looked at her son. "You'll have so much to tell her, all about Christmas and all about our new house."

"And about the big long car for special party night," added Alice, kicking her feet in excitement. "Put me in, put me in, put me in!"

Maria smiled at the chauffeur who stood ready to open the door on command.

"Sweets!" screamed Alice, diving into the car and running onto the soft leather.

"And fizzy pop!" added Noah, spotting the brightly lit minibar.

Maria cleared her throat. "Maybe we *should* send them in to Mrs Honey tomorrow so she can deal with their inevitable sleep deprived come down from tonight's night of sugar and dancing."

Connie lifted her long gown and stepped into the car. "We won't be dancing, will we?"

Maria shrugged. "I don't know. I've never been to a book launch before."

****

Connie took a deep breath and clutched the little fingers in her own, Noah one side and Alice the other. She could feel Maria behind her, hands on her waist guiding her into the welcoming room.

The voice spoke again. "And here she is now. Miss Connie Parker with her two beautiful children and supportive life partner, Maria."

Connie cringed. It had sounded much better on paper when she'd handed it to her publisher earlier that evening. They'd insisted on officially introducing her to the small crowd of people, and going into detail about their familial connection or calling Maria her girlfriend hadn't sounded quite right, so she'd chosen to keep it simple, albeit saccharine.

Connie smiled at the sea of faces. Everyone was there who mattered. Even Earth Mother and Crusty had taken a night off from the kids. Her emotion-filled eyes gazed around at the well-wishers' smiles before being drawn to the huge billboard on the stage. *"The Adventures of Bonnie Blythe. By Miss Connie Parker."* Her heart skipped a beat. How had this happened? How had everything fallen so perfectly into place?

The disembodied voice continued. "Who'd like to hear a few words from the talented lady herself?"

Connie laughed loudly. "No, I've got my hands full." She wiggled the little arms.

"We'll take care of them," said two men, reaching down to pick up the children.

"Higher!" squealed Noah, as he was thrown into the air.

"Me too, Ry Ry!" shouted Alice, desperate to join in the fun.

Connie waited for the catch before wrapping her arms around Karl's shoulders. "You made it!"

"Of course I did. I wasn't going to miss your big moment."

"But Canada's such a huge flight!"

Karl lifted Noah further up on his hip and tilted his head to the woman standing behind him. "Erin insisted we came."

"Erin, hello!" Connie stepped forwards and kissed the pretty woman on the cheek. "It's lovely to see you again. Thank you so much!"

She smiled. "It was Karl's idea."

Karl ruffled the little boy's shirt. "Gives me chance to catch up with this big man. How have you been, mate? How's Ryan been treating you?"

"Ry Ry's just great," said Noah with a smile.

Karl nodded and shook the hand of the man standing beside him. "I know he is, son."

THE END.

About the author:

Kiki Archer is a UK-based lesbian fiction novelist and winner of the Ultimate Planet's Independent Author of the Year Award 2013.

Her debut novel, the best-selling "**But She is My Student**," won the UK's 2012 SoSoGay Best Book Award.

Its sequel, "**Instigations**," took just 12 hours from its release to reach the top of the UK lesbian fiction chart.

Kiki also topped the lesbian fiction charts in 2013 with her best-selling third novel, "**Binding Devotion**," which was a 2013 Rainbow Awards finalist.

"**One Foot Onto The Ice**" has been her most successful novel to date, breaking into the American contemporary fiction top 100 as well as achieving the US and UK lesbian fiction number one.

Kiki received an honourable mention in the 2014 Author of the Year category at the Lesbian Oscars.

Novels by Kiki Archer:

BUT SHE IS MY STUDENT - March 2012

INSTIGATIONS - August 2012

BINDING DEVOTION - February 2013

ONE FOOT ONTO THE ICE - September 2013

WHEN YOU KNOW - April 2014

TOO LATE... I LOVE YOU - June 2015

Connect with Kiki:

www.kikiarcher.com
Twitter: @kikiarcherbooks
www.facebook.com/kiki.archer
www.youtube.com/kikiarcherbooks

Printed in Great Britain
by Amazon.co.uk, Ltd.,
Marston Gate.